The Innocent of
Falkland Road

The Innocent of
Falkland Road

Carlo Gébler

NEW ISLAND

THE INNOCENT OF FALKLAND ROAD
First published in 2017 by
New Island Books
16 Priory Hall Office Park
Stillorgan
County Dublin
Republic of Ireland

www.newisland.ie

Print ISBN: 978-1-84840-630-8
Epub ISBN: 978-1-84840-631-5
Mobi ISBN: 978-1-84840-632-2

Typeset by JVR Creative India
Cover design by Anna Morrison

New Island received financial assistance from The Arts Council (An Chomhairle Ealaíon), 70 Merrion Square, Dublin 2, Ireland.

New Island Books is a member of Publishing Ireland.

This is for Glenn Patterson, the only begetter

'Aristotle could not divine what
an autumn night might do.'

Irish proverb

August

Ralph woke and remembered. Yes. The last Sunday of the month. Today was the day.

He got up and pulled open his curtains. His bedroom was on the ground floor by the front door and all comings and goings in and out of the house could either be seen or heard from here, or both. Outside their front gate, in Falkland Road, a black woman and her two girls went by. They all wore mauve hats and white gloves and he knew they were headed for the corrugated-iron church up on Putney Bridge Road. Most Sundays Ralph could hear their congregation singing.

He dressed and went down to the kitchen, full of modern fittings, unlike anyone else's in the neighbourhood, then under the arch at the rear and through to the extension his mother had added, known as the River room. Polished wooden floor, gleaming white walls, open fire with exposed brick chimney breast, and, at the back, a wall of glass.

He opened the sliding doors at the rear and went out. Three steps glittering with mica led down to a gravelled patio. The day – mild, dry, no wind. Ahead of him, the garden – his mother's creation, she was a landscape designer – comprising a set of descending terraces ending at the flood wall, with the River Thames beyond.

He went forward, downward, past planters, hedges, animal sculptures and Mediterranean terracotta pots. At the bottom he smelt the Thames' familiar smell of slime, silt and rot as he leant on the rough old concrete of the wall and peered over.

A few feet below, floating on the river's shiny black surface, a huge dirty brown carpet of froth, while farther out, logs, crates, bottles and pieces of furniture hurtled past, carried by the tide that was rushing furiously in.

The noise of a train rattling and clattering on its tracks. He turned and looked inland. Halfway up Falkland Road an iron bridge spanned the river, underground carriages hurtling over it. He let them lead his eye across to the other side, which was north London, quite far away, and full of buildings and trees.

Then he looked rightward, seaward, at Wandsworth Park, which began where Falkland Road ended. The leaves on the park's trees, he noticed, had lost their summer lustre. He had never paid much attention to the seasons changing when he was younger but this year he had. In the far distance Wandsworth Bridge stretched from one bank to the other.

Ralph turned, wandered back up to the top of the garden. Under the River room ahead, a line of little windows close to the ground. These let light into the basement bedroom where their housekeeper, Doreen, slept along with her husband, Tom.

Slender wiry Tom, bow-legged and strong. Pointed nose and dark eyes. The skin on his jaw and neck was stretched and polished smooth and looked like cheese rind. When Tom was in the Irish army his tank caught fire. His whole body was burnt.

After his accident, Tom left the army and came to London and worked on building sites. He met Doreen in an Irish dance hall in Cricklewood. A clerk in a Kilburn bookies, she was from Waterford like him. Doreen and Tom married in 1959.

Two years later Ralph's newly divorced mother saw their card in the glass box outside Pritchard's, their local newsagents, with its message printed in Biro:

> Irish Couple, good refs, clean, tidy, honest, v. hard-working & trustworthy, seek accommodation in return for housekeeping duties, minding children, cooking, cleaning, gardening, et cetera. No job too hard. Phone Cam 9084 any evening after 7 p.m. and ask for Doreen MacGraw.

His mother rang and a week later the MacGraws moved in to Falkland Road.

Doreen and Tom had no children. Doreen and his mother often talked about this in low, confidential voices that they assumed Ralph wouldn't be able to hear. They were wrong. He was able to hear what they said and in that way he learned that Tom couldn't give Doreen a baby because of being burnt all over his body when his tank went on fire on the Curragh Plains and that Doreen, when she married, knew there would be no children and accepted this. At the same time she wished it was otherwise. It mattered to her that she didn't have children. It mattered very much. Adoption was mooted but

Doreen, he'd learnt, hadn't the heart for that. The thing she wanted was a child of her own, if she could have one, but Tom couldn't give her one, and that was that. She had made her bed and she would lie in it and she wasn't one for regrets or complaints.

From his eavesdropping, Ralph also understood how much the MacGraws liked his mother, and how grateful his mother was to them, how much she relied on them, and how much she liked them. He liked them too and for the same reasons she did, Tom because of his humour, which was sharp and novel, and Doreen because she was always kind and thoughtful, always interested, always interesting, and because she cared for him.

He thought of the MacGraws now, as he was about to climb the steps, lying asleep downstairs in the back room of the basement. He mustn't wake them, so he crept in and slid the River room door shut behind with slow, gentle care.

★

It was afternoon. They were in the kitchen, Ralph, his mother, Doreen and Tom. His mother wore suede boots and a check dress with a fur collar she had bought in the Mary Quant shop in Chelsea for the journey. Her hair was newly bobbed.

'Right,' said his mother. 'Here's all the contacts.'

She straightened the three badly typed pages on the table that listed all the names and addresses Doreen might need while she was away:

Mrs Moody next door.

Ginny Boscombe, mother of Ralph's best friend, Benedict, who lived at 56 Falkland Road.

Other neighbours and friends.

His father, Peter, who lived in the north of England.

The GP, Dr O'Dwyer.

The dentist, Mr Phillips.

The secretary at St David's school, Mrs Beadle-Collins.

The gardener, Mr Cameron.

The local shops where his mother had opened accounts.

The branch of Lloyds on Putney High Street where his mother banked.

The utility companies.

The insurance company.

The family's solicitor.

And so on.

Ralph had looked through the typed list earlier and beside his father's address his mother had scribbled in biro, 'Only to be contacted in the event of death or emergency'. Ralph hadn't seen his father for many years and he thought his mother was probably right.

At the top of each sheet, in capitals, his mother had typed her own details: her address in the United States where she could be reached by telegram, and the telephone number, where she could be rung in the event of a crisis, until she returned in a year, in good time, as she had promised him, for his next birthday. He'd turned twelve nine days earlier.

'And here's two hundred pounds,' his mother continued. She touched the bundle of notes fastened with one of his father's old bulldog clips on which were scratched his initials, 'PG' for Peter Goswell. 'Hide the money somewhere safe.'

Doreen nodded. 'Will do.'

His mother touched the two green chequebooks.

'All signed,' she said. 'And don't forget to fill in the stubs when you write them. And get receipts. For everything.'

Doreen nodded. She knew. His mother had been over everything with her many times.

'Hide them too as soon as I've gone.'

Doreen nodded again. 'Will do.'

Ralph knew Doreen's hiding places. These included inside the hollow stem of the cake display stand on the dresser, the box under the sink down among the bars of carbolic soap, and inside the rice canister on the shelf over the stove. She would put things so deep within the hard grey grains that she could only retrieve them with a tongs. Doreen was an accomplished hider.

Two peeps from outside. His mother's taxi.

'Mustn't dilly-dally,' she said.

She put on her red coat and matching beret.

'I'll do the honours,' said Tom.

He stood between her two huge square suitcases with new luggage labels tied to the handles with the address of the estate where she would be based written on them in her big looping handwriting on one side and her home address on the other: 88 Falkland Road, Putney, London SW15, England.

'They weigh a ton,' his mother said.

'I'm used to donkey work,' said Tom.

Tom lifted the suitcases.

'What's in here?' he asked. 'Bricks!'

'I warned you they were heavy,' said his mother.

His mother pulled on her gloves. They were leather, black and smooth. The taxi horn sounded again.

'We'd better get a move on,' she said.

Doreen opened the side door to the passage between their house and Mrs Moody's next door. Doreen went out first, then Tom, then his mother. Ralph was last.

Ralph followed the adults up the passage to the privet hedge at the end that separated theirs and Mrs Moody's front gardens, and then went left. His mother's taxi was parked at the kerb beyond the gate, its engine ticking.

Ralph went through the gate and out to the pavement. His mother and Doreen were standing waiting and Tom was on the other side of the taxi trying to load the luggage into the open hold where the front passenger door and seat would otherwise have been. The taxi man was sitting beside the hold in the driver's seat, holding the steering wheel. He had a very pink face and curly hair and was chewing a toothpick.

The taxi man turned to Doreen and his mother.

'Does he need help?' asked the taxi man. He pointed at Tom.

'Ask him yourself,' said his mother.

The taxi man took the toothpick out of his mouth and then put it back in again. He swung the door open and got out. On his seat was an orange cushion and a raffia back support, both shiny from wear.

The taxi man went round. He helped Tom heave the suitcases into the luggage hold and secure them with straps. Ralph noticed his mother and Doreen were not talking. Strange. They usually talked a lot. They just want this moment to be over, he thought.

The luggage secured, the taxi man came back, followed by Tom, who was wiping his hands.

'Job done,' said Tom.

'Waterloo, Miss?' asked the taxi man.

His mother was catching the train to Southampton where she'd board her liner for New York.

'Yes, please,' his mother said.

The taxi man threw himself onto the orange cushion and tugged the leather strap to close the door.

His mother turned and looked at him.

'Ralph,' she said, 'you remember what I've said, don't you? If anything goes wrong, anything at all, big, medium or small, the size really doesn't matter, you are not to keep it to yourself. You are to go to Doreen. Do you understand?

And you tell her everything. Or if Doreen isn't about, you go down to Ginny. Do you understand?'

'Yes,' he said.

'Your father I wouldn't bank on but Doreen will always be here and so will Ginny. Isn't that right, Doreen?'

'Yes,' said Doreen.

'So, no secrets. Any worries of any kind, any kind, you know where to go.'

'I do,' said Ralph, in the tone he knew she wanted to hear – loud, direct, forthright.

'Right, let's not string this out,' said his mother.

She seized him by the ears and kissed him loudly on each cheek. His ears rang. Then she kissed Doreen quickly and shook hands with Tom. The taxi man reached round and opened the passenger door for her. A thick smell of hot leather and boiled sweets came out from inside the back of the cab. He would remember that, he thought.

His mother ducked in and threw herself on the long seat that ran along below the back window. Tom swung the door and it closed with a deep clunk. From the dark rear his mother leant forward into the light and waved. The indicator clicked. The taxi man spat out his toothpick. The taxi pulled away from the kerb and began to move off down Falkland Road. His mother turned to the rear window and her hand was beside her face and she was waving as she looked back at them. He waved and called goodbye. Doreen waved. Tom stood, his hands in his trousers pockets. It didn't surprise Ralph that he wasn't waving. Tom always said he didn't like goodbyes or scenes of any kind.

The taxi passed under the railway bridge arching over the rooftops of Falkland Road, carried on to the end, turned left and vanished.

Ralph looked down at the toothpick. The chewed end was swollen by the driver's saliva but the other was still pointed and sharp.

'Right, Buster,' said Doreen.

He turned to face her.

She was plump and small, with a smooth neat face. She wore glasses, the lenses set in a thin blue frame. Her cheeks were rosy. Her two front teeth stuck out over her bottom lip, so her mouth was always a bit open and a sliver of white always showed. It was attractive somehow. Her hands were small and beautiful. They were her best feature, she said. She wore a Claddagh ring on her ring finger with the heart turned in to signal, as she had told Ralph, that she was married. The term she used was 'spoken for'. Doreen had a warm, cheerful and charming manner, was an inde-fatigable and endlessly interesting talker, and he never tired of her company - never.

'What happens tomorrow?' she asked.

Until this moment he'd managed to keep all thoughts of school out of his head but now, before his inner eye, the image flashed of his satchel in his bedroom packed with his pen box, a few exercise books and the necessary per-mission slips, and beside the satchel his bulging drawstring kit-bag with his name on the outside in indelible ink, his gym clothes, plimsolls and towel packed inside.

'First day of term?' said Ralph.

Term started at St David's the next day, the last day of August.

'No, wrong,' said Doreen. 'Not school. No. The first day of a year of fun, slow coach. So let's go in. If I'm not mis-taken, I've got to sew up the bottom of your tie, haven't I?'

'I think so.'

'And then,' said Doreen, 'you know what we're going to do?'

'No.'

'Well, guess.'

'Dunno.'

'He's not in a guessing mood,' said Tom.

'We're going to the Wimpy bar, and you can have whatever you want, but only on one condition.'

'What?'

'You don't tell your mother.'

She gave him one of her funny Doreen winks. Rather than the top lid coming down, the bottom lid came up.

'You coming, Tom?'

'I haven't read the paper yet.'

'The paper will keep. Come with us,' she said. 'My treat.'

★

They went out and had hamburgers and sweet fried onions and thin French fries and thick gluey milkshakes and came back. Ralph checked he had everything in his satchel and his kit-bag one last time. Then he brushed his teeth, put on his pyjamas and got into bed. Doreen came in and bent over him.

'Sleep tight,' she said.

Her lips brushed the top of his head.

'You're going to have to wash your hair tomorrow night, Buster,' she said. 'Or the bugs will move in.'

She switched off the bedside light, walked out and closed the door.

Ralph lay staring upward. Yellow light from the street lamp leaked in around the edges of his curtains and spread over his ceiling. Through the floor, coming from the basement, the sound of fiddles. Tom always listened to Irish radio in the evenings. The day was done.

★

Early next morning, Ralph heard O'Neill's van at their gate which would take Tom and other labourers to the tunnel for the new line to Victoria Station they were digging and Tom getting in. Later he heard Doreen's alarm clock through the floor ringing in the basement below and a few minutes after that he felt Doreen shaking him.

'Come on sleepy head,' she said.

Ralph opened his eyes. Doreen wore a puffy blue housecoat over her nightdress. She hadn't her make-up or her glasses on yet. Her eyes were small, round and blue, like pebbles.

'How are you?' she asked. 'Ready for school. Get washed and dressed. Hot milk with your cornflakes? I'll take that as a yes.'

Doreen padded out. He heard her in the kitchen. Ralph went upstairs and washed his face and hands and brushed his teeth and then combed his hair flat. Then he came back and dressed. His shirt smelt of starch and his school trousers and blazer, which had both been dry-cleaned in the summer, were stiff and smelt of chemicals.

Ralph got his satchel and kit-bag and carried them to the kitchen. His cereal was on the table, the milk steaming. Doreen stood at the stove, staring at the kettle, waiting for the whistle.

'Cup of tea? Toast? Do I hear, "Yes please, Mrs MacGraw, thank you so much"?'

'You do.'

'Go on then. Manners cost nothing.'

'Yes please, Mrs MacGraw, thank you so much.'

Ralph heard the rasp of a match as it was struck and the whump of the grill catching and smelt the vague sour milk smell that came when the gas was on. He heard the tray being slid under the grill with the bread for toasting. He sat at the table and began to eat. The milk was frothy and warm, the cereal limp and yeasty. As he ate Ralph felt his stomach warming. When he was nearly finished he got a whiff of burnt toast. He heard the noise as the scorch on the bread was scraped into the sink and the sound of butter being spread. The whistle went and boiling water glugged into the teapot.

Doreen set a mug of tea and a plate of toast in front of him.

'There we go,' said Doreen. 'And there's your bus money.'

She pointed at a pile with the correct change.

'Put it in your pocket,' she said.

Ralph put the money in the inside pocket of his jacket and closed the zip at the top.

'I'm not a morning girl, you know.' Doreen set her own mug of tea on the table and sat. 'When I was girl at home, all my brothers and sisters would get up when they were called but would I? No. I never wanted to get out of my lovely warm bed. I'd just pull the covers over my head and think, just another minute and then I'll get up. Just another minute. And a minute would become two would become five would become ten and suddenly our neighbour Mr O'Dennehy's car would be coming down the avenue to lift us to school in Tramore and I'd have to jump up and throw on my uniform and rush out, sleep in my eyes, hair uncombed. And more than once the car would be driving, actually driving away, slowly by the time I got down. Mr O'Dennehy would know I'd be coming and he'd just be wanting to make the point, and there'd be me running after him shouting, "Stop! Wait, Mr O'Dennehy!" And then he'd stop and I'd hop in and he'd go, "Morning, Miss Furlong. Nice of you to join us."'

Doreen took a sip of tea. 'This tea made with London water it's not a patch on the tea we have at home. Doesn't have the bite. But it's all there is, so I make do.'

She took another sip. 'You're not a morning man either, as we know, but you haven't a patch on me.'

'Will you take me?' he asked.

'Where?'

'You know. Waterford.'

'Yeah, yeah.'

'When?'

'Christmas, maybe.'

She glanced round at the murmuring grill.

'Forgot to turn the gas off. Nip across and turn it off would you?'

Ralph went and turned the Bakelite knob to the off position and came back and sat.

'It's going to be good you know, this year,' Doreen said. 'It's going to be a laugh.'

★

Ralph pulled on his navy school raincoat but didn't do the buttons up and put his school cap on. He got his satchel and kitbag.

'Bye,' he said.

'I'll see you later, unless you see me first,' said Doreen.

He went out onto Falkland Road. He began to walk. Mrs Moody's house next door was just like theirs; tall, narrow, three storeys over a basement, redbrick, semi-detached. So was the next house and the next. All the houses were the same on their side. The houses across the road were smaller. They were all two-storey.

He squinted ahead. Benedict was outside his house staring along the pavement toward him. Ralph waved casually. Benedict waved back. Ralph drew closer.

'Hello, sordid,' Benedict called.

'Sordid yourself,' said Ralph.

They began to walk up the road, heading for the railway bridge.

'I got such a long dreary lecture this morning,' said Benedict. 'I thought I was going to die.'

'What have you done now?' asked Ralph.

'I haven't done anything. The lecture was about you, and let me tell you, it was sordid.'

'Who gave you the lecture?' Ralph asked. 'Was it your mum?'

'No,' said his friend. 'It was Clive.'

Clive was Benedict's father and he was always Clive and never Father, whereas Ginny was always Mother or Mum and never Ginny. Quite why this was, Ralph had no idea. It was just one of those Boscombe things that he accepted but never understood.

'So Clive stayed over last night?' asked Ralph, hoping he sounded unconcerned, even indifferent.

Though Clive and Ginny were still married, Clive did not live at home in 56 Falkland Road anymore. He lived in a flat in White City near Television Centre where he worked as a scriptwriter and a producer. Ginny and Clive's arrangement, as Benedict had once pedantically explained to him, wasn't the same as his situation: Ralph's mother and father were divorced, Benedict had said, whereas Clive and Ginny had something called an open marriage. This was why his father was not only living in White City but was also in and out of 56 Falkland Road all the time and sometimes even stayed the night, which presumably, Ralph reasoned now, he must have done the night before in order to deliver the lecture to Benedict that morning.

'Yep, Clive stayed last night,' said Benedict.

They reached the steps at the side of the bridge and began to climb. They were concrete and had a lattice pattern of lines scored deeply into them to stop water pooling and forming ice sheets in the winter.

'So what was he saying about me?' asked Ralph carefully.

'Ah, so you're interested. Well you would be desperate to know I suppose. No surprise there.'

'Actually,' said Ralph slowly, 'you raised the subject in the first place and you haven't stopped going on about it ever since. I think the desperate one is you.'

They came to the top of the steps. The footbridge, with its pulpy, soft skim of ancient asphalt, ran ahead; to their left, the railway tracks; to their right, the high cast-iron safety fence topped with a bulky rail; below them, the black river; above them, the huge sky; and ahead of them, on the far bank, three enormous seven-storey mansion blocks like three great castles.

They walked on.

'Apparently, according to Clive,' said Benedict, 'you're going to be weepy this morning because your mother's just gone away to America to work.'

'I'm not weepy,' said Ralph carefully. 'I'm not anything.'

He hoped he sounded defiant but not strident.

'Yes,' Benedict continued. 'You'd deny it. That's exactly what Clive warned me about.' His friend sounded very pleased with this. 'But deep down, Clive said, you'd be in the dumps and absolutely soggy.'

'Soggy? What does that mean?'

'It's what happens, my mum says, when you cry. "Oh that bastard of a husband of mine, Clive, he knows just how to make your mother cry, and once I've cried my fill I'm positively soggy with tears."'

Benedict was an excellent mimic, and his Ginny take-off spot on.

'Well, I don't want to cry,' said Ralph.

On the river a tug pulling a line of coal-filled barges was nosing toward them, smoke pluming from its funnel. Its hooter sounded. Ralph felt the noise right in the middle of his being, throbbing and deeply stirring.

'According to Clive, the more you say you don't want to cry, the more it means you really do want to cry. You're denying it so strongly, I'd say you must be very unhappy, and, that being so, Clive said, I've got to be kind. So, I'm radiating kindness. Can you feel it? Do you feel better, knowing I'm being kind?'

'Do you know what you are?' asked Ralph.

'No.'

'Beyond sordid.'

'What does that mean?'

'It means worse than sordid. Surely even a simpleton like you can understand that.'

Without saying a word, both stopped at the same time, stuck their feet into the spaces in the lattice, scrambled a foot or so up the fence, leaned over the rail and stared down at the tug and barges passing directly beneath.

'Do you ever think what it would be like to jump down into the back of a barge if it was full of mattresses?'

'No,' said Ralph.

The last barge disappeared beneath them. There was no more to see, just the wake with its beer-coloured lines of froth and little round waves radiating backwards and outwards. The boys got down and resumed walking.

'By the way,' said Benedict, 'Mum's collecting us. She's got to see Maud. Remember Mopey Maud?'

How could he forget? She lived near their school in Barnes in a big house with a huge garden filled with her husband's gigantic sculptures, multi-coloured fibreglass pipes, crimped and crunched into weird arrangements. Maud's

husband called them 'worm casts for the nuclear age'. They
baffled Ralph. What was the point of enormous fibreglass
rods in bright colours going everywhere like the lines on the
Underground map? They were great to climb on though.

'Course I remember Maud,' said Ralph.

'Well Mum has to see her, so she'll pick us up after
school and we'll all go. Mum said she'll ring Doreen and
tell her.'

Ralph was joyful. He could spend the bus fare he
would save on sweets.

★

The boys boarded their bus at the depot beside Putney
Bridge Underground Station. It carried them over Putney
Bridge, up the High Street, round Putney Heath and on
to Roehampton. They got out in the middle of the Lark
Hill council estate and followed a little road past high grey
tower blocks to a wooden door in the fence at the back
of St David's grounds. They opened the door and stepped
through and the door clanged shut behind.

They were in the school's grounds now, walking past
the compost heap where sometimes foxes from Richmond
Common were spotted scavenging, the greenhouse where
pupils grew tomatoes and herbs, the tool shed, the garage
where the mowers were parked, and finally the gardener's
hut. Luigi was sitting inside at his table drinking tea from a
mug. He sat there at the start and end of every day moni-
toring who came in and went out.

'Morning,' he shouted.

The boys waved back. They began to follow the path.
Their shoes scrunched on the gravel as they ambled. On
either side were stands of oak, chestnut and elm. Everyone
at St David's called this area 'The Park'. The school's

swimming pool lay away to their left, a sunken blue lozenge filled with still water. Swimming would carry on until the October half-term holiday and then the pool would be drained for the winter.

They came to a set of old brick steps. They climbed up. Now they were in 'The High Garden' as it was called. Here were flowerbeds, ornamental ponds, neat hedges and paths of warped stone flags. The long Queen Anne mansion that housed the school was ahead. They heard the school bell clanging.

Benedict looked at his watch. 'Crikey. Better leg it.'

The boys held their satchels and kit-bags to stop them from bouncing and began to trot.

★

Ralph's classroom was long and shallow, with windows at one end, and the door at the other, and three long rows of desks strung between at which the class were seated. Ralph's desk was in the front row by the window and his teacher, Miss Loudon's desk was in front of him.

Miss Loudon had arrived the previous September and this was the start of their second year with her. On her very first day with them and within the first hour she had told the class her age: twenty-six. They had found this incredible on two counts. One, that she was so young. Two, that she'd told them. On her twenty-seventh birthday, Lisa Griffiths got the whole class to sign a card. Everyone liked Miss Loudon.

Miss Loudon had green eyes and black hair that hung down to the middle of her back. Today she wore a red skirt and a huge black necklace. None of the other lady teachers would have dressed this way.

Miss Loudon put a pile of books on Ralph's desk.

'Pass these round please.'

Ralph took one and slid the pile sideways to the next desk. The book was a paperback, used and worn, its front cover creased at the corners and the pages stained brown on their edges. Ralph knew many children had read it already.

He studied the jacket front. Most of it was covered with a strange drawing of small boys, some naked, some in bits of their school uniform, several carrying spears, moving round in a forest of weird plants with gigantic rubbery leaves. Ralph understood it was supposed to be a tropical forest but he didn't believe this was what a tropical forest looked like in real life. The space above the drawing was filled with writing – *Lord of the Flies* – and above the title, slightly smaller, was the author's name, William Golding.

'Has everyone got a book?'

'Yes, Miss Loudon.'

'Right, boys and girls. You hold in your hands a remarkable novel. The story it tells will appeal because it concerns children, like yourselves. Indeed, as you will find when you start reading, these children are so like yourselves that one of them, he's the book's hero in a way, even has the same name as one of you: his name is Ralph.'

Ralph felt his face redden slightly but there were no titters. He realised then that Miss Loudon had done him a service saying what she had said. When the book was read aloud and Ralph was sounded out, there'd be no mocking.

'Now,' Miss Loudon continued, 'at the same time as being a story about a group of boys who get marooned on a desert island, it is also a story about humanity, and the way people organise themselves in the world in what we call society, and whether we do this by consent, or not …'

Miss Loudon then explained that they would read the entire book aloud in class and discuss it over the following weeks.

The opening pages were then read, with different children taking different passages. The pages described two of the marooned schoolboys meeting on a beach. Neither had a name at the beginning. That came later. One was blond. He was Ralph and he was exactly Ralph's age – twelve. The other was plump. He was Piggy. There was not a lot of action, and certainly nothing interesting or exciting. Just descriptions of the beach, the shore, the sea, mingled with the strange stop-start conversation of boys. It was quite hard-going. At the same time there was something about the way the two boys talked, following their own different trains of thought, not listening to each another, not understanding each another, and then just clicking and hearing each another, before diverging again, which struck him as true. During the class discussion that followed, he talked about this – or tried to.

'When I read sometimes I think, this isn't true. Well, no. I know it isn't true. It isn't. The story and that. It's made up. I know that. But sometimes I know that I believe and other times I know I don't. That's what I mean. Especially when it comes to talking. With dialogue sometimes I go, no, that doesn't sound right. And sometimes I go, yes, that's how people talk. And with the bit we just did, with Ralph and Piggy meeting, I thought, yes, that's how they'd talk.'

'Ah,' said Miss Loudon, 'because of the writer's skill you've suspended disbelief here, whereas elsewhere you don't – is that it?'

She'd put it so much better than he could.

'Yes,' he said.

At the end of the class everyone put their copy in their desk where it would lie until the next class, but he put his copy in his satchel to bring home.

★

The last bell of the day clanged, rung by hand by the school secretary, Mrs Beadle-Collins, standing in the hall by the front door. The form stood and set their chairs under their desks. Miss Loudon got up from her desk and came forward.

The bell stopped.

'Good afternoon, children,' Miss Loudon said.

'Good afternoon, Miss Loudon,' the children said.

'Dismiss,' Miss Loudon said.

The class began to file out. The children nearest the door in the back row went first and because of his position at the front by the window, Ralph was always last to leave. He heard jostling by the door as his classmates squeezed out.

'No shoving now,' Miss Loudon called. 'Did you hear? No shoving, Corbett.'

'Sorry, Miss,' Corbett called back.

'Well, Ralph,' said Miss Loudon, 'anything planned for this evening? Are you popping off to see a Bach concert at the South Bank perhaps?'

She was always posing questions like this. He didn't quite understand them but he liked them.

'I'm not going to a concert, Miss,' he said, 'although I am going out as it happens.'

'Oh, really?'

'Benedict's mother …'

'Benedict Boscombe?' asked Miss Loudon.

'Yeah, Miss.'

'Yes,' she corrected him.

'Yes, Miss,' he said.

'He's in the other class?'

'Yes, Miss.'

This was school policy. Close friends were kept apart because it was believed they would interfere with each other's capacity to learn if they were together all day.

'She's collecting us, Miss – Benedict's mother – so we won't have to take the bus home.'

'I wish I was being collected,' said Miss Loudon. 'I live in Nunhead. That's a bus, the tube, the train and another bus. It takes for ever.'

'We're going out for tea, Miss,' he said. 'To a friend of Benedict's mother.'

'Oh very nice,' Miss Loudon spoke through her nose in a funny accent.

He look puzzled. He was puzzled. This was another thing of hers: she put on funny voices.

'Kenneth Williams,' Miss Loudon said.

Who? He was none the wiser. He wondered should he ask Miss Loudon to explain who Kenneth Williams was but then he sensed the quiet, everyone having left the classroom, and remembered Ginny was waiting outside.

'I have to go,' Ralph said, though he also wanted to stay. He liked talking to Miss Loudon.

'Yes, you do.' Miss Loudon smiled. Her front upper teeth were small, like a child's. 'Don't eat too much cake.'

★

When he got out into Crescent Lane, he found a few St David's pupils waiting for late parents, plus Ginny standing beside her red Saab with Benedict already in the back pointing at his wrist watch and mouthing, 'You're late!'

'Come on, slow coach,' she shouted. Her voice was light, joshing, cheerful.

He ran up to her. She had a long face and an enormous mouth and a great tumult of curly dark blonde hair.

'In you hop.'

She was wearing something with an Arab name he couldn't remember that went all the way to her ankles and was fastened at the front with clasps made of stiffened fabric and decorated with swirling lines and bits of mirror held on with bright red thread. He knew Ginny had bought it in the souk in Marrakesh. She had bought a similar garment for his mother but his mother didn't like it and she only wore it as a nightdress.

He got into his seat and as Ginny closed the door he put on his safety belt. Ginny went round to the driver's side, lifted her skirts high over her knees and got in.

'All stations active,' she said in a bad American accent. 'Thunderbirds are go.'

They drove off. Over the next few minutes Ginny asked about their day and they replied laconically. They stopped at a red light and she pulled her skirts higher. The skin on her thighs was taut and white. On her feet she wore red tennis shoes. She cleared her throat as she did when she had something important to say.

'Here's the score, lads,' she said. 'Things aren't going well for Maud at the moment. Arnold's done something very stupid.'

Arnold was Maud's husband, the sculptor.

'What's he done?' asked Benedict from the back.

'He's got himself into trouble with the police. He might go to prison. Actually, he is in prison, but he might have to stay there.'

'Did he rob a bank?' asked Benedict.

'No. Don't be ridiculous.'

'Did he murder someone?'

'Of course not. You know Arnold. He wouldn't hurt a fly. Of course he wouldn't do something like that.'

'Did he glass someone then?'

Glassing had entered Benedict's vocabulary when Peter, the son of Ginny's housekeeper, Jeannie, and a Mod, had stabbed a man in the eye with a pint glass in a brawl outside a pub in Streatham. He had been convicted of GBH and got three years and was currently in HMP Wandsworth. The offence fascinated Benedict and he had quizzed Jeannie about it at length. This was inevitable. All kinds of youth violence fascinated him – especially the pitched battles between Mods and Rockers during bank holidays.

'I wish you wouldn't say that word,' said Ginny.

'What word?' asked Benedict.

'You know the one I mean.'

'Glassed?'

'Yes.'

'What's wrong with it?'

'I just don't like it,' said Ginny.

'Why?'

'I just don't. It's not a very nice word.'

'So what did Arnold do?' asked Benedict.

'He's accused of smuggling,' said Ginny. 'Smuggling drugs.'

The lights turned green. Ginny drove on.

'So just try to be sensitive and be nice to Maud, all right lads?' said Ginny. 'Will you do that for me?'

'Does that mean we're not allowed to talk?' said Benedict.

'It means showing compassion,' said Ginny. 'And if you see Maud crying, you could try giving her a hug.'

'A hug,' the boys said in unison. 'Uh. Sordid!'

★

They were all inside, sitting in Maud's kitchen at her table. It was pine, scrubbed white, and enormous. Ralph and Benedict were sipping hot Ribena. Ginny and Maud were drinking white wine.

'Arnold drove his van down to Morocco,' said Maud, 'took the panels off, filled the voids with hash, put the panels back on. They said in court how much he had but I can't remember. It was a lot. The van was well down on its axle. I know that much. Not that anyone noticed mind you. Not when he crossed from Morocco to Spain. Not when he drove up through France to Calais. But when he got to Dover, they noticed all right. Too fucking right they noticed.'

Maud described the van being searched, the discovery of the drugs, Arnold being charged, his first appearance in court and his being remanded to HMP Lewes.

'What was he thinking?' asked Ginny.

'He wasn't thinking,' said Maud, 'that's the point. He just had this notion. Smuggle the gear, flog it, retire on the proceeds. Easy-peasy lemon squeezy. That was the plan. Stupid cunt. Stupid, stupid fucking cunt.'

'What happens now?' Ginny asked.

'The judge set bail. Arnold wants me to find it. He's screaming to get of jail. Can't stand it of course. Can you imagine Arnold locked up with a whole bunch of criminals? Of course he hates it but he should have thought about that, shouldn't he, before he got himself arrested.'

'How much?'

'Ten thousand,' Maud said.

'What!'

'Yeah. Ten thousand fucking pounds.'

'And ...' Ginny rolled her hands helplessly in the air.

'I don't have ten thousand lying round,' said Maud, 'if that's what you're asking. I'll have to put the house up.'

'Really?'

'Yeah,' said Maud. 'I could fucking kill him. I could you know. It's just as well he's in Lewes because if he walked in here now, I'd get the fucking bread knife and I'd run him through. I'd fucking run him through.'

She shook her head as if she'd just remembered something and then turned toward Benedict and Ralph.

'You all right there, boys?' she asked. 'Want a top up? Biscuit? Don't pay any attention to what I said. That's what sometimes happens in life, as you'll find out. Sometimes you just have to let it out. You know. Ventilate. Let rip. And that was me, just now. But I wouldn't really stab him, you know. That was just words, stupid words. Wasn't it, Ginny?'

'Just words,' said Ginny.

'I love him really, don't I?'

'Yes, of course you do,' said Ginny, 'of course you love Arnold very much.'

★

In bed that night he read a few pages of *Lord of the Flies*. He would have kept reading but Doreen came, told him he must go to sleep and turned out the light.

September

The following night he read a few more pages of the novel and again the night after and that was the pattern established. Thereafter he got a few pages read every night, not that he told anyone at school that he was racing ahead and would have *Lord of the Flies* finished long before they managed this feat in class. He might be a swot but he didn't want anyone thinking he was one.

He got in from school. A telegram was sitting on the kitchen table waiting for him when he got in. It was a square of coarse paper with white strips of paper stuck on it and on the strips was the message typed in capitals:

'Docked New York safe and sound. Love Mum'

A few days later a letter arrived from America:

Dear Ralph,

As we came in closer to New York all the passengers crowded out on deck to gawp, including yours truly of course. We were premature. What was on offer was mostly a lot of sea, choppy and grey and not very nice (like Brighton when we went there and it rained the whole weekend – remember?) and then very far away on the horizon, nothing more than a little smudge really, the city itself. It was pretty inconsequential at first and didn't seem like much but then we got closer and the blur gradually became defined. First I could see the skyline and then the buildings and finally, which really told me I'd arrived, the Statue of Liberty, which, strangely, I have to tell you, was a bit disappointing. It's this business of seeing in the flesh for the first time what you know so well from photographs and the sad fact is, after the photographs, the real thing just isn't so good somehow. Isn't that why they say you should never meet the film stars you admire? You're going to be disappointed.

The docking and tying up took an age (there was a tug involved, a marvellously trim vessel and not like the grimy tugs we're used to seeing on the river from our garden) but was rather wonderful – to get the huge ship to go precisely where it was supposed to go without any mishaps was achieved entirely by human beings making very precise judgments. It's amazing what talents people have.

Then I got off the boat and found, for a few moments, I could barely stand. My land legs had been replaced by sea legs. I was certain I'd topple and I had to actually sit down on one of my suitcases and wait for the gyroscopes inside my head to right themselves before I could stand up and go on. I've never known anything like it.

After I'd checked in to my hotel I went back out into the city. No plan at all, other than simply to gawp. My hotel was over on 53rd and I walked along to 5th and then headed off, going north. It was like being in a river only instead of water shoving down a channel it was cars and New York cabs with their distinctive yellow livery and people. People, people, people. Hurrying, hurrying, hurrying. All in a rush. None of them looking at each other. Hardly any of them talking to each other. Just rushing wherever they were going. To work I suppose. Extraordinary. A torrent. And I was like a cork bobbing along. At first I thought I'd be bashed about or even go under. But I got the hang of the flow and the intensity and the density of people and after a few minutes I was quite content I would survive without mishap. It's incredible how quickly one adjusts.

And now I was in the swing of things I could take in my environment and specifically the shops. And oh my lord. Huge windows. Incredible displays. The amount and quality of goods on display – overwhelming. There was one shop that particularly caught my eye. It sold kitchen stuff for hotels and restaurants. I had to stop and stare. Fabulous pans and skewers and knives and utensils as you'd expect. All lovely bright stainless steel. But then, most marvellous of all, the uniforms, especially the chef's whites, double-breasted jackets, houndstooth-patterned trousers, and the high hats, the toques blanches, so white and clean and glorious. I stared at them and I actually thought for a moment I would go in and buy one for you. Then I thought better of it. Really, if I got it, what would happen to it? It would sit in the kitchen in Falkland Road gathering dust and only get worn to a fancy dress party if they still happen anymore – they were a feature of my childhood but I sense they've died out – but once a year.

I'm going to sign off now. I'm writing this in the hotel lobby on their slightly yellow notepaper – I've been told technically it's lemon – and feeling a little woozy after pounding the streets and soaking up the sights and the sounds but I'm scheduled to meet an old friend for supper.

Love, Mum xx

★

The Friday afternoon of the second week of term Ralph entered number 88 by the side door after school. The kitchen was steamy and smelt of salt. An enormous gammon simmered in a huge pot on the stove. This was to clean the salt out before it went into the oven for roasting.

'Afternoon,' Doreen called without looking up.

She sat at the table stripping parsley leaves from their stalks for the white sauce she would make for the gammon. This was a task that required patience and dexterity and she excelled at it.

On the table beside her was a box filled with cabbages and potatoes with earth-covered skins, while under the table was tucked the delivery from the off-licence, including boxes of Babycham, crates of Guinness and Carling Black Label, bottles of Paddy whiskey and Martell brandy, half a dozen soda siphons and his treat, which Doreen had got in specially for him, a dark orange bottle of Tizer with a black stopper in the neck. It was a drink that normally he wasn't allowed because his mother thought it was bad for his teeth.

The MacGraws were having a poker evening the next night, which was Saturday, and he had agreed to help as he always did, with preparations and with the guests when they were there. Doreen had promised he would be well-rewarded for his services. Now, after he changed out of his uniform, his first job would be to unpack the alcohol and set up the bottles on the shelf that would act as a bar. On the night itself he would stand beside it and serve the guests.

★

On Saturday morning he peeled the potatoes and sliced the cabbages and then together with Doreen he made mounds of sandwiches with white shop bread and then wrapped these carefully in greaseproof paper to stop the bread from going stale. He would serve these around midnight. It would be his last job of the night.

★

He only had a few pages of *Lord of the Flies* to go. Doreen said she didn't need any help for a while, so he went to his room, stretched on his bed, opened the book and resumed reading, and he read on without stopping, right to the terrible end where the boys were chasing the hero, Ralph, along the beach, hoping to catch him and kill him. Fortunately, a passing battleship, having seen smoke – the island was on fire – had sent a landing party ashore and the commanding officer was there on the beach as the boys were about to close in. Ralph ran into him, literally, his harriers right behind – and so was saved. His pursuers, seeing the naval officer, stopped in their tracks and began to weep. The officer was embarrassed. He turned away. His ship, a cruiser, was moored in the distance, and he let his eyes rest on her and that was it. That was the end.

Ralph lifted his own eyes and stared out his bay window. In his mind's eye he saw the crying filthy schoolboys, the baffled officer in his immaculate white drill, the lovely warship anchored in the distance. And as he saw these he was filled up with the marvellous entranced feeling of pleasure that he always had when pictures from a book flooded his mind.

Then the sensation of blissful absorption and the pictures that went with it waned and the world rushed in. He saw Mrs Moody's Morris 1000 with its round roof parked at the kerb near their gate. He saw the roof tiles of the smaller, two-storey houses opposite glistening from a fine invisible fog. He saw a sliver of moon, so pale and thin he could easily believe it was a piece of paper cut out and laid down across a corner of the sky. He smelt the burnt sugar and cloves smell of the gammon Doreen had roasting in the oven.

'Ralph!' It was Doreen.

'Yeah.'

'Can you come?'

He got off his bed and went down.

As he came into the kitchen he registered the usual smell of gas. He saw the sandwiches in their greaseproof paper covers on the platters, the bottles he'd laid out on the shelf ready for the evening, Doreen at the stove. He went over. A vast pot of sliced cabbage stood at the back waiting to be boiled. She was stirring white sauce in a pan. The sauce gave off a buttery, floury smell.

'Ralph,' said Doreen. 'Can you do me a favour?'

'It depends.'

'Don't you start with "It depends,"' said Doreen. 'I haven't the time. I need a hand.'

'Absolutely. There you go.'

Ralph held out his right hand. It was a school joke. He thought it was good.

'It wasn't funny the first time, last year,' said Doreen, 'and it hasn't got funny since.'

'Devastating. What do you want me to do?'

'I need nutmeg,' said Doreen, 'for the cabbage. I thought we had some but we don't. Run down and ask Ginny.'

'Okey-doke,' he said.

He went out, walked up Falkland Road and turned through the Boscombes' gate. Clive's Vespa was parked against the hedge. Though he no longer lived there, Clive still kept it at Falkland Road because in White City he'd have had to keep it in the street where it was very likely to have had its mirrors snapped off and its tyres slashed by an angry Rocker who would have assumed its owner was a hated Mod.

Ralph stopped to look at it. It had a blue body, masses of glistening chrome trim and small wheels. It reminded Ralph of the horses in *King Arthur and his Knights of the Round Table* by Roger Lancelyn Green, one of his favourite books when he was younger: the scooter's blue bodywork resembled the barding horses wore, the seat with its rear bars was like the high-cantled saddle that held knights upright and stopped them from being knocked off, and the high poles that stuck up into the air at the back with pennants and rabbits' feet attached were the lances.

When he had lived at Falkland Road, Clive had ridden on his scooter to Television Centre in Shepherd's Bush for a while, dressed in a suit, an old-fashioned motorcycle helmet jammed on his head, the old leather suitcase that had belonged to his grandfather, a Lloyd's underwriter, stuffed with scripts and lashed to the back. His huge frame on the small machine had always struck Ralph as comic – a fact he had never shared with Benedict.

Nor would he or had he ever disclosed his other feelings connected to this machine, specifically to the Mods who typically rode about on scooters just like Clive's and their arch-enemies with whom they clashed violently, the

Greasers or Rockers, who rode motorbikes. These two might fascinate Benedict but they terrified Ralph, especially since he had seen three brutal fights with stomach-churning screaming and swollen faces and blood on the ground between Mods and Rockers over the preceding summer, in the park at the end of Falkland Road, on Putney High Street outside Woolworths, and on Wimbledon Common.

He hadn't been the only one to see these fights. There had been other people about and he had seen from their faces that they were clearly as frightened at what was happening and what they were seeing as he had been, and remembering these frightened onlookers now, as he stared at Clive's Vespa, he found himself again asking a question he had asked himself many times before: Why did Clive want to risk association with any of this by having a scooter which was so obviously connected with all this? He didn't understand it.

Ralph slipped down the passage, opened the side door and stepped into the Boscombes' kitchen. It was a long space stretching from front to back, divided by a partial partition, and it had not been modernised like theirs. He closed the door behind. In front of him there was a huge square dining table with odd chairs set round it. Ranged around the walls were old pine cupboards and an enormous Welsh dresser, all salvaged from old houses and stripped down to the wood by Clive, a What the Butler Saw viewing machine, and Clive's cider cask with a porcelain cup hanging by a wire handle from its wooden tap to catch any drips.

On the far side of the partition, he heard the tap running and he guessed Jeannie was in there. Jeannie was Ginny's help and she did all the cooking, cleaning and laundering. Her husband had been a carter at Young's brewery in Wandsworth and had been dead many years. It was her only son, Peter – a Mod with excellent contacts in the second-hand scooter market – who had sourced Clive's scooter before he went to prison for the glassing offence Benedict found so fascinating.

'Jeannie,' he called.

'That's me,' he heard from the other side of the partition.

She came out drying her hands on her apron. She was a huge, heavy woman with sovereign rings on her fingers, a sovereign on a necklace round her neck and huge hoop earrings dangling from her ears. She had a broad flat face, slightly yellow skin, huge moist brown eyes and big strong teeth.

'Well, Ralph,' said Jeannie. 'How are you my old china? Except you're not old and you're not china are you?'

This was how she always greeted him. He had no idea why.

'Hello, Jeannie,' he said.

'You keeping all right?'

'Yes, I think so.'

'Heard from your Mum?'

'Yeah. Got a telegram and a letter.'

'You must be missing her I'd say.'

'I don't know,' said Ralph.

Was he? He knew he had feelings but they were stored deep inside and the tap to let them out was closed tight. He believed that one day it could be loosened and then they could come out but he had no idea how or why this would happen, or even when. It was a mystery, the way his mind worked.

'Well, not yet,' he added, which was the truth.

'What can I do you for?' asked Jeannie.

'Have you any nutmeg?'

'Nutmeg?'

'Yes.'

'Nutmeg. What do you want nutmeg for? You're not going to smoke it, are you?'

'Ah, no,' said Ralph. What sort of a question was that? 'Doreen needs it. For cabbage.'

'Nutmeg for cabbage,' said Jeannie. 'I like white pepper and butter myself but what do I know? Let's see.'

Jeannie, despite her size, moved to the food cupboard with great speed and incredible lightness. This fleetness intrigued him and he always noticed it. She pulled the doors open. Inside the shelves were jammed with tins of Golden Syrup, molasses and baking powder, packets of flour, porridge, pasta, sugar and Bird's custard, sacks of lentils and pulses, bottles of vanilla essence, dozens of spice jars and all sorts of other things.

'Nutmeg,' she said. 'Now let's have a look.'

While he waited Ralph gazed at the shelves of the Welsh dresser. They were filled with Victorian plates, cups, beer bottles, tins, cartridge boxes, lamps and irons. Ginny and Clive had a huge collection. Then he looked at the walls crowded with railway signs, pub mirrors, religious prints, old-fashioned advertisements, World War One recruitment posters and a life-sized painting of a sash window through which a garden could be seen. Maud's husband, Arnold, had painted it at Art School before the war.

'Is Benedict about?' asked Ralph.

'Yeah,' said Jeannie. 'He's doing a bit of mudlarking with his father.'

Clive had recently bought a metal detector to search for metal at low tide on the Thames mud flats.

'Tell you what,' said Jeannie. 'Go and say hello to Benedict and by the time you get back I'll have found what you want.'

Ralph slipped round the partition into the back half of the kitchen. There was a door with a lot of glass at the rear. He opened it and went down three steps.

The Boscombes' garden sloped away from him. It was filled with crowded unruly beds, crooked old fruit trees and blackcurrant bushes. He walked to the bottom. There was a hut here where Clive had worked when he lived in Falkland Road and where he still came to write his scripts.

Ralph climbed up three metal steps onto the flood wall and stared out. He saw the black sticky mud flats littered with debris. Benedict and his father were in the distance. Benedict was short and stocky while his father was six foot five with a vast head and improbably wide shoulders. Benedict had the metal detector and was waving it backward and forward. It looked as if he were vacuuming.

Ralph waved but they didn't see him. He called. They didn't hear. He turned about and went down the slippery metal rungs of the ladder on the other side. The Boscombes' was the only house on Falkland Road with a ladder that went down to the Thames foreshore. It had been put in by the previous owner who had kept a boat moored at the end of the garden.

From the ladder's last rung Ralph jumped down onto the shingle strip that lay snug against the flood wall at the bottom. Then he ran along the band of loose stones that shifted and scrunched underfoot as he went until he drew level with Benedict and his father. He shouted and waved again. They heard him this time and looked up. Benedict passed the metal detector to his father and came over.

'What are you doing here?' asked Benedict.

'Getting something for Doreen.'

'Want to see what I found?'

Benedict drew something from his pocket and held his hand out.

In the centre of his palm was a dark metal frame a couple of inches wide with a bar across the middle.

'It's a shoe buckle,' he said. 'Clive says a drunk was on a boat and lost his shoe and the shoe sank into the mud and rotted and the buckle lay there till we found it. What about that?'

'You don't know that's what happened,' said Ralph. It annoyed him the way Benedict automatically accepted whatever his father said. 'For all you know the boat sank and the man with the shoe that came from, he drowned because he couldn't swim, and that's how come his shoe ended up in the mud. He was never drunk.'

'Maybe,' said Benedict. He didn't sound convinced.

'Hey, Benedict,' Clive shouted over the flats.

'I'm wanted,' said Benedict, smiling, happy. Whenever Clive paid him attention he was always like this. 'All right, see you Monday.' He turned towards his father. 'Coming, Clive,' Benedict shouted cheerfully.

He set off, splashing over the mud in his Wellingtons, sending spurts of black ooze flying upward with every step. Ralph watched. He wanted from his father what Benedict got from Clive but he also suspected, since there had been no contact for such a long time between him and Peter, this was never going to happen.

Ralph turned and ran back along the shingle, climbed up the ladder, jogged through the garden and went in by the rear door. Jeannie was at the sink, washing up.

'You're in luck,' she said.

'That you Ralph?' Ginny called from beyond the partition.

He went through to the front part. Ginny was standing at the food cupboard, tidying one of the packed shelves.

'Hello there,' said Ginny.

He went up to her. She wore a long dress and a headscarf round her head. It wasn't the kind of headscarf that Jeannie and other older women wore, the kind that protected hair from the rain and tied under the chin. Ginny's was bright red and tied at the back of her head. The only other women he knew who wore anything like this were the gypsy women who sold bunches of lavender house-to-house.

'On the hunt for nutmeg?'

'Yes,' said Ralph. 'For cabbage.'

'And the good news is, I found some.'

Ginny had grown up in a mansion in Marlow on the Thames but when she talked she affected to sound not as she had when she was growing up, but as the students in her WEA classes talked.

'It's not much, just half, but half's better than none.'

She held up half a brown nut with a flat side where it had been grated.

'Smell that,' she said.

She held the rough grated side under his nose. He sniffed.

'Oh yeah, nutmeg,' he said, as if he recognised it.

He didn't but he thought it would impress her if he pretended he did.

'"He's of the colour of the nutmeg,"' she began, speaking now not in her usual everyday voice but in her own authentic voice, the one that had caused her once to describe herself to him as a cut-price Fenella Fielding, though he didn't understand what she had meant, and that she only used when she spoke to her parents, or to certain people she felt at ease with, or when she recited from literature, as she was now, and which Ralph loved because it was deep and throaty and rich.

'That's the Duke of Orleans,' she said, 'who's just spoken, and the Dauphin replies, "And of the heat of the ginger. It is a beast for Perseus: he is pure air and fire; and the dull elements of earth and water never appear in him, but only in patient stillness while his rider mounts him: he is indeed a horse; and all other jades you may call beasts."'

She reverted to her everyday non-posh voice, 'Henry the fifth, act three, scene seven. Now you understand, Orleans and the Dauphin are speaking of a horse that is this colour.' She popped the hard brown nut into his hand. 'There you go, and don't be smoking it.'

First Jeannie and now Ginny. What was this obsession with smoking nutmeg? Where did it come from?

'Can you smoke it?' he asked.

'Malcolm X smoked it in prison,' she said.

He made a puzzled expression.

'Don't you know who he is?'

'No.'

'Malcolm X is the most important political leader in the United States if not the world at this moment: he is the only one who is standing up for the oppressed black minority but don't let a policeman hear you saying that.'

'Malcolm X?'

'Yes.'

'Is he really called X?'

'Yes.'

'Like you're …'

'Boscombe, yes.'

'So instead of Ralph Goswell, I could be Ralph Y?'

'Oh no, don't you muck about with your name. Just leave it alone.'

It was Jeannie, carrying a dish in from the back kitchen and wiping it as she went.

'Malcolm X,' she said, 'ridiculous. Everyone's mucking about with their names nowadays and I don't like it. I'm Jeannie Russell and that's done me since I was sixteen, and you're Ralph Goswell and that'll do you nicely till they bury you. Mark my words.'

'What was your name before you married?' he asked. He felt pleased to have thought of that.

'Winters. I was Jeannie Winters and then I got married to the bane of my bloody life, may the Lord have mercy on him, my lord and bloody master, and I became Russell. I've loved being Russell but you know what? If I could have had the name Russell without the husband that came with it, that would have been just perfect. But, that wasn't to be. You take the name, you get the man.'

He left, the nutmeg held tight in his hand. Once he was out on the pavement, he began to run. He ran all the way back, threw the side door open and flew in.

'I was beginning to wonder where you were,' said Doreen from the stove.

She slid the roasting dish with the huge gammon backward onto the oven shelf and as she did he heard the fat in the bottom spitting. She closed the oven door and straightened up. He handed her the nutmeg.

'Bit small,' she said.

'All Ginny had.'

'It'll do. It's enough. Thank you.'

Doreen smiled. Ralph thought she had a lovely smile. He smelt his hand. It smelt of nutmeg.

'Strong stuff, nutmeg,' he said.

Doreen asked him to polish the glasses and gave him the special cloth for the job. He sat, took a glass, turned it and then held it up to the electric light to check it was smear free. At the other end of the table Doreen stood polishing cutlery and then folding paper napkins round each knife, fork and spoon set. He heard footsteps in the passage, turned and saw a shape through the frosted panes in the side door. He knew who it was. The door opened.

'Greetings,' said Clive.

He ducked in and then straightened up and assumed his full height. His face was unusually broad and he had incredibly bushy sideburns that grew all the way down to his jaw. He'd changed since Ralph saw him on the mud flats. He was wearing a short reefer jacket with a couple of badges on the lapels and underneath this a dark suit, a white shirt and a thin tie. Clive was clearly going out.

'Hello, Doreen,' he said. 'Young Ralph.' He smiled at Doreen. 'Look what Ginny found.'

He held up an entire nutmeg.

'Oh excellent,' said Doreen.

'Oh lovely …' Clive sniffed the air. He put the nutmeg on the table. 'Roast ham. Smells great.'

'There'll be plenty if you want to stay,' said Doreen.

Ralph felt a throb of anxiety. What was Doreen thinking? Clive and her friends together. Neither would know how to talk to one another. It was an appalling idea.

'Well Doreen, thank you. Perhaps another time.' Clive beamed. His smile when he was happy was marvellous. Ralph felt a surge of relief. 'Tonight I'm going out,' said Clive.

'Somewhere special?' asked Doreen.

'The Gay Hussar in Soho.'

'Posh?' asked Doreen. 'Or just expensive?'

'Not too expensive, I hope,' said Clive. 'I'm actually going …' He hesitated. 'Why am I hesitating? I don't belief in dissembling or repressing. I believe in the truth, I believe that it's the truth that sets you free. So I should practise what I believe, shouldn't I?'

He looked directly at Doreen.

'If you say so,' she said.

'I'm going on a date,' he said. 'Yes. Someone's set us up. She's called Yvonne. Never met her before. She's from the

Beeb. She's in radio, so we won't be stuck for conversation. And, ah, all I know is she has lovely long blonde hair and will be wearing a wool coat, very bright, patches sewn together. And I have to say I'm quite excited. So wish me luck.'

'Right,' said Doreen. 'Good luck.' The words may have been positive but to Ralph's ears she sounded doubtful, not that their visitor seemed to notice that.

'Thanks,' said Clive and he smiled again.

He backed out of the kitchen, swung the side door shut and stomped away up the passage.

'Well, I've heard it all now,' said Doreen. 'Isn't he and Ginny still married, yet he's going on a date?'

'I think so,' said Ralph.

He gave the glass he was holding another wipe. The glass squeaked.

'You might be desperate, but why would you want to advertise what you're doing like he just did?' said Doreen.

She glanced at the tiny watch on her wrist.

'Where's that husband of mine? He'd better not be going on a date tonight I can tell you.'

★

Tom returned from work a bit later wearing mud-caked overalls and a donkey jacket. He went up to the bathroom and washed and then down to the basement and changed and when he returned to the kitchen he was in a suit and tie and he'd wet his hair and slicked it back and this had the double effect, Ralph thought, of making his face seem more pointed and his burnt skin seem shinier.

★

Ralph was sitting quietly at the kitchen table. There were different chairs around it – brought from all over the house – as well as its own matching ones. The guests appeared about seven and Ralph served them drinks from the shelf. First to come were two couples, the Maguires and the Quinns, then Mary Kinahan and Deidre Flynn who were sharing a room in Colliers Wood, and then another married couple, the Yeatses. Ralph had met them all at one time or another at these Saturday night sessions. Last to stride in though was someone he hadn't met before. He was a labourer in Tom's gang, from Monaghan, and he was unlike all the other men there. They wore their hair short but his was long, very long, and covered not only his collar but his shoulders as well. They were clean-shaven but he had a moustache that not only covered his top lip but drooped down on either side of his mouth. They wore tightly fitting suits, white shirts and narrow ties but he wore a loose-fitting brown suit, a cream waistcoat, a black shirt and a red knitted woollen tie. Ralph didn't know what he thought about this. On the one hand he valued conformity. He liked convention. The out-of-the-ordinary troubled him. On the other hand, he could tell this man had something the others hadn't got. He compelled attention. Tom and the other men, of course, kept their interest hidden behind an attitude of slightly mocking cool appraisal but the women made no attempt to hide their feelings. They gathered around him and admiringly praised his clothes, his hair, his moustache.

'I wonder what a kiss from a man with such a moustache would be like?' said Mary Kinahan.

'Dynamite,' said Deirdre Flynn.

'Is right,' he said.

Mary asked if she and Deirdre might be allowed to touch his hair.

'Be my guest,' he said, and they both stroked his hair at the back where it flowed over his shoulders.

A few minutes later the visitor came over to Ralph who was sitting at the table again.

'And who might you be, young fellow?'

'Ralph,' he said.

The visitor put out a hand and Ralph shook it. The hand was large and, to touch, warm and rough.

'Kit,' he said. 'Kit McCreesh.'

'You weren't always Kit though were you?' said Mary Kinahan. 'You were Kevin before, weren't you?'

Kit released Ralph's hand and turned to Mary Kinahan. 'That's right,' he said. His tone was calm and from the way he spoke it didn't seem to Ralph that he minded this being brought up in the least. 'Yes, I was Kevin. But why'd you want to be a Kevin? I mean, there's dozens, probably hundreds of Kevins. Why'd I want to be one of them? Kit on the other hand – how many Kits do you know?'

'Just the one.'

'And you won't forget him,' he said. 'You won't forget this Kit.'

He took a box out of his pocket and removed a knobbly brown cheroot.

'You don't smoke them?' Ralph heard someone say. 'Oh Christ, they're disgusting.'

'The cheroot is the epitome of sophistication,' Kit said.

Kit lit the end of the cheroot, inhaled and exhaled. Ralph smelt the heavy dark bitter smoke.

'Where does he get it from?' said Doreen. 'Gas you are Kit McCreesh, pure gas.'

★

The gammon came out of the oven and went on a wooden chopping board. Tom rubbed the carving knife up and down a honing iron and began to cut the meat. He worked quickly. The meat when it fell sideways was dark red like a human tongue and the tiny crust of fat on the edge was pale white like icing.

Once he'd carved, Tom forked the sliced meat onto the plates. Each visitor carried their plate to Doreen and she added cabbage, mashed, boiled and roast potatoes, and then ladled white sauce mixed with chopped parsley over everything. Each visitor then took a knife and fork and a paper serviette and sat at the kitchen table and began to eat.

Ralph replenished everyone's drinks and then got his dinner and a glass of chilled Tizer. The dinner eaten and the plates put to soak in the sink – he would wash, dry and put them away later – he and Doreen dished up apple pie with slices of Wall's vanilla ice cream cut from a block, along with cups of dark sweet tea. Then the guests went down to the front basement room underneath Ralph's bedroom, each carrying a chair with them, and sat at the card table. It was covered with an oilcloth and dotted with coaster mats with pictures of the Ring of Kerry on them and half-a-dozen clean glass ashtrays. Two new decks of Waddington's cards were unwrapped and cut and the visitors began their game.

While they played, Ralph replenished their drinks, washed their glasses, emptied their ashtrays, made more tea and passed the cups and then carried round the milk and sugar so each guest could sweeten and milk their tea exactly as they desired with the exception of Kit who drank his tea black. Around midnight Doreen asked him to get the sandwiches. He fetched little plates from the kitchen and the sandwich platters and passed them out. He washed and dried everyone's teacup and made more tea in the teapot in the kitchen upstairs and carried it down and poured it into the washed cups and then made another circuit and gave everyone milk and sugar except Kit of course.

And throughout, the visitors went on playing cards, placing stakes, losing, winning, joking, shouting, laughing, all without breaking from the game except when they had to use the toilet or when they turned to Ralph and gave him money or told him what a good lad he was, how capable he was, and how far he would go in the world.

★

About midnight he sat on the step at the bottom of the stairs that connected the basement to the ground floor. He looked at the table and the eleven people seated round it. Kit was cool and calm. He still had his jacket on. The other ten were hot and red-faced. All the men had taken off their jackets and hung them over the backs of their seats and loosened their ties. All the women had shrugged off their cardigans to expose their white or freckled arms and taken off their shoes to reveal their stockinged feet. Everyone, apart from Kit, had drunk a lot. Everyone, apart from Kit, was happy and warm and generous as well as raucous and boisterous and apt to repeat themselves. Everyone, apart from Kit, had bright eyes and was talking too loudly and making big imprecise gestures when they moved their arms and were unsteady when they got up to use the toilet. It was always like that at this point in these evenings. Doreen called it the sloppy time.

He yawned.

'Off to bed now, Buster.' It was Doreen.

He was happy to go. He stood. Everyone called, 'Good night.' Everyone thanked him for all he had done.

'Don't spend all your money in one go,' Mary Kinahan shouted.

She had changed the most over the evening. She was the noisiest out of everyone.

He went up to the kitchen. The shillings, florins, and two-and-sixes that the visitors had given him at various points during the evening were on the table. He counted them up. Nineteen shillings and sixpence. Another six-pence and he'd have a quid. It was a good haul. Maybe even the best ever.

He filled a glass with water and carried everything to his bedroom. He put the money in the H. Upmann cigar box in which he kept his money. He decided not to bother brushing his teeth. He put on his pyjamas, got into bed and turned out the light beside his bed.

Through the floor came the voices of poker players, bursts of laughter, and queer bangs as cards were slapped on the oilcloth. It was marvellous hearing everything coming from below while drifting off. He was very tired. He closed his eyes. He fell asleep.

★

He woke. It was still dark. He couldn't tell how long he had been asleep. Someone was shouting and laughing. It was a woman he thought. He heard another woman talk-ing back. He thought perhaps it was Doreen. Someone was drumming on the table. More shouting and more laughter unlike anything he'd ever heard coming from downstairs before. What were they doing? He felt curi-ous. Deeply, hungrily curious. They thought he was asleep. But he was light-footed. He was nimble. He could creep along the hall and see what was happening down there and not be seen.

He slid out of bed. He heard a woman shout, 'Pay the forfeit.' He slipped along the front hall and down the four steps at the back. More laughter from downstairs and the clicking of fingers. A different woman shouting, 'Come on, come on,' and Doreen shouting back, 'The best things in life are worth waiting for.'

He lay on the linoleum-covered floor and peered down the basement stairs. Because of the angle he could see only part of the scene. The only person he could see properly was Kit. He was sitting on his chair with his back to the wall, looking up and smoking. Doreen was standing on the table in her stockinged feet. He knew it was Doreen even though he only saw her from the waist down. Doreen's bare legs at the top of her stockings were red at the back because she'd been sitting down so long, he guessed. A hand was trying to tug her knickers down over the straps of her suspender belt. It was Mary Kinahan's hand, he thought. Doreen batted her hand away. He heard Doreen laugh. Mary sank back onto her seat.

'That'll teach you,' someone shouted. 'Don't mess with Doreen.'

More laughter. Doreen shrugged her knickers down over her stockings and kicked them away. They hit the wall behind Kit's head and landed on his shoulder. Kit applauded. The others applauded. Doreen turned slowly on the spot. She clicked her fingers. She was triumphant. Kit reached up to his shoulder to get the knickers and as he did he turned his head slightly in the direction of the stairs, and Ralph, knowing he might be seen, rolled quickly sideways. Then he was straight up onto his feet, up the four steps, along the front hall, into his bedroom, and under his covers. Downstairs, he could hear someone talking. There was a thread of anxiety in their voice. He heard a chair scraping back, someone standing, someone on the basement stairs, and a man's voice coming from the back of the house.

'Hello. Anyone there?'

He lay very still with his eyes closed. Footsteps on the four steps at the back and then coming up the front hall towards his bedroom door. He expected the hall light to click on. Instead he heard his door swing open. He heard a match strike.

'Ralph?' It was Kit at his door. 'Are you asleep?'

He breathed slowly and evenly as if he were asleep. He heard the sound of Kit blowing out the match and closing his door. Then the sound of Kit going back down the front hall, descending the four stairs, and going down the basement stairs.

His stomach trembled. His thighs felt weak. The middle of his being went on churning and roiling. Beads of wet appeared on his forehead. He was aware vaguely of the facts of life, of men and women alone in bed together. But all his knowledge up until now had been theoretical. Now, for the first time in his twelve years on earth, he had seen grown-ups with his own eyes doing something that he knew was connected with the mysterious business of love. Doreen had stood on the table and they'd all looked at her, especially Kit.

★

He fell asleep again. His sleep was fitful. At some point he heard visitors slipping out by the side door, moving up the passage and across the garden, and, amidst laughter and farewells, piling into mini-cabs. After that he heard the side door closing and the bolts being drawn, and Tom and Doreen talking in the kitchen.

Later, much later, he sensed the light coming round the edge of the curtains and he heard Doreen going out by the front door, and the clack of her heels as she crossed the garden, went out the gate and started along Falkland Road. She was going to first Mass.

He went back to sleep and woke when he heard the key going into the Yale lock and the front door opening. Doreen was back. He hoped she would pass by his room and go down to the kitchen but he also knew she wasn't going to do that. Her custom when she got back from Mass was always to come in and rouse him. Sure enough she opened the door, the door Kit had pulled to the night before. He smelt the cigarette smoke and rancid beer smell that always filled the house after one of the Saturday night card sessions.

'Morning, Buster.'

He pretended to wriggle as if he were waking from a deep sleep and opened his eyes.

'Oh hello,' he said, in a mock-sluggish voice.

She was wearing lipstick and mascara and she had her Mass outfit on, coat, dress, shoes, hat, gloves – all black. Her eyes were smaller and her skin looked paler than usual. She had an Irish newspaper under one arm.

'I'm going to make a fry. Come on, upski.'

When she was cheerful Doreen added 'ski' to some of her words to make a nonsense language. She wouldn't be so cheerful if she thought he had seen what he saw. A great sense of relief surged over him.

'Yesski,' he said.

'Open your windows, will you, when you're up?'

'Yes,' he said.

'Fried or scrambled eggski?'

'Friedski.'

She went along the hall and down the back stairs. He heard her shouting down into the basement, 'Tom. Wakey-wakey. I got your paper.'

He sat up in his bed, swung his feet round and put them on the floor and gave out a long slow yawn.

Dear Ralph,

Train from Grand Central to Rye Station. I was told I'd be met by a chauffeur. There he was. Ancient man, heavy accent. His name was Charles. And there was his car. Huge. Black. Vulgar. And when I say vulgar, I mean vulgar. I got in. The rear was cavernous, hideous. 'What kind of a car is this?' I asked. Charles didn't understand. Yes, it's really true, the English and the Americans really are two peoples separated by a common language. Eventually Charles grasped what I was asking and he answered. Now it was my turn to be mystified. It took him four tries before I had it. I was in a Lincoln Continental Sedan. 'Like your Rolls-Royce but American made, ma'am,' he added. Ma'am. That's what they say here to show respect but that makes me think I'm a dried-up old schoolmistress who doesn't like children. I am planning to have a badge made (they're badge mad the Americans) with 'Please don't call me ma'am'.

We purred through the countryside for half an hour and got to the Old Partridge Estate – to use its full name. Gates, trees, gravel, an American colonial mansion (although it may not actually be as old as it looks, it may be a nineteenth-century copy), residence of my employers, Mr and Mrs Michael Scobie-Jeffries, whose money comes from the grandfather (his) having been the biggest manufacturer of tools in the world. But we didn't stop at the house. We went around it and on, past fields, woods, a lake (substantial, jetties, diving platforms, boat houses, boats, et cetera, these people are seriously rich) until eventually we came to a little cottage, small, single-storey, more a cabin actually, very Hansel and Gretel, surrounded by woods, my home until next year. Charlie heaved my bags in. Inside, I found a nice sitting room with a fireplace and American rustic furniture and chintzy curtains, a bedroom with more of the same, a kitchen, more up to date, big stainless steel stove, a breakfast counter, stools, a fridge so big I could probably live in it, and a bathroom with a huge white bath and robust American plumbing (not like ours, no shaking pipes here) – all in all, a little home that is and will be perfect for my needs. Charlie went off promising to return to whisk me up to the house for dinner with my employers. I didn't unpack but hurried out into the woods behind, anxious to see and to smell and to experience this world, this new world that I had found myself in for the first time in my life, ever. And I was not disappointed. Out there, in the woods, I found different trees to what I am used to, different light, different birdsong, different everything. Oh yes, or do I mean no, this was not England; this was unmistakably the New World.

I went back to unpack and found while I had been out that a small bird, I didn't recognise the species (I really must improve my bird identifying skills), had got in down the chimney and was sitting, looking a bit stunned, on the hearth. I went to the kitchen to find a tea towel to catch it with and when I came back it was up on the mantelpiece. I tried to catch it there but it eluded me and flew up to the curtain pelmet and thereafter led me a merry dance. Eventually, I opened all the doors and the windows and – get this – it slowly walked itself out. Through the front door.

When I told the story at dinner to Mr and Mrs MSJ (as they are universally known as I had just discovered) they said that the bird (a finch, they told me) was once a pet of the previous occupier of the cottage (he worked in the estate stables) and when he left he set it free; but of course, having been used to human company it has a habit of wandering into the cottage. They said it was a symbol of good luck it was there to meet me on my first day. Dinner was rather dull and stodgy (prawn cocktail, big steaks, potato dauphinoise, several types of ice cream). Tomorrow I move into my office and take a look at the land, virgin ground as of now, at the back of the estate where I am to establish a kitchen garden, an orchard, a maze and all sorts of other delights. There's ten acres to transform. A huge project. We start hiring labourers next week.

Love, Mum xx

★

Their bus stop in Lark Hill was beside the community centre, the parade with the shops and the doctor's surgery. When the boys arrived they found their bus waiting, its engine idling.

The conductress was on the platform at the back. She was often on their route. Her hair was tucked under her hat though several wisps had come free. Her face was hot and red. She wore a jacket over her white blouse and a straight skirt. A small brown suitcase full of rolls of blank paper, levers and keys lay open at her feet while her ticket machine was hanging from her neck with its lid up and mechanism exposed.

'Either of you mechanical?' she asked.

She was trying to move a handle but it wouldn't budge.

'Not really,' Benedict said.

'Pity.'

'Does it need oil?' Ralph asked.

'Yeah, maybe. Dunno.'

She yanked the cord vigorously and the bell rang in the driver's cab.

'Come here, Roy,' she shouted down the bus. 'This ticket machine is leading me a merry dance.'

Roy, the driver, opened his door and climbed out and began to make his way along the side. Ralph saw him through the downstairs side windows making his way along the outside of the bus, a small old man in shirt sleeves, smoking.

'Can we get on?' Benedict asked the conductress.

'Or we can wait,' said Ralph. 'If you prefer.'

He wanted to watch and listen.

'No, hop aboard,' she said.

Ralph and Benedict got onto the platform and climbed the narrow twisting stairs to the upper deck. It stank of tobacco. There were butts and old tickets all over the filthy floor. They could hear banging below as Roy hammered at the ticket machine.

'Let's see if today's our lucky day,' said Benedict.

They grabbed the back seat tucked behind the stairs – there was a knack but they had done it so many times they were experts at this – and wrenched it away. The well underneath was a dusty grimy oblong. They saw discarded bus tickets with serrated edges and smeared blue writing, an empty Park Drive packet for five cigarettes, a page torn from a magazine of a naked blonde holding a beach ball, and, lying right at the back, two big pennies and a brass thrupenny bit that had fallen from some hapless passenger's pocket, as often happened.

'You take the pennies,' said Benedict.

'And leave you the thruppence?' said Ralph. 'I don't think so.' He scooped up the money. 'I'll be banker. We'll buy five pennies worth of Black Jacks and divide them.'

They slotted the seat back into its housing and went and sat at the front on the right directly over the driver's cab – the best seats on the bus in their opinion.

'Come on,' said Benedict. '*Show me the way to go home, I'm tired and I want to go to bed,*' he sang, quoting a song they'd both heard at a children's Saturday morning cinema matinee.

Ralph looked out at the nearest tower block. On a balcony a woman was shaking a blanket. He heard girls racing up the stairs and along the aisle and then there they were in the seat directly across from them. He took a quick side-ways glance. They were teenagers, fifteen or sixteen, not in uniform. He heard a kerfuffle behind. It sounded like someone at the back seat. He turned and looked. He was right. The back seat was off and a man was rummaging in the well. The man wore a brown hat and a brown raincoat. Ralph knew him well. He was often on the upper deck at this time. He had a habit of staring at him and Benedict and once or twice he'd said things, nasty things, and they hadn't liked what they'd heard. It had been embarrassing. Ralph turned back.

'Red alert,' he said. 'Dennis the menace.' This was their nickname for him.

The bell rang. The bus pulled away. Ralph was sure Dennis had returned the back seat to its housing and was now sitting and staring at them. The nerves and flesh of his back felt vulnerable and sensitive because he knew he was being watched, but other than going downstairs, which they weren't going to do, there was no way to escape either the man or this feeling.

The conductress came, took everyone's fares, issued tickets, left. Another stop. More passengers. The bell again. One of the girls across the aisle lit a cigarette and shared it with the other girl. The smoke was blue.

A third stop, more passengers, the bell again, but nobody came up to the top deck. It was still just them and the girls and Dennis.

Ralph heard the sound of someone settling in the seat directly behind, then the rustle as the person leant for-ward, and then Dennis had his head right between him and Benedict.

'Hello, boys,' said Dennis. 'Are we well today?'

Ralph felt his mouth dry. Deep inside himself he felt the tightening that came when he was frightened.

'Nice day at school?' asked Dennis. 'I didn't really like school myself. Didn't see the point. Didn't like the rules. And I didn't like all them bossy women that were in charge, did I? Don't like bossy women. Bet you boys don't like them either. Am I right? You don't like them bossy women? You going to answer my question? Or are you going to sit there like shop dummies. Are you shop dummies? I don't think you are. I think you're two full-blooded youngsters on the cusp of manhood. That's what I think you two lovely lads are. Two full-flooded … What do I mean full-flooded? Two full-blooded youngsters on the cusp of manhood. And seeing as what you are, I've got something to show you.'

Dennis pushed his arm between them. In his hand he had the page from the magazine that had been under the back seat and what he was showing them was not what they'd already seen but the reverse – the same woman, no beach ball, on a towel, her legs wide. Ralph's face went hot and red. He stared at the road ahead, the cars coming at them, the buildings on either side, the people on the pavements.

'What about that eh? She making you hard? You know what it is to be hard don't you? Of course you do. You're at the age it starts. You often wake up in the night or in the early morning, don't you, and find your cock absolutely rigid, like a rod of steel, don't you? Has anyone told you why you go rigid? I doubt those bossy women at school have. Of course they haven't. They hate men, don't they? And why's that? Cos men men don't pay them attention, do they? Well, why would they? They're bossy women and, as we've established, men don't like bossy women.'

Ralph was vaguely aware of the girls staring across the aisle at them.

'What are you looking at?' Dennis screamed across the aisle. 'Why don't you fuck off?'

He heard the girls bolting down the aisle and jumping down the steps two at a time.

'Nosy parkers. Good riddance,' Dennis shouted after them. His head came back between their shoulders. 'Now, where was I? Oh yes. Young men, like you, you mustn't start life all ignorant like poor old me because the bossy women haven't told you what's what. You need to be told what to do with them lovely hard cocks of yours. You see this picture. Hey, boys, look at the picture. Look at her. See her cunt? See it? Yes. That's where you stick your cock, in her cunt …'

'Oi!' It was the conductress at the top of the stairs. 'You, get off, now! Or I press the bell and I will press the bell and I'll get Roy up and he'll put you off and I tell you he won't be gentle about it.'

'There, another bossy woman,' said Dennis. 'The whole world is run by them.' Dennis folded the photograph from the magazine and stood. 'Bossy bloody cunts. They run the world.'

'Come on, come on,' shouted the conductress, 'you're getting off and you can count yourself lucky I haven't called the police. I know what you're up to and it's filthy, disgusting. Those boys could be your grandchildren.'

Ralph turned and looked back. He saw Dennis's brown back descending the stairs, the conductress waving at him and Benedict, then turning and following Dennis down the stairs. The bus stopped. Ralph rushed across to the window on the pavement side and looked out and back. He saw Dennis on the pavement. He had his handkerchief out and he was blowing his nose.

'He's off,' said Ralph. 'Hooray, hooray.'

Two stops later the bus stopped near a huge secondary school and the upper deck was soon filled with its pupils, boys and girls in maroon blazers.

'This is what Dennis dreams of I'd say,' said Benedict. 'A whole busload of school children.'

'Are you going to tell your Mum?'

'Are you going to tell Doreen?'

'Don't be stupid,' said Ralph. 'Of course not.'

The maroon uniforms were shouting and jeering at one another. The noise they made was incredible. Benedict leaned close and spoke into his ear, confidentially.

'I think Clive has met someone,' said Benedict, slowly and bleakly.

'A girlfriend?' asked Ralph carefully.

'Dunno if she's a girlfriend exactly,' said Benedict, 'but she's someone he's met on a date.'

Ralph remembered when Clive dropped the nutmeg over. Was this girlfriend the woman he met that evening in the Gay Hussar?

'Mum said I'm to prepare myself,' said Benedict.

The bus trundled on. The maroon uniforms screeched. Ralph and Benedict sat in silence. The noise around them made their not talking seem all right. As they sat, Ralph thought about what he'd just been told. There was something about the way that grown-ups organised their affections that he found both terrifying and baffling.

Twenty minutes later the bus stopped at the depot at Putney Underground Station. Ralph and Benedict stood and followed the other passengers down the aisle of the upper deck to the stairs. When they eventually got to the bottom they found the conductress on the platform reading numbers off her ticket machine and writing them in a book.

'That bloke who was bothering you,' she said, 'he's definitely ...' she touched the pencil stub she was using to her right temple '... and if it happens again, stamp on the floor, three times, I'll hear, or ring the bell, ding, ding, ding and

Roy'll stop. He's not a big bloke Roy but he's more than a match for that bloke.'

They left the bus, bought five pennies worth of Black Jacks at the kiosk, climbed the steps to the footbridge, and began to amble across, stuffing the chews into their mouths as they went and throwing the wrappers into the river.

Once they had eaten the Black Jacks, they dumped their satchels, scrambled up the fence and stared down at the Thames flowing far below.

'Bombs away,' Benedict shouted and spat.

His spit was a deep black from the chews. Ralph watched Benedict's globule curve forward, lose trajectory and start to fall. Ralph curled his tongue, gathered saliva at the back of his mouth and launched his own ball of spit. It went forward and then plummeted. He watched it until eventually it dropped out of sight.

They picked up their bags and went on.

When they got to Benedict's gate his friend said, 'See you tomorrow.'

Ralph said, 'Unless I see you first.'

Benedict went through his gate. Ralph walked on. He thought about Doreen at home in the house. As soon as he got in she'd be off, talking about whatever came into her head and her words would put him into a kind of trance and his anxieties would vanish and he would forget everything. The bus and Dennis and what happened would not matter.

Ralph passed Florian Street, a small little street on his right with Pritchard's the newsagents at the top. He wondered what was for supper. Would he do his homework before? All depended on what was on the box. Then Ralph remembered. *The Avengers*, his favourite programme, was on later. He'd have to do his homework first. Definitely. Everything must be done before his favourite programme started.

He'd just come to the end of this thought when he saw movement up ahead. He was some way away from his house but if he wasn't mistaken it was in their front garden. There was someone there. And now that someone was coming out their gate. And it wasn't a someone anymore. It was a man. The man didn't see him. He turned left and began to hurry up Falkland Road away from him. He had an incredible stride. He had hair as well. Long hair. Hair that lifted from his collar and shoulders and floated behind as he hurried off. Ralph hadn't recognised the person at first but now he saw the hair he knew who it was. Oh yes. The man who he could see hurtling away from their house was Kit McCreesh.

He went the gate and down to the side door. He heard the kettle whistling inside. He stepped in. Doreen was at the stove turning the knob that controlled the burner. As the gas stopped there was a pop.

'Oh hello,' she said, lifting the kettle from the hob.

She was in her dressing gown and her hair was astray.

'I wasn't feeling very well,' she said. 'I must have got a bug. I had to lie down. Do you want a cup of tea?'

'No thanks.'

He looked at Doreen's face. Her eyes were shining. Her skin glowed. Her lips seemed fatter than he remembered, though her two small white front teeth still showed between them. She didn't look ill. She looked happy, he thought, radiant.

'I think I'll have a bath after my cuppa,' she said. 'That'll get me right.'

★

Homework. Sometimes he worked at the kitchen table. Sometimes at the desk in his room. This evening it was the desk. Banging pipes overhead. Doreen's bath emptying.

Then clattering in the kitchen as she started dinner. Tom's boots outside as he crossed the front garden and went down the passage. The side door banging. He had a way of closing the door very hard. Doreen's voice, raised. She was telling her husband to close the door more gently as she did every evening when he came home. More pipe-banging overhead. Tom rinsing himself in the bath. Doreen calling him to dinner. He put the lid on his fountain pen and went down.

As he came into the kitchen, Ralph smelt lamb chops and saw that the walls were drenched with steam from the potatoes and peas. There was a smell of potato and pea as well. The side door was ajar to let the heat out.

'Call Tom up,' she said.

He went back to the top of the basement stairs.

'Tom,' he called down. 'Dinner.'

He went back into the kitchen and sat at his place. Doreen was at the sink rinsing a pan. He picked up his knife and fork and cut a potato in half, skewered one of the steaming halves, blew on it and put it in his mouth. It was hot and he panted hard so it wouldn't burn his tongue. Tom came in and sat.

'Anything strange?' Doreen said.

'McCreesh bunked off at lunchtime for a pint and didn't come back.' Tom picked up his knife and fork. 'What was he thinking?'

Ralph felt his heart speed up.

'You can't just walk out, not when you're a team like we are, sure you can't, can you, Ralph?' asked Tom.

'No,' he said.

Ralph began trimming the fat off the side of a chop. He didn't like the fat because it gave him horrible burps that tasted of lamb grease.

'I thought he was a good worker,' said Doreen. She sat at her place.

'So did I,' said Tom. 'But this afternoon he just vanished.'

Doreen took a blob of butter from the dish in the middle of the table and dropped it on her potatoes.

'And how are you, young Master Ralph?' asked Tom.

'I'm all right,' he said.

He hoped he sounded quiet and nonchalant but inside he was fizzing on account of what he'd heard. Neither knew he'd seen Kit earlier.

'Just all right?' said Tom.

'Well you know how it is,' Ralph said. 'School, school, school. Not much to write home about.'

'No I don't,' said Tom. 'I hated school. Couldn't wait to get out. But you want my advice? Stick with it or you'll end like yours truly here, digging holes in the London ground.'

Ralph kept his eyes down and focused on his food. He would eat slowly and listen. And then, when he had finished, instead of rushing off to the television in the River room to watch *The Avengers* as he normally would, he would stay and listen some more.

October

The Boscombes' kitchen, the front part. Jeannie was at the table peeling potatoes. Ginny was delving in her purse. She wore the dress from the souk in Marrakesh.

'That's the money exactly,' said Ginny.

She handed the change for two tickets for the children's Saturday morning cinema matinee to Benedict.

'What about something for a lolly?' asked Benedict.

'Not today,' said Ginny. 'There's Jeannie's shepherd's pie for lunch and we don't want you spoiling your appetite, do we, Jeannie?'

'Don't drag me into this,' said Jeannie quietly.

'Timothy's bringing someone for lunch,' she said.

Timothy was a friend of Ginny's, a journalist. Ginny revered him as a truth-teller and a radical but he could also be difficult and cruel. He'd lost his left hand and had a stainless steel claw that Ralph found impossible not to stare at.

'So don't drag your feet after you come out of the cinema. I want you back here by one o'clock sharp.'

'You can be sure we'll be back unless we aren't,' said Benedict. 'In which case you'll know we've run away.'

'And you can drop that tone while you're at it.'

Ralph hoped her mood would have improved by the time they returned.

★

The whole of the auditorium of the Odeon Cinema on Putney High Street was filled with noisy children. Ralph stared forward at the rich red velvet curtains and the small stage that jutted out in front. The house lights faded, the stage lights came on and a heavy man in a suit ran out.

'Ho, ho, ho,' he shouted, 'it's yo-yo time, boys and girls.'

He pulled a string out of his pocket and began yo-yoing the attached spool up and down its length. Next he began to move the yo-yo through the air and round his body. Then he added a second, a third and finally a fourth yo-yo to the display, all of which he kept going at the same time. After a blizzard of tricks that lasted, Ralph guessed, ten or fifteen minutes, the demonstrator ended by releasing his yo-yos into the air one after the other and catching them in turn in his jacket pockets. Every child in the auditorium began to clap. It had been impressive. The man bowed, ran off and came back with a box full of yo-yos that he proceeded to toss into the auditorium. Ralph and Benedict made a few attempts to catch one but they were unlucky. All the yo-yos passed over their heads. They were too close to the front.

The demonstrator left the stage. A tremendous ripple of organ music boomed out and from somewhere under the stage a huge gold organ began to rise slowly while simultaneously the velvet curtains opened to reveal the white screen that the films were shown on. The organ man wore a dinner jacket and a bow tie like someone in an old black and white film. He spoke into a microphone, his voice coming over the PA system and filling the cinema.

'"Happy Days Are Here Again,"' he shouted. 'Come on boys and girls, sing your lungs out.'

The words of the song were now there on the screen above and behind the organ man and as he played the song a ball landed on each word at the exact moment it was to be sung and the whole auditorium including Ralph and Benedict followed the ball and belted the words out. After 'Happy Days', several more songs followed and then the auditorium lights began to brighten and the organ sank slowly from view and the screen that had showed the words of the songs was covered over by the velvet curtains again. The music continued, though the volume was lower than before. Waves of silver and gold washed over the cinema's walls and ceiling. The usherettes appeared and sauntered down the aisles. They wore white shoes and white socks and orange dresses with skirts that stuck out stiffly and had buttons up the front, and they all carried white trays full of soft drinks, chocolates, ice creams and lollies that hung by a strap that went behind their necks. When they got to the bottom of the aisle they turned their backs to the front and faced the auditorium and children swarmed round them. Ralph and Benedict, having no money, did not leave their seats.

'Mum could have spared a shilling,' said Benedict. 'We could have bought some gumdrops at least.'

Ralph thought about the money in his H. Upmann cigar box. For the previous matinee Ginny gave them each enough spending money to buy a Butterkist popcorn, a Kia-Ora orange drink and a Lyons Maid strawberry Mivvi and he'd assumed she'd do the same today, which was why he hadn't raided his box that morning. He wouldn't make the same mistake next time.

The usherettes, their trays empty, began to make their way back up the aisles. The house lights dimmed. The curtains swished open revealing the cinema screen behind. The faint whirr of the projector somewhere far behind. A shaft of bright light in the dark overhead and a certificate from the British Board of Film Censors on the screen. The films were about to start. Ralph read the first film was classified U, suitable for viewers of any age. The Censors' certificate faded. The speakers crackled and music sounded, perky, raucous and thrilling. Ralph felt a throb of pleasure, as he always did the moment a screening began. He settled back in his seat to watch. He was happy

The matinee began with a run of cartoons, *Tom and Jerry*, *Merrie Melodies* and *Looney Tunes*. These were followed by episodes from the serials *Ali and the Camel*, *Five on a Treasure Island* and *Masters of Venus*. The morning finished with a children's feature, *The Flood*. Ralph was rapt throughout.

The boys rolled out into the street with the rest of the audience at twelve-thirty. After the darkness of the auditorium their eyes hurt in the light. It was raining. A miasma of droplets floated in the air. The paving stones glistened. They buttoned their duffle coats, threw the hoods over their heads and started to tramp home.

When they reached the Boscombes' side door, Ralph could hear Timothy inside. His voice, loud, angry and posh – unlike Ginny, he made no attempt to talk in a different way from the way he had grown up talking – was instantly recognizable.

Benedict opened the door.

'Hello there, Benedict,' drawled Timothy.

Benedict went in. Ralph followed and closed the door. Timothy had removed his claw and set it on the table. It was a metal thing, vicious-looking, fascinating, and dangerous. In his working hand Timothy held a tankard of cider. Ginny sat opposite. She'd combed her hair and put on lipstick. There were plates, glasses and cutlery piled in front of her. A man with unruly black hair and bright blue eyes sat on the other side of the table between them.

'This is my son, Benedict,' said Ginny, addressing the stranger. 'That's his friend, Ralph, who lives down the road.' She pointed at the stranger. 'Lads, this is Douglas. He's a friend of Timothy's.'

Ralph decided Ginny's strained behaviour earlier must be on account of this visitor.

Douglas called a greeting across.

'So,' Timothy said, 'what have you been up to, boys?'

Ralph stared at his stump, so smooth and red, and, a couple of inches above, the wristwatch held in place with a silver expandable strap, which somehow made the stump even more compelling.

'Children's matinee,' said Ralph.

To divert himself from staring, Ralph took off his duffle coat and hung it on the back of a chair.

'Oh, children's matinees, they're still going are they?' asked Timothy.

'Yes.'

'Mostly crap films I suppose?'

Ralph squirmed. If he said no and Timothy would go on the attack. If he said yes and Timothy would denounce him for watching rubbish, or something like that.

What was he to do? He looked sideways at Ginny but she was staring at Douglas and if he didn't catch her eye, he couldn't enlist her help.

'I'll take that as a yes,' said Timothy. 'Films mostly crap.'

'Give the boy a chance,' said the visitor. His voice had a Scottish burr. 'He's only in the door.'

'I'll ask the defendant again,' said Timothy. 'Films mostly crap were they?'

'I liked the Hollywood cartoons, especially the *Tom and Jerrys*,' said Ralph.

'Oh Sweet Christ,' said Timothy, 'we've got a bloody apologist for the Yanks.' He looked down the table at Ginny. 'I don't know if I can actually trust this one, Ginny. He could be dangerous. He could be a fucking Tory.'

Ralph stared at Arnold's painting on the wall showing the window overlooking the garden and pretended he hadn't heard.

'Shut up, Timothy,' said Ginny. She said this in her gentle coaxing voice.

'What else did you see, other than the cartoons?' asked Douglas.

Ralph listed them.

'Plus we had a yo-yo demonstration and a sing-along,' Benedict added.

'Sounds like Butlins,' said Timothy. 'Whatever you do, keep the proles happy.'

Jeannie carried the shepherd's pie to the table on a breadboard. Ralph and Benedict sat. They all ate together, including Jeannie, though she didn't join in the conversation much. When everyone had eaten, Jeannie piled the plates and stood.

'I'll take this.' Ralph grabbed the pie dish. 'I'll give you a hand.'

'Thank you very much, young Ralph,' Jeannie said.

'Sordid,' whispered Benedict. 'Crawler.'

'Right, Benedict,' said Ginny. 'You can help too.'

'Child cruelty, child cruelty.' Benedict stood.

'My hearing,' said Ginny. 'Never underestimate my hearing.'

'Oh my,' said Jeannie, 'two helpers today. It's my lucky day.'

Jeannie hefted the plates and cutlery and darted away to the back kitchen. Here she went to the enormous sink and began to wash up. Ralph dried the first plate and Benedict the next and they took it in turns until everything was done. After the drying everything was put away and then tea was made in a Brown Betty. That done, the boys and Jeannie carried the teapot, a clutch of mugs, a bottle of milk and the biscuit barrel back to the table.

Douglas was talking. Ralph sat in his chair and tuned in to what he was saying.

'I did English and French at Edinburgh,' he said. 'Then a year at a school in Dieppe as a language assistant, helping the children improve their English. Then teacher training in Leeds. I did my teaching practice in a Secondary Modern in Barnsley. Most of the pupils were the children of miners. It was my first encounter with the working classes; I mean my first proper encounter. I got my eyes opened. Oh Christ, the squalor, the poverty, the misery. Saw it all at first hand. Of course conditions were a lot better than they were when Orwell visited the north to research *The Road to Wigan Pier* but still, they were still pretty awful.

'After I finished teacher training, I went to Liverpool. I taught in an all-male Grammar School. Very different to Barnsley. The children were mostly the offspring of professionals or civil servants. They had a confidence that came from their position in the class system which the children in Barnsley didn't. After two years in Liverpool I came to London. I'm in Plaistow now. Another Secondary Modern. Grim. Horrible. Depressing. But also strangely thrilling. I have no idea what the future holds. I can't stand the idea of teaching for the rest of my life but I have no idea what else I could do instead. So I'm treading water in Plaistow and waiting to see what turns up and in the meantime I've written a few articles about my experiences which Timothy is trying to place.'

'Those I would love to read,' said Ginny.

'No you wouldn't,' said Timothy. 'He's only started. He's only finding his voice. It's far too early to start on his stuff. He's still writing rubbish. Give him time to improve.'

'There's a vote of confidence,' said Ginny.

When they finished their tea and biscuits, Ginny suggested a walk in the park.

'Do we have to?' asked Benedict.

'Yes. You do. Absolutely,' said Ginny. 'You haven't had any air today. You've only been here or the cinema. It'll do you good.'

Ralph put on his duffle coat and followed everyone out the side door and along Falkland Road and round the corner and through the big green gates and into Wandsworth Park. There was a board here with the bye-laws and a frame at the bottom that had different numbers slotted into it every day giving notice of the park's closing time: tonight it was six o'clock.

'Why don't they have the place open all the time?' asked Timothy. 'We own it. It should be available anytime, day or night.'

'Why don't you stop being so bloody belligerent all the time?' said Douglas.

They began to walk. The asphalt path was smooth and grey. On either side there were stretches of thin grass with black London earth showing round the edges and stands of trees. The trees were mostly planes and their trunks were olive green and grey but here and there it looked as if plates of bark had been peeled off to reveal the skin below, smooth and white like a nut. Their leaves were thick and spongy and they were turning orange and yellow. They passed a park attendant in a brown uniform and a round brown hat raking leaves that had fallen into a drift, and then a second man gathering piled up leaves and transferring them into a cart.

'I worked in a park for a while when I was in Leeds,' said Douglas. 'You wouldn't believe how many leaves trees shed and how long it takes to pick them up.'

They passed the painted bandstand and turned down to the river and followed the path that ran beside the wall that separated the park from the Thames. The adults were ahead of Ralph and Benedict. They were talking about the closure of the *Daily Herald* and its replacement by *The Sun* and then the general election and the narrow victory for Labour and the new Prime Minister Harold Wilson, whom Ralph knew had grey hair and a square head and smoked a pipe. The talk bored him so he stopped listening though he remained aware of the drone of the adults' voices and he stared at the river instead. It was low tide. The exposed mud flats were grey this afternoon. The shrunken Thames flowing out to sea was a similar grey. Clayey. The sky overhead was grey too, the grey of old putty.

'Ginny alert!' said Benedict.

Ralph swivelled his gaze from the river to the grown-ups in front of them. He saw Ginny had slipped her arm through Douglas's and put her shoulder right against his.

'Sordid!' said Benedict.

Ralph felt his face redden and his scalp go hot. This was his standard reaction to any overt display of affection but this situation was horribly complicated by its being his friend's mother who was the offender, and even worse that his friend had drawn his attention to it. Why oh why did he have to be here now with Benedict seeing this? It was simply sickening. He wanted to say something. Something dismissive. Something blasé. Something that showed that, contrary to the way he was feeling, he was actually indifferent. He didn't care. He really didn't. But as always happened in situations like this, the words would not come. Not even one. All he knew was how hot he was and how red-faced he was and how empty his head was.

'I might be sick right now,' said Benedict. 'I might upchuck the shepherd's pie all over the park you know.'

'There's a bin there if you want to be sick,' said Ralph, pointing ahead.

'Not actually sick you idiot,' said Benedict. 'It's a figure of speech, you retard, if you know what that is.'

'When you say something for effect which isn't necessarily true,' said Ralph. 'Covered that last year. Of course I know.'

'I wish they'd just get on, Mum and Clive,' said Benedict, 'and not have "friends". God I hate it.'

Ginny put her head on Douglas's shoulder and began to laugh.

'What do you think they're laughing about?' asked Ralph.

'Don't know,' said Benedict, 'and I don't care either.'

Ralph had hoped to be able to cheer up his friend by agreeing with whatever he said but that wasn't to be. They walked on in silence.

★

The following Monday morning. The kitchen cold and dark when he entered, having got dressed. Rain droplets chattering on the frosted panes in the side door. The electric light was on, its light insipid and depressing. The oven doors open and the gas jets burning blue within. This would make some heat until the paraffin heater, sighing and ticking in the corner, got properly going. The fishy smell of burning paraffin. On the table, at his place, a slice of toast with strawberry jam. He sat and began to nibble. He felt the gassy heated air from the oven wafting round him. Beads of perspiration swelled up along his hairline.

Breakfast done, Ralph pulled on his navy blue raincoat and school cap and opened the side door. He looked out. The concrete floor of the passage outside was slick with wet and the channel at the side was full of running water.

'Take an umbrella,' Doreen said.

He thought not. He'd only forget it on the bus.

'Nah, I'll be all right,' he said, and plunged out.

On Falkland Road, rain striking his face so sharply he had to narrow his eyes. Ropes of water banging on the pavement and exploding. Plodding forward, peering ahead, no sign of Benedict outside his gate. He'd be waiting under the porch by his front door, Ralph decided. That was what he always did in atrocious weather. But when Ralph got to the Boscombes' and looked through the gate, there was no sign of Benedict sheltering under the porch.

Ralph went down the passage and in through the side door. Ginny at the big table.

'Ah, Ralph,' she said. 'Bad out there is it?'

For a second he hoped she'd drive him to school but then he saw the pile of essays in front of her.

'No, it's all right really,' he said. 'Just a bit of water.' He was pleased with this show of indifference.

'Give this to Mrs Beadle-Collins, will you?' Ginny held out an envelope. 'It's a note. Benedict's not going to school today. He isn't well.'

He unfastened his satchel, stowed the envelope.

'You won't forget?'

'No.'

'Of course you won't. You're totally reliable, which means one day you're going to make some woman very happy.'

He concentrated on doing the fasteners up carefully, which allowed him to ignore what she had said.

'Call in will you and say hello to Benedict on your way home,' she said.

'Okay.'

He was soaked by the time he got to St David's. With at least half the school – the half who weren't driven there – it was the same and like them his first task on arriving was to find a length of hot pipe to drape his coat over. All morning the school was filled first with the smell of damp clothes drying and then the sharp odour of the bone dry clothes scorching and browning. By the end of the day the whole school smelt as if there had been a fire.

★

He called in to see Benedict after school. He found Ginny and Maud talking in the kitchen when he came in. Ginny made him mugs of Horlicks to bring up.

'He's in my bed,' Ginny said.

He went up slowly, a mug in each hand. Ginny's bedroom was the same room that his mother used as her office at home. Ralph found it strange to enter. The door, the window, the picture rail, the shape of the room, these were all identical to his mother's study except it wasn't his mother's study. It was Ginny's bedroom.

'Hello, sordid,' he said.

'Sordid yourself,' said Benedict.

His friend was in his mother's brass bed, propped up by a bank of pillows. The eiderdown on top was puffy and green, and over the bottom of the bed was laid a patchwork quilt made of hexagonal pieces of bright fabric. Ginny had once told Ralph it was special because it had been made in Wales by the widows of drowned fisherman and was two hundred years old. Ginny collected quilts along with all the other things.

Ralph put the mugs on the bureau by the bed and sat on the nearby rocking chair. He sat well back so the chair wouldn't move and took his Horlicks. Benedict took his too. Each boy stirred and sipped. There was a strong malt smell.

'You know who I met in the kitchen when I came in?' said Ralph.

'Tell me,' said Benedict.

'Mopey Maud.'

'What's she doing here?'

'Talking to your Mum.'

'They never stop. What were they on about?'

Ralph had heard enough while he waited in the kitchen for the milk to boil to answer and it was so that he could give this answer that he'd started the conversation in the first place.

'She's sorting Arnold's bail,' said Ralph, 'so he can get out of prison and come home. She's putting the house up as surety, or something.'

'Yes, that's right,' said Benedict. His voice was slow and syrupy as it always was when he was showing off his knowledge. 'You put up something that's the value of the bail, "surety", so the judge knows if you ever have to pay up, you can, so it's their house.'

Ralph took another hot, milky sip. Little grains of Horlicks stuck to his front teeth. He wiped them off with his tongue. Benedict might know what surety was but he knew something his friend didn't.

'Maud's really pissed off,' Ralph said. 'That's what she actually said. She's pissed off.'

He hoped this would impress Benedict but if it did he didn't say anything. A silence followed. Ralph heard rainwater gurgling in the gutter outside.

'Was school sordid?' asked Benedict.

'What do you think?' said Ralph.

In truth he'd enjoyed it.

'Did you get wet?'

'Soaked. Yeah. Going *and* coming.'

His trousers, shirt cuffs and shoulders were sodden from the journey home.

'It's been raining all day,' said Benedict. 'I know. I've been looking out the window.'

Ralph glanced over and saw the glass was smeared with condensation inside and water drops outside. Each boy stirred and sipped again. A small ball of malt came into his mouth. He used his tongue to flatten it against his bumpy palate. The bead broke and malt powder, dry and highly absorbent, was speckled everywhere.

'What's actually the matter with you?' asked Ralph.

'I'm sick.'

'Yeah, but what kind of sick?'

'Sore eyes. Sore throat.'

'Sore eyes! Really?'

'Yeah.'

'Sore eyes?'

'Didn't you hear? That's what I said.'

'When was this you got ill?'

'Saturday, after the park. Mum says I picked something up there.'

'You picked something up? In the park? On our walk?'

'Yeah.'

'But *I* didn't get sick.'

'So! I got the germ, you didn't. That's all. And Mum packed me off here.'

When he was sick, Benedict always went to his mother's bed, never his own. Both Benedict and his mother said he got better more quickly there than in his own bed upstairs. Ralph didn't believe this. He thought the truth was that Benedict wanted to be fussed over and Ginny wanted to fuss over him and this idea about Ginny's bed making him better was just their excuse to allow this. Ralph also found the idea appalling. He would never have wanted to be sick in his mother's bed, lying there at night with her lying beside him. The very idea made him queasy.

'You on for school tomorrow?'

'Could be. We'll see. Might get another day off.'

'Ralph?' It was Ginny shouting from downstairs. 'Toast is ready. Can you come down?'

'Coming,' Ralph bellowed back.

He put his Horlicks on the bureau by the bed and went downstairs to the kitchen. He found Maud still at the table. Her face looked red, her eyes puffy. While he'd been upstairs she'd obviously been crying. Ginny was in the back kitchen doing he didn't know what.

'There's your toast,' said Maud, pointing at a plate with four rounds of white bread smeared with brown salty anchovy paste.

Ralph nodded briefly as a sign of thanks.

'And don't bother to ask me how I am because the answer's shit!' she said. 'That's how I am. Shit. Absolute shit. Have you got that.'

He took the plate. He wanted to get away as quickly as possible.

'I'll bring this up to Benedict,' he said.

He shot out into the hall and climbed the stairs two at a time. If anything would impress Benedict, this would.

★

The postcard from America showed trees with orange and brown leaves. The caption read, 'Another glorious fall.' On the reverse his mother had written:

Dear Ralph,
The autumn glories on offer at the Old Partridge Estate are ten times better than this picture. The little bird – named Ralph in your honour – now comes regular as clockwork every morning for the crumbs and other surprises I leave out for him.

The MSJs have lent me a Ford Country Squire Station Wagon (curious name when you think this is a country with no country squires) to potter about in.

Love, Mum xx

November

Thursday evening. He was in the kitchen with Doreen.

'See you, Dor,' he said.

'Bye, Ral,' she said.

'It's Ralph,' he said.

'It's Doreen,' she said.

He left by the side door and went out to Falkland Road. It was dark. The street lights were on. A dead rocket lay on the roof of Mrs Moody's car. He lifted it off by the white splintery stick attached to the cardboard body. He sniffed the tube and smelt gunpowder. It was a smell he loved, one of his favourites. He threw the firework into the garden of Mrs Moody's neighbour. Two bangs faraway and then a whoosh overhead. He looked up and saw gold and red streaks which appeared to hang in the sky. Then a gigantic bang which he felt in the middle of his being and thousands of small silver balls were tumbling, turning and roiling earthward and there was a fierce crackling noise. Guy Fawkes night.

Ralph traipsed up the street. As he got closer to the Boscombes' he heard the sound of the party inside. He turned through the gate. Inside the front room, people and flashing lights, and flooding out to him the sound of voices and music. 'Hit the Road Jack' by Ray Charles. It was a song he knew.

He crossed the garden, slipped round the privet hedge and went down the passage. The closer to the side door he got, the louder the noise of the party inside became. He opened the side door and it was as if the volume had been turned right up. Incredible noise of talk and laughter and people crammed together. He stepped in and closed the door. The first person he saw was Maud, talking to a man he didn't know. The man wore glasses with thick black frames.

'Oh hello, Ralph,' Maud said.

On the table, glasses, bottles of drink and Clive's cider cask but no sign of Coca-Cola or anything like that. Maud turned back to the man with the glasses.

'Made it myself,' she said, pointing at her dress.

It was long and straight and white with cubes of red, black and green placed randomly across the front and back without any apparent pattern.

'It's Kazimir Malevich inspired,' said Maud. 'My art school hero.'

The man in glasses nodded and took a drink from a tankard. Arnold was standing slightly behind his wife. He was a lot thinner than the last time Ralph had seen him, which was before he was arrested. His hair was shorter too and shot through with streaks of white. He was staring up at the ceiling.

'Hello, Arnold,' said Ralph.

'Who are you?' asked Arnold.

Maud heard and turned. 'This is Ralph. You know, Ralph, Benedict's friend. He's been to our house. Often.'

'Oh yes,' said Arnold. 'Sorry, Ralph. I was a million miles away. Got a lot on my mind as they say.'

'Do you know where I'll find Benedict?' Ralph asked.

'In the garden,' Maud said.

He wove his way through the guests and got out to the back. There was a brazier burning outside the back door. The coals were red and hot and packed in between them were potatoes in silver foil, baking. Ginny was there tending the food with Douglas beside her. She wore a furry Russian hat and a long dress made of some dark heavy thick material and a shawl. Douglas was in a donkey jacket and a top hat.

'Hello, Ralph,' she said. 'Benedict's at the bottom, getting everything ready.'

Ralph looked down the length of the garden. There were jam jars everywhere with candles burning inside. Some were standing on the ground and some were hanging from the trees. The river beyond was streaked with silvers and blues and the sky overhead was a livid purple with rockets streaking across here and there leaving trails of gold and green and red behind.

He found his way to the end. Clive and a stranger were nailing Catherine Wheels to a temporary trellis. Milk bottles were lined along the flood wall and Benedict was setting rockets into each one. A tarpaulin that had been soaked in water and was dripping had been draped over Clive's writing shed to protect it from sparks.

'Hello, Ralph,' said Clive. 'We are going to have quite a show and you are just in time. This is Lee by the way. Lee, Ralph, friend of the son.'

Lee nodded and grunted. He had a tack between his teeth and with a small hammer he was driving another tack through a Catherine Wheel. Job done, Lee gave the wheel a turn to check it rotated freely. He had short hair, wore a suit and tie, and he made Ralph feel nervous.

There wasn't anything for Ralph to do so he simply stood and watched as the final preparations for the fireworks display were made. Then, when it was done, Clive sent him and Benedict to tell Ginny to get everyone out of the house and into the garden because in five minutes he and Lee were going to let off the fireworks. As they meandered up, Benedict whispered, 'You see Lee?'

'Yeah,' he said.

'He's a bank robber.'

'What?'

'Yeah. Clive's doing some programme on bank robbers. That's how he knows him. He's been in prison. Many times. Armed robbery. Firearms offences. He's quite dangerous you know.'

They gave the message to Ginny and everyone was brought outside, including Jeannie. She complained her knees were sore and he and Benedict had to carry out a chair for her to sit on.

Clive and Lee lit the fireworks and the guests watched them exploding at the end of the garden and in the sky above the river and while they watched they clapped and shouted. After a while Ralph decided one firework was very much like another and he turned his attention to the upturned faces of the guests. They all shared the same expression. They were rapt and filled with wonder. Ginny was beaming, he noticed. Douglas had put his hand under her shawl and was rubbing her back.

The fireworks finished. Clive and Lee came up. The guests shouted 'Bravo!' and applauded even more loudly and several slapped the new arrivals on their backs. Clive and Douglas, Ralph noticed, began a long intense conversation.

The baked potatoes were ready and every guest got one, wrapped in a napkin, quartered and filled with melted butter and cheese. Everyone stood round the garden eating and when they had finished they threw their potato skins and their napkins into the brazier. Timothy appeared and got up on Jeannie's chair. He was in a dinner jacket with a cummerbund underneath and a velvet bow tie.

'All right everybody,' he shouted. 'Attention please. The auction will commence inside in two minutes. Two minutes, ladies and gentlemen.'

Everyone crowded into the front kitchen. Ralph wiggled his way to the front. He wanted to see. There was a screen print on a chair. It wasn't big. About three foot wide and two foot high. It was silvery and showed a room with no windows and in the middle of the room there was a chair with straps and a cable curling out from under it and a sign in the top right corner that read 'Silence'. Ralph didn't know what he was looking at and he didn't think what he was seeing was particularly interesting.

'All right, everyone, you can all shut up,' Timothy shouted.

As the room grew quieter, he dragged over the stool that the cider cask would ordinarily have stood on. He got up on the stool.

'Good evening. Welcome.'

The guests fell silent.

'This,' Timothy continued, 'is a screen print called *Electric Chair*.'

He pointed at the print with his claw. Ralph looked back and realised that the straps on the chair must be to hold the condemned down before execution while the thick cable that snaked along the floor must be for the electric charge that killed them.

'This work of art by the artist Andy Warhol has been generously donated for us to auction for a good cause at this Guy Fawkes night with a difference through the good offices of a private individual who is here but who wishes to remain anonymous. Private individual – you have our thanks.

'The electric chair that you see is based on a photograph that was in the papers on January 13, 1953, in America, land of the free, home of the brave, a photograph of the death chamber in Sing Sing Prison, New York, wherein Julius and Ethel Rosenberg were fried for passing information about the atomic bomb to the Soviet Union during the Second World War. If the Allies were to have it, then it should be all the Allies who defeated Fascism, and that meant the Russians too, that was the Rosenbergs' thinking, since you asked, but our Uncle Sam didn't see it that way.

'Now before we get down to the actual business of the evening, that is the relieving of one of you of your cash for a good cause, I'd like to tell you a story. It's about me, a subject of inexhaustible interest to me obviously, but it also relates to something bigger: what's wrong with this dung heap of a country and what's wrong with the world for that matter. My little tale is a kind of Everyman tale, and I beg you to listen, it won't take long, and believe me, because this is true, I've the scars to back me up …' Timothy waved his claw '… and once I conclude, you will understand why I have told you what I'm about to tell you and what it has to do with this screen print and what we're trying to do tonight.

'I was a clergyman's son. I grew up in a nice rectory in Leicestershire. Neither rich nor poor. Very comfy. Small "c" conservative. The war comes. I get a couple of years in at university but then the conscription notice plops through the Leicestershire rectory letterbox. Get thee to the recruiting station, Timothy. Now, this is not as terrible as it sounds. It's 1945. *La guerre est finis.* Just. More or less. But though the fighting's done, rules is rules. You have to do your duty. So: I enlist; and in short order, training, troopship, Libya.

'Now, Libya. Or Italian Libya as it was officially known then, run by the British Military Administration of Libya, there's been fighting there, heavy fighting and it's wrecked. The place is full of mines, barbed wire, debris, blown-up tanks, ordnance, it's a mess, a fucking mess. And that's just the landscape. Politically it's feudal. There's a king, a bastard, he's not there, he's in Cairo, but he pops over now and again, and there are some civil servants, Italians, and us, running the show, and the result, utterly predictably, is poverty, crippling poverty. There's no work, no industry, no commerce, most of the population live in squalor and have no access to doctors, teachers, schools, toilets, running water, electricity, sanitary towels, toothpaste, et cetera, although I can't help noticing there are plenty of fags and Coca-Cola. So basically, Libya, just after the war, it's like the Middle Ages and it's got nothing. Oh, sorry, tell a lie. It's got one thing and we, and the French who are occupying the south, I forgot to mention them, we are very interested in this one thing, and it's oil.

'Anyhow, it's a shithole. A complete and utter fucking shithole. Did I mention it's a shithole?'

'You did,' shouted someone in the audience.

'I did.'

'Less preaching and more narrative please,' called the heckler. It was Douglas, Ralph realised.

'And try not to swear quite so much,' said Ginny.

'Sorry. Right, don't fucking swear. Got it. No fucking swearing. The best jokes are the old ones. Ba, boom.

'Now, I'm in a garrison at a fuel dump deep in the desert but quite close to the Egyptian border. I'm a guard.

That's what I do. I guard the dump day and night. A couple of months into this tour of duty, this bent sergeant from the garrison makes an approach. One night when I'm on duty, he says, it would be really handy if I could stay in my hut between midnight and two or something, and have a little shut-eye or something and pay no attention to the sound of the perimeter wire being cut, fuel drums being loaded onto a flatbed, and the lorry driving these away. Once it's sold in Egypt, the sergeant says, I'll get a few quid. I'll get paid, in other words, for sleeping. He thinks the offer is fucking irresistible.

'I'm not so sure. I think, I don't know this guy. Why's he asking me? This is a set up. So I'm just going to act dumb. Clergyman's son, I know, but no flies on me.

'I don't know, I say. I have to do a perimeter check every hour. I have to fill in the log. If I don't fill it in I'll get into trouble and I don't want to get into trouble.

'The sergeant eventually loses the rag. Says I'm a bloody fool. He storms off.

'And then the fuel is stolen. Not on my watch. Different night. And then, and then, the sergeant, the bent one, who knows I know and so I'm a threat, and who's got the ears of the officers and the military police, he makes a statement. And you know what he says? He says it was me. I'm the fuel thief. I had the Egyptian contacts and I corrupted the guard on the night of the robbery. Now actually he was the one who corrupted that sentry but the sergeant has him by the balls and he has to go along with this.

'I'm court-martialled. Plead not guilty. Defended by some wanker. Found guilty. I get eighteen months. The glasshouse is out in the desert. The regime is punitive and includes regular forced runs in the boiling sun, supervised by the military policemen in charge. They're all lunatics but the worst is this corporal from Hull, pointy and sinewy like a ferret, and he loves nothing better than being in an open Land Rover at the back of the line of runners, and if he thinks you aren't going fast enough, or need encouraging, he comes up behind you, slows down and then, one hand on the wheel, Mabel in the other – Mabel is a length of rubber piping – he fucking belts you. Whack, whack, whack, and as he does he shouts, "Mabel loves you. Mabel loves you." Imagine it. You're in your singlet and shorts, pouring with sweat, dying of thirst, blinded by the sun, on the verge of dropping and this lunatic is behind you shouting, "Mabel loves you, you little toe-rag," whack, whack, whack.

'Then one day, we're out, I'm staggering, I've got dysentery or something, I'm really not well, he's behind, he comes up, "Mabel loves you. Mabel loves you," whack, whack, whack, and as he lashes me the world goes white and I go down, bosh, like that, face down on the boiling sand.

'Of course he's very surprised. One moment he was driving along, he had his victim, and then the next moment, no one. I'm not there to hit anymore and he was having such a good time.

'He slams on the brakes, looks round. There I am. On the sand behind. Arms out like so. Into reverse, foot to the floor, back he hurtles, doesn't look where he's going, course he fucking doesn't, he crushes my hand. Breaks every single little bone. "Oh sorry, diddums. Did I hurt your hand?" Did you like the Hull accent?

'Anyway, me, military hospital, Benghazi. It can't be saved, my hand. They cut it off.

'Now, you're thinking, he must be in trouble, Mabel's boyfriend. No. He's praised by the glasshouse OC for getting the prisoner who fainted to hospital and who otherwise would have died owing to injuries sustained in a vehicular accident. As for me, I'm mutilated and nothing – no redress, no compensation, no apology even. I'm meant to be thankful. I'm supposed to be thankful that the fucking sadist who ran me over in the first place saved my life. Mad or what this world of British justice?

'And the madness didn't end there. All the officers knew about Mabel and what the corporal did on the punishment runs, and they all knew about all the other little extras that he and the other NCOs dreamt up, beating prisoners in the block, pissing in their food, salting their water, and so on. Of course they knew. But they did nothing. They believed there was no other way to straighten out a bad soldier. Brutality was the only way, that was their thinking, and if a prisoner lost a hand in the process, or worse, died, so what? And going by their way of thinking, I got off light. Several died in that Libyan glasshouse, murdered, in effect, by the NCOs. I'd only lost a hand, so in a way they were right, I had got off light. But did it work, all this brutality? Of course it didn't. Look at me now. It did me no good whatsoever except to make me a revolutionary.

'Now what I saw, what I'm describing, was done by whites to whites. But just imagine, if you will, what we did to those who weren't white, in our colonies. They lost much more than a hand. But do we admit this? No, we, the English, are such a nation of self-deceivers.

'We did a bit of bad, in the Empire, back in the day, we grudgingly admit that, but we gave them Shakespeare and the rule of law and the railways and a few other things, which evens things up a bit, doesn't it? That's what we say, don't we?

'And then, which is the other great bulwark we have against the truth of how horrible we actually were, we have our record, as we laughingly call it. Look! we proclaim. We fight a just war against Hitler and then the story just gets

better and better, because all our benighted colonial subjects, apart from those in Rhodesia, but let's not go there,
we give them their freedom, we give them their nation-
hood. One after the other, just like that. Oh, aren't we just
marvellous? That's what we say.

'But are we or were we? Really! We've exploited them.
We've annihilated their culture. Is there any mention of
this? Or apology? Or reparation for what we did in our
colonies? No. Nothing. Nothing. Just as in the glasshouse,
and I know of what I speak, in our Empire power was
ruthlessly exercised over millions and our sometime colonial subjects were beaten, brutalised, exploited, destroyed
and then they were let go, given their own flag and their
own currency and their own parliament, and expected to
say "Thank you so much" for all that we supposedly did
for them and gave them. But the best part, now we've set
them free, is that all that which happened in the past has
been erased. It never happened just like everything in my
glasshouse never happened.

'That's the way we do it here in Blighty but don't imagine for a second this level of denial is peculiar to us here
in England. It's universal. The black population of the US,
the descendants of slaves, who incidentally we shipped to
the New World when we were getting our own colonies
up and running, has anyone in the US ever said to them,
"Sorry. That slavery malarkey really wasn't very nice"? Of
course not. Indeed, the awful truth has never been admitted over there, just as it has never been admitted over here.
But it must be. It has to be. And it will be.

'Now, here in England, in Africa and America and
Asia, those peoples whom we oppressed, while technically
or theoretically free, are still suffering because of what we
did and continue to do. We might have set them free, ha
ha, but we're still world class in the oppression department.

So they're organising, why wouldn't they, to defend them-selves against us. It's happening everywhere, notably in the United States under Malcolm X and it is to help that great, forward-thinking leader who is struggling to improve the conditions of his fellow black Americans that we are gath-ered here tonight. He has recently founded the Organisation for African-American Unity to seek independence for those still called Negroes in polite society, and to raise funds for his organisation we are going to auction, here, tonight, this print of the most famous American electric chair, oh they do so love capital punishment in the land of the free and the brave and they particularly love executing black men, don't they? God bless America, and all over Vietnam I'm sure those words are on the lips of every peasant tonight.

'I will now open the bidding. Do I hear fifty pounds? Fifty pounds, ladies and gentlemen, fifty pounds …'

★

After the auction Clive announced that if anyone wanted to see What the Butler Saw they must pay. He pulled his harmonium into the middle of the room and said he would play whatever song was wanted but again guests must pay. All the money so raised would also go to the Organisation for African-American Unity. Ralph was designated to stand by the What the Butler Saw machine and take the money. First in the queue was Maud.

'Shilling,' he said.

She turned to Arnold. 'Right. This'll perk you up.'

'It won't be anything I haven't seen already in life class,' he said.

'Now, now.' Maud opened her handbag.

'Oh,' Maud said.

Ralph looked at her face as she looked down into the inside of her bag.

'My purse,' she said.

She moved items here and there in the bottom of the bag.

'My purse,' she said, 'it's not here!'

'Could you have put it in your coat pocket?' asked Arnold.

'No. It's been taken. My purse has been taken. Someone's only gone and bloody taken my purse.'

Guests near Maud turned.

One said, 'Oh how awful!'

Another asked, 'Are you sure?'

'Yes,' said Maud.

News of Maud's loss spread. Women checked their handbags. Men checked the inside pockets of the jackets they'd left down. Maud was not alone, it was discovered. Many of the guests had been robbed during the auction.

The room fell quiet. Who was the thief? Everyone was looking round trying to spot who had been there earlier and was now gone as that person was the most likely candidate. Eventually a culprit was identified and named and then Clive spoke:

'I've done so much for Lee and this is how he rewards me?' he said. 'I am apoplectic with rage.'

'How do you know that *he* did it?' This was Maud's husband. 'It could have been me for all you know.'

'But it wasn't,' said Maud. 'You were standing beside me during the auction.'

'Well then, if you prefer, I think it was Lee,' said Clive.

'We should call 999.' This was the man with black-rimmed glasses. 'And report him.'

'You can suspect whatever you want,' said Timothy. 'The question is, did you actually see him do it? No, you didn't. So if you didn't, don't call the police. It won't do any good.'

Some guests murmured in agreement. Others scowled and shook their heads.

'If I had him here, I'd hit him so hard,' someone said.

'I wouldn't do that if I was you,' said Jeannie.

She set a tray of clean glasses down on the table.

'So what do you propose,' said the man in the black-rimmed glasses, 'if we don't call the police?'

'Have a look in the street outside,' said Jeannie. 'He'll only have taken the cash. He'll have chucked everything else once he's got the money.'

'Jeannie, you're right,' shouted Timothy. 'I'm on it. And you can help.' He waved at Ralph and Benedict. 'Got some torches, Ginny?'

Ginny gave them torches and a cloth bag each to carry anything they found. Ralph and Benedict followed Timothy outside into Falkland Road. It was cold but dry. In the distance Ralph could hear fireworks going off. Timothy issued instructions. Benedict and Ralph would search toward the railway bridge, Benedict taking the pavement on the opposite side, and he'd search the other way.

They turned on their torches and moved off. Ralph's torch was black and heavy and encased in ribbed rubber and it gave off a strong chemical smell. The beam was white and narrow and strong. He swept it along the first stretch of gutter and picked out a brown wallet lying weirdly with one half right on the edge of the kerb and the other hanging down so for a moment he thought it was a bird.

'Found something,' Ralph shouted.

When he bent down to pick up the wallet he saw a purse lying a bit farther along the gulley.

'Timothy,' Ralph shouted.

He dropped his finds in the bag. Timothy returned, Benedict too, and together they searched gutters, below cars, front gardens, heading toward the bridge. Every few yards they found a wallet or a purse lying as it had fallen. When they got to the steps leading up to the footbridge they saw that was the way the thief had gone for there was a purse halfway up. On the footbridge itself they found two more purses lying on the asphalt, dark humps lit by the white lights that shone down every few yards, but thereafter it was smooth and grey and empty as far as they were able to see.

'Well, that's our lot,' said Timothy.

In the sky overhead a solitary rocket exploded.

'Any more he'll have chucked into the river I'd say,' said Timothy.

They carried their haul back to number 56 and piled it on the kitchen table. Guests milled about and retrieved their property. They had retrieved every stolen purse and wallet with the exception of Maud's.

'I feel so terrible about this,' said Clive. 'Really Maud, I do. I feel responsible.'

'You're not responsible for the actions of a sneak thief,' said Maud quietly.

'Yeah, but if I hadn't asked Lee, would it have happened? I don't think so. Tell me what was in your purse and I'll make it up to you now.'

'No,' said Maud, 'that wouldn't be right. It's not your fault.'

'Look, why don't you borrow it?' asked Arnold. 'We need to fill your car tomorrow, for a start. And then you can forget to pay Clive back and then everyone will be happy.'

As he watched Clive pass Maud a ten pound note, Ralph's thoughts went back to the beginning of the

evening at the bottom of the garden. He remembered
Lee nailing up a Catherine Wheel. Lee had troubled him
then. He remembered the auction. Ralph had been at
the front near the screen print which was still there on
the chair. He hadn't taken his eyes off Timothy while he
made his speech and his sense, as he remembered now,
was that no one else had either. As he considered this,
a thought that was as surprising as it was inadmissible
came to him. It had taken great cool and cunning to do
what Lee had done and then vanish. As much as Lee disturbed him, Lee also impressed him. He actually admired
Lee. This idea was so terrifying he blushed. The flush was
deep and fierce and scorching. He stared at the floor and
pretended to be looking for something he'd dropped. He
kept this going until the party hubbub resumed and the
music started. Ray Charles again. Nobody saw the blush,
he thought. His secret was safe.

★

He left the Boscombes' party and walked home. As he
came down the side passage, he saw light through the
frosted glass in their side door. In the kitchen he found
Doreen sitting at the table. Her back was toward him. It
was curved. She was looking down at the table he guessed.
The lamp on the shelf in the corner was on. The ceiling
light was off.

'Hello,' he said.

He saw Doreen shake her head in acknowledgement
but she didn't speak. Something was amiss.

He closed the door.

'Nice time at the party?'

'We were robbed,' he said.

'What?'

Doreen turned. There wasn't much light but there was enough for him to see. Her face seemed to have shrunk and he thought she looked unhappy.

'This man Clive asked to the party, a bank robber, he went into everyone's handbags and jackets. Took all the purses and wallets and scarpered.'

Ralph pulled out one of the high-backed Swedish chairs and sat. Doreen stared over at him. Her eyes were narrowed, her brow furrowed.

'You're codding me?'

'No. Everyone was robbed. Well, not everyone. But a lot of people. Then I went out and helped to find the purses and the wallets in the street that Lee, the thief, had thrown away.'

'Any money in them?'

'No.'

'I didn't think so.'

She peered down. There was a magazine in front of her. She was doing the crossword. She'd solved only a few clues.

'Where's Tom?' he asked.

He couldn't hear the radio in the basement which Tom normally had on at that time.

'I think he's at his sister's.'

Tom's sister Veronica lived in Willesden.

'He should be back soon then,' said Ralph. 'Doesn't he have to get up in the morning?'

'He does. And so do you. Go on. Teeth, bed.'

'Maybe I will have something.'

'Like a Horlicks?'

'Yes.'

'Well go and get your jim-jams on and come back.'

She stood up and sighed.

'Okay?'

'Okay,' he said.

Much later he heard Tom cross the garden and click down the passage. He heard the side door open and close. He heard the bolts being drawn. He heard Doreen and Tom's voices. They didn't sound friendly. They didn't talk for long either. Then he heard them going one after the other to the bathroom upstairs and the pipes knocking and whooshing. He felt a cramping feeling behind his solar plexus come on. He wished he was asleep because if he was he wouldn't have to endure what he was feeling, which was a sense that something awful was looming. He closed his eyes and, unbidden, the image sprung up – Kit McCreesh shooting out of their gate and hurtling away down Falkland Road. He opened his eyes. Voices from below. Tom and Doreen were quarrelling.

★

Evening, Wednesday, the week after Guy Fawkes. Ralph was lying on his bed. He had heard Tom come home earlier and go in by the side door.

'Hello, my name's Steed, John Steed,' said Ralph slowly.

He liked to practice talking like the suave secret agent played by Patrick Macnee in *The Avengers*.

'Yes, Steed as in horse,' he continued.

He imagined this was the sort of witty quip Steed would come up with when he was in danger yet wished to appear unperturbed and cool. When he grew up, more than anyone else, Ralph wanted to be like Steed.

Tapping on his window, sharp and alarming. Tom was outside the window closest to the front door.

'Ralph!' Tom called.

He got off his bed and went to the window.

'Get your coat and come to Pritchard's,' said Tom through the glass. 'And go out the front door here, not the side door.'

Ralph put on his duffle coat, opened the heavy front door and stepped out. Tom was waiting on the step.

'Quicker coming out this way than going round by the kitchen,' Tom said.

This didn't sound right to Ralph. He always went down to the kitchen and out that way. Always. He never went out the front door. In fact none of them used the front door really except Doreen on Sundays when she went out and came back from Mass. It was always the side door they used. Why was Tom anxious he shouldn't use it now? He didn't understand.

He closed the door and stepped forward. There was a mizzle: tiny raindrops hovered in the air. It was also very cold. He felt the cold with his cheekbones. He pulled up the hood of his duffle coat.

'I've been ordered to get milk,' said Tom, 'and I thought to bring you and we'd have a chat.'

He followed Tom through the gate and over the road to the far pavement. The street lamps were on. In the front room of the first house they passed a schoolgirl in uniform was playing the piano. The notes spilled out. As he heard them, he also heard Tom sniffling as he always did when he was nervous.

Ralph felt a curdling in his stomach. He dreaded hearing whatever was coming but he also wanted to know as soon as possible.

'I just wanted you to know,' said Tom. 'I'm going up to stay with my sister for a bit.'

'Is it because of work?' asked Ralph. 'Is your sister's closer to the tunnel?'

He only asked because he thought he must say something.

'No, not really.'

They reached the corner and turned into Florian Street. The houses were small. The road smelt of anthracite.

'Then why do you have to move?' A perfectly reason-able question, he thought.

'How old are you, Ralph?'

'Twelve.'

Ralph felt the pavement was slimy under his feet.

'Do you understand the way adults, you know, get on and that?' asked Tom.

'Oh yes,' said Ralph. 'I'm told I'm very mature for my age.'

'Says the innocent of Falkland Road,' said Tom.

Ralph shrugged.

'One day you'll get married, so you might as well know,' said Tom. 'It's not a bed of roses, marriage.'

They reached the junction of Florian Street and Putney Bridge Road. Pritchard's shop was right on the corner. Its windows were steamed up.

Tom opened the door. The bell pinged. He went in. Ralph followed. Instant smell of newspaper ink, hot bread crust, saltpetre and sugar. The door closed behind. A second ping. Ralph pushed his hood off. Counters on three sides displaying chocolate bars and sweets, the evening papers and a dozen gaudy boxes of fireworks with a handwritten sign on top reading 'Reduced to clear'. The walls behind were lined with painted shelves, their edges worn and chipped. They were loaded with tins and packets, tubes and jars, and all kinds of dry goods. Mr Pritchard stood oppo-site the door. He was thin and bony and what little hair he had was carefully combed over the top of his head. The skin below, which showed through, was red and dotted with large brown patches like squashed toffees. He wore a beautifully ironed shop coat the colour of cardboard with the enamel badge of a London rifle regiment pinned to the lapel and a Remembrance Day poppy threaded through the buttonhole.

'Evening,' said Mr Pritchard. 'Wet out?'

He spoke carefully, enunciating each word fully. Mr Pritchard, Ginny had once said to Ralph, spoke in the same way as the Londoners in Charles Dickens' novels and was one of a dying breed.

'Not really,' Tom said. 'Just spotting.'

'It's giving it bad.'

The rain was a subject of which Mr Pritchard never tired of talking.

'Later, maybe,' Tom agreed.

Behind Mr Pritchard was the doorway to the Pritchards' kitchen. Coloured plastic strips hung from the lintel to stop customers seeing through. A radio voice was speaking behind and Ralph presumed that Mr Pritchard's wife, a small bird-like woman with spun white hair and huge blue eyes was, at that moment, sitting in there and smoking as she listened. As he had often heard Mrs Pritchard say, she ate Woodbines.

'What can I do you for?' asked Mr Pritchard.

'Pint,' said Tom.

Mr Pritchard disappeared through the plastic strips and returned with a milk bottle. The bottle was dripping. To stop it spoiling, Mr Pritchard kept the milk he sold in his sink, which was filled with cold water. He wiped the bottle dry on a piece of old flannel that he kept under the counter for this purpose.

'Go on, Ralph,' said Tom. 'Pick something. What do you want?'

Ralph hadn't expected this. If he'd known he'd have worked out in advance what he really wanted. There wasn't really time now.

'Kit Kat.'

This was what he always picked when he hadn't prepared and he had to make a quick decision.

'Please,' Mr Pritchard said. 'Kit Kat please.'

'Please,' Ralph murmured.

Mr Pritchard took an oblong bar in its distinctive red wrapping and set it beside the milk bottle.

Tom settled up. He took the pint and slipped it into the deep pocket of his donkey jacket. Ralph lifted his Kit Kat.

'Don't have it now,' said Tom. 'It'll spoil your dinner. Put it in your pocket.'

Tom opened the door. Another ping. He went out. Ralph followed. As soon as he was outside, Ralph felt rain on his face. While he'd been in Pritchard's it had started to lash. He pulled his hood up and thrust his hands into his pockets. The two began to walk. Ralph fingered the wrapper of his Kit Kat. Would he eat it later? No, he'd bring it to school tomorrow. He'd share it with Benedict on the bus.

'You won't tell Doreen we've had this chat, will you?'

He wasn't surprised by the request but he didn't like it. He was a bad liar and if Doreen asked him directly, he wouldn't be able to hold out. He'd tell her. He could hardly say this now though. Of course not. He must tell Tom what he wanted to hear. Nothing else for it.

'No,' he said.

'Promise?'

'Promise,' he said.

'I knew I could rely on you,' said Tom. 'You're a good boy.'

They walked to the bottom of Florian Street and turned right. Tom wriggled and snuffled beside him. The talk wasn't over yet, Ralph realised.

'Now I'm going to ask you something else,' Tom said. 'This is just between us. You mustn't breathe a word of this to Doreen. She'd kill me if she knew. Understand?'

What could he do? He had to agree.

'I understand,' he said.

'I've got my sister's number on a piece of paper in my pocket. Actually it isn't *her* number. She doesn't have a phone. It's the neighbour's. You call her Betty.'

Ralph knew the name. Betty the neighbour with the phone who lived in the house beside Veronica's.

They waited to cross the road. A car crashed by, the beams of its headlamps needling forward and illuminating the threads of falling rain.

'If you ring, Betty will take a message, or else get my sister or me if we're home.'

The car had passed. He heard the tyres sloshing through the water lying on the tarmac. But they stayed where they were.

'And why are you giving me this number?' asked Ralph, though he had a fairly good idea what was looming.

'If anything happens to Doreen, if you're worried, if anything's wrong, you ring me, yes?'

'You mean if she's sick, or something?'

'Yes, if she's sick. Definitely. You ring if she's sick, that's exactly right,' said Tom.

'Is she sick now?'

'No.'

'Is she going to be sick?'

'I don't know. Maybe,' said Tom. 'Actually yes, later, she might be.'

She might be. So why was he going away?

He followed Tom across the road and in through their gate. He looked at his bedroom window and saw that the electric light was still on in the room behind. He'd forgotten to turn it off.

'Let's go under the porch,' said Tom.

They made their way past the dripping terracotta pots and planters that filled the front garden and slipped under the porch.

'Here it is.'

Tom handed him a sheaf of writing paper folded in four.

'Where are you going to put that?' Tom asked as Ralph took it.

'With my money,' he said. 'In my cigar box.'

'That sounds good.'

Tom had his front door key in his hand.

'I'll let you in the front here.'

He inserted the key gently and pushed the door back carefully. He made no noise. The house smell of polish and potato steam and gas came out to Ralph straight away and folded round him.

'Go and hide Betty's number straightaway,' said Tom. 'And not a word about this little chat. Or the Kit Kat.'

Ralph went in. Tom closed the door silently behind. Ralph stood in the dark hall. He heard him going round the bay window and crossing the garden toward the passage. Now he understood why Tom had got him in and out through the front door. He'd done it so Doreen, who was in the kitchen cooking the dinner, wouldn't know they'd been out together.

He went into his bedroom, opened the piece of paper and read:

'Mrs Betty Mottram – lives next door to the sister Veronica and Ronnie Sharpe – Phone WIL 3286.'

It was Basildon Bond paper and he knew the words were woven into the paper itself. Ralph guessed Tom had torn it from the pad Doreen used for the letters she wrote home most Sunday afternoons. Tom, unlike Doreen, did not write to his family very much. He preferred to send messages with people going home.

He got his H. Upmann cigar box out from his sock drawer, refolded the sheet and slipped it under the money. Then he returned the box to its place under his socks.

★

They were eating dinner. He took a long careful look at Doreen but she didn't seem any different tonight from any other night. What on earth had Tom meant when he said she might get sick? Then he remembered there was another kind of sick that happened to women that didn't involve illness but something else entirely. Could it be that? He found the idea preposterous because of what had happened to Tom in the army. She couldn't …

Then, before his mind's eye, he saw Kit shooting out of their gate, loping away up Falkland Road, his lolloping swaggering stride. He felt a weird tremble inside, very deep. He'd got it, hadn't he?

★

Ralph was at the kitchen table on Sunday morning trying to learn the past tense of some French verbs when the side door opened and Ronnie Sharpe, Veronica's husband, came in.

Ronnie was from Walsall. He was bald, square, muscular and had enormous feet. He was a plasterer and he always smelt of plaster dust, even on Sundays.

'All right, Ralph?' he asked.

Ronnie gave him a big smile. There was a gap on the left lower side. The tooth had been knocked out in a fracas after a darts match and when he smiled broadly, as he did now, it showed. His assailant, Ronnie had told Ralph once, was a Mason and the tooth was dislodged by his Mason's ring. 'Never trust a fucking Mason,' Ronnie had added, though because Ralph was not entirely certain what a Mason was, he didn't follow.

'Hello, Ronnie,' Ralph said.

'Tom about?'

'I'll give him a shout.'

Ralph went out to the back hall and leaned over the basement stairs. At the bottom he could see Tom's bulging plastic suitcase tied shut with twine. Both clasps were broken and stuck up like tongues.

'Tom?' he called down.

Tom appeared below, his face whiter, tighter and shinier than usual, or so it looked to Ralph. He was in a suit and tie, as if about to make a journey.

'Ronnie's here.'

'Tell him I'll be there in a tick.'

As Ralph turned he heard Tom say to Doreen, who was out of sight, 'I'll be off then.' It sounded as if he was telling her he was about to leave for work rather than moving to his sister's. The matter-of-factness surprised Ralph but perhaps, he thought, that's how adults did these tricky things. They got through by not acknowledging what was happening.

Ralph went back to the kitchen and a few moments later Tom followed him, lugging the suitcase. Doreen followed behind. She was in the black dress she wore to Mass.

'If you hadn't the car, I don't know how I'd have got this up to you,' said Tom.

He put the suitcase down.

'What do you mean?' said Ronnie. 'Didn't you hear? I couldn't get the lend of a motor. We'll have to use the tube.'

'What!' said Tom.

'Only joking.' Ronnie waggled a key on a ring.

'Hilarious,' said Doreen.

Ronnie went out side door first, Tom followed with the suitcase, Ralph and Doreen were last.

The car was parked by the gate. It was a cream Vauxhall Victor, the body scuffed, the chrome spotted. Ronnie opened the boot and helped Tom to lift in the suitcase.

'What you got in there, bloody bricks?'

'No,' said Tom, 'just my things.'

Ronnie closed the boot. The mechanism made a tinny click.

'Bye, Dor,' Tom said.

Doreen offered her face and he kissed her cheeks briefly.

'Look after her Ralph,' he said. 'I'm relying on you.'

Ralph nodded. Tom and Doreen's calm was baffling. Surely, at this point, they must show something. They must show some real feelings, they must show some anger, or something. He'd have thought so. But no. Nothing. Nothing at all. Perhaps he was right in what he'd thought earlier. It was only by pretending that what was happening wasn't happening that they were able to get through this. It occurred to him that perhaps grown-ups did this all the time but that he had never really noticed till now.

Tom went round and got into the passenger seat.

Ronnie stepped swiftly up to Doreen. On his face Ralph saw what he'd never seen on Ronnie's face before – anxiety.

'It's none of my business,' Ronnie said quietly and speaking very quickly, 'but I just want you to know I'm sorry and if you want my opinion I think Veronica's stirring but what would I know? I'm only her fucking husband.'

He jumped behind the wheel, closed the door and wound the window down.

'Ralph,' Ronnie called.

He had something between his fingers, silver, gleaming.

Ralph bounded across. It was a florin.

'Don't spend it all at once.'

'Thanks.' Ralph took the coin.

The engine fired up with a low harrumph. Ronnie put the car in first gear and sped away.

'Just you and me now, Buster,' said Doreen.

Ralph looked at Doreen. She was staring after the car. He tried to work out what her face said. There wasn't much colour in it but otherwise she looked the same.

'You'll have to be very nice to me,' said Doreen. 'Will you be nice to me?'

'I'm always nice,' he said.

'I suppose you are.'

The Vauxhall Victor passed under the railway bridge.

'Do we have to tell my Mum?'

'We?'

'Are you going to tell her, I mean, about Tom?'

At the very end of the road the small speck that was Ronnie's borrowed car turned and vanished.

'I'll mention it.'

'I don't think it'll matter to her.'

Ralph hoped he sounded grown up. He also believed this. Doreen was the woman tasked to look after him, not Tom, so surely it didn't matter whether Tom was there or not. He didn't think so.

'Probably not,' Doreen said.

Her voice wavered slightly. He knew that wobble in the voice from when his mother was going through her divorce. He wondered if Doreen was going to cry. In his experience that was what usually followed the tremble. He would have to say something nice if that happened. What though? As he waited for an answer to come to him, he saw Doreen close her eyes, slip two fingers behind the lenses of her glasses and then press on the lids. That was a way to stop tears. He had observed his mother do the same.

'We just have to make the best of the hand we're dealt,' said Doreen, still pressing on her lids.

She turned away from him. She didn't want him to see her tears. There was another gesture he recognised. She dropped her hand and went in through the gate. He followed after her.

★

Tom had been gone a few hours.

'Can you eat them?' asked Doreen.

Ralph looked at the fish fingers on his plate. He knew the batter should be caramel-coloured and moist but tonight it was dark brown and baked dry.

'Left them under the grill too long,' said Doreen. 'Wasn't really concentrating.'

Ralph took a knife and went to cut an end off one of the fish fingers. The brittle carapace split and the piece shot off the plate. He lifted the piece from the table and popped it in his mouth and brought his teeth down. A feeling of hardness yielding, not so different from crunching on a boiled sweet and then incredible heat from the small flakes of fish inside. He breathed out quickly to cool the mouthful.

'No, it's all right, it's fine,' he said.

'Very forgiving you are, Ralph,' said Doreen. 'It's a virtue we should all cultivate.'

Ralph took this as a compliment to him. But later, lying in bed and waiting for sleep, he wondered if her comment was really meant for Tom, though he hadn't been there to hear it. Ralph considered this for a while and the more he pondered, the more he thought he was right. Then it occurred to Ralph that he had never had a thought like this before. Never. Where had it come from? And why had it come? It was a question he couldn't answer.

★

When he got in from school there was a blue airmail envelope sitting on the kitchen table with his name and address in his mother's writing. He opened the envelope and pulled out the letter from inside.

Dear Ralph,
Well, we're hard at it – trees are coming down, trees are going in, earth is being moved, ground is being cleared, paths being laid, foundations are going down – you know the sort of thing. I have half a dozen men working for me out on the estate and another two – one a draughtsman, the other a clerk who does the orders, pays the bills, et cetera – in my office at the back of my employers' house. I spend my days giving orders and I'm quite often hoarse by close of play.

Because of where my little house is, I see a lot of animals. The little bird mentioned in previous dispatches has been in and out a lot and I've also seen red squirrels, porcupines, skunk, and deer. The woods are absolutely teeming with life.

I had hoped – vaguely – that maybe I'd be released for Christmas and I could get back to see you, but no, it's not to be. They don't take proper Christmas holidays here like we do. You just get a couple of days. I hope you won't be too down-hearted by this news. We'll have to work out where you'll be and what you'll do. It'll be fun whatever it is. Perhaps Doreen will take you home. She has mentioned this. We'll see. Keep bright, keep happy, keep going.

Love, Mum xx

When he finished reading the letter, he was struck by the silence of the house. Was he on his own?

'Doreen?' he shouted.

No reply.

Then he noticed the ashtray on the table with two mangled cheroot butts lying amidst the dark ash. There was only one person he knew who smoked cheroots.

He went to the top of the basement stairs.

'Doreen?' he called. 'Doreen, are you there?'

He descended, stamping his feet to advertise his coming. At the bottom he turned towards the back. The basement bedroom door was open. The room beyond was dark.

'Doreen?'

'Yes.' Her voice was weary, croaky, crumpled.

He went to the door and looked in. He saw the double bed had a bump in the middle. It was Doreen curled up.

'Are you sick?' he asked. 'I could get you a Disprin.'

'I'm all right, just a bit tired. Just need a lie down,' said Doreen. 'Go up and put on the kettle. I'll be up in a tick.'

He went up, filled the kettle and turned on the gas. Doreen shuffled in. Her hair was tangled, her skirt creased.

'I don't know what's the matter,' she said. 'It must be the winter. It's wearing me out.'

She flopped down heavily. He stared at the kettle.

'Toast or something?'

'Nah,' she said, 'you're all right.'

★

On Sunday morning he did not hear Doreen returning from Mass. When he got up she was still in bed in the basement. He brought her down a cup of tea. Her bedroom was dark and smelt of sweat.

Doreen didn't get up until the afternoon. She was sick, he thought. He was sure of it. And what was it Tom had said? If she was sick he was to get in touch. He would definitely have to ring the number on the piece of paper Tom had given him. He took out the sheet of Basildon Bond and put it in the middle of an empty *Bryant & May* matchbox he had. It would be safe there. He would bring the matchbox to school. That's where he'd ring from.

★

St David's. Lunchtime. Monday. Ralph in the dining hall at a table that was old, gouged and coated in layers of yellow varnish, children crowded round, their voices echoing off the green walls. He had chosen to sit alone in order to eat quickly and get away. In front of him – a metal cup with water and a Pyrex dinner plate with a portion of cauliflower cheese. The food had a metal taste that put his teeth on edge.

He finished, handed his crockery through the hatch to Mrs King, one of the dinner ladies, and left. The hallway outside was a long space with panelled walls and gilt-framed paintings of past school heads hanging along its length. There was a large round wet patch in the middle of the floor and a nasty disinfectant smell lurking in the air. He guessed someone must have been sick here earlier, which the caretaker had then cleaned up. This explained the patch and the tang of Dettol.

He made his way to the front hall and the office door of the school secretary, Mrs Beadle-Collins. He knocked. He heard the typewriter going inside.

'Yes?' shouted Mrs Beadle-Collins.

He went in.

'Yes, Mr Goswell?' she said.

She was typing up a stencil from which she would later print smudged copies using the inky Gestetner machine in the corner. All the school's printed materials were produced using this system.

'Can I use the phone?' Ralph asked.

On request – if supported by a credible explanation – pupils were allowed to make emergency telephone calls during the lunch break.

'It's "May I use the phone?" Not "can",' said Mrs Beadle-Collins. 'And if you don't know even that I can hardly see you passing your Common Entrance.'

'May I use the phone?'

She took her hands off the typewriter keys and looked at him.

'Why?'

He'd prepared an excuse.

'The lady who looks after me, Doreen, isn't well. I need to ring her husband, urgently.'

Mrs Beadle-Collins appraised him. Her eyes were dark. Her mouth was red with neatly applied lipstick. Her short curly hair looked as if it were glued to her head. He felt a flush spreading under his chin.

'But won't he know this already?'

The flush moved toward his cheeks.

'He goes to work very early,' he said. 'She got sick after he left. He's building the Underground.'

'He is?'

'Yes, the line to Victoria.'

It was a relief to say something he knew to be true.

Mrs Beadle-Collins turned back to the keyboard and resumed typing.

'Is there a phone in the tunnel he's digging?' she asked. 'Is that how you'll get him?'

His cheekbones went red.

'No,' he said. 'I ring his sister and she gets the message to him.'

'Your housekeeper, Mrs MacGraw, is that the right name?'

'Yes.'

'Why doesn't she phone? You've a phone at home haven't you?'

'It's broken,' the words flew out.

Mrs Beadle-Collins stopped typing, turned and stared again.

His whole head was burning now and he was sure she saw this.

'Is something wrong, Ralph?'

He had only one option.

'They had a big row,' he said.

'Who?'

'Tom and Doreen. He moved out. He's staying with his sister. If I ring and tell him she isn't well, I think he'll come back. And he did ask me to ring if she got sick. And she is sick. So I'd be doing what he asked, if I do ring.'

There was a long pause.

'Your mother's in America, isn't she, Ralph?'

'Yes.'

'Is everything all right at home with Mrs MacGraw?'

'Yes,' he said.

'Are you sure?'

He nodded.

'All right, seeing as you've asked so nicely,' Mrs Beadle-Collins nodded at the door to the headmistress's study. There was a phone by Mrs Beadle-Collins but when pupils made a lunchtime call they used the extension on the headmistress's desk. 'You've got five minutes. Leave the door open.'

Mrs Beadle-Collins resumed typing. He opened the heavy door and stepped in. The study was a large book-lined room. It smelt vaguely of ammonia, and strongly of book glue, dust, ink and scent. The phone was Bakelite, large and black, and it crouched on the desk like an animal.

Ralph sat on the headmistress' chair. Through the doorway he saw Mrs Beadle-Collins front-on, her face tilted downward as she typed, brown buttons as big as stones running up the front of her dress and a thick necklace comprised of angular green shapes round her neck.

Ralph took the matchbox from his blazer pocket, got out the sheet of Basildon Bond and dialled. Through the earpiece he heard ringing at the other end. Then someone picked up.

'Hello.'

'Hello,' he said. 'This is Ralph.'

'Who?'

'The Ralph that Doreen and Tom look after.'

'Who?'

'Tom,' he said. 'Tom next door.'

'Oh, Tom next door, Veronica's brother, yes.'

'Well I'm Ralph. His wife looks after me.'

'His wife?'

'Doreen.'

'Oh right, you're that Ralph.'

'Yes,' he said.

'Well Tom's off at work, son, you won't get him now. I'd get you Veronica but she's working as a stitcher. Over in Harrow. And Ronnie's at work. So there isn't anyone at home. I'll have to take a message. Go on. I've pen and paper.'

Ralph stared out the window. He saw a weather-worn bench and a sundial.

'Doreen's sick.'

'Doreen is sick. Is that all?'

Well, no. He wanted to say, tell him Doreen's in bed all the time and cries a lot, and if he could just come back it would make such a difference. But he couldn't of course.

'Yes, that's it,' he said.

'All right. Will do. Bye for now.'

He heard the click as Betty put the handset back on the cradle at her end.

He refolded the sheet of paper and stuck it back in the matchbox. He stood, put the matchbox in his pocket and went through to the outer office where Mrs Beadle-Collins was hammering on.

'Success?'

'Yes, thank you.'

'I don't know if I believe you,' said Mrs Beadle-Collins, still typing away, 'but if you need the phone again and come back, I'll probably say yes, providing you ask properly.'

★

The week had passed. No word from Tom. It was now Friday afternoon. He and Benedict approached the gate of 56. His matchbox was in his pocket, the sheet stowed inside.

'Need to come in and use your phone,' he said.

'What!'

Benedict got into the gateway, turned and blocked Ralph's way.

'The phone's very expensive, you know,' said Benedict. 'Go home and use your own.'

'It's an emergency.'

'Really. Go on, tell me about it. You can trust your old friend Benedict.'

Ralph looked up. Low cloud, pigeon grey.

'Tom's moved out to his sister's,' said Ralph.

'Oh dear, trouble at t'mill,' said Benedict in a Yorkshire accent.

He was copying Clive, who liked to say this, though Benedict's accent was rather better than his father's.

'I need to ring Tom,' said Ralph, 'but I can't from home, can I? Doreen will know and I don't want her to know. That's why I need to come in and use *your* phone.'

Benedict stepped back and swept his arm towards the side passage, 'Be my guest.'

Ralph went across the garden and through the Boscombes' side door. Ginny and Jeannie were at the kitchen table drinking tea.

'He wants to use the phone,' said Benedict, coming in behind.

'That's all right, he's welcome to it.'

Ginny was in a dress covered with swirls and braiding.

'You know where it is, don't you, Ralph?'

It was in the front room, the one he slept in at home on the ground floor by the front door. He found his way there and went in. There was a chaise lounge covered in green velvet, an eight-sided table and dark red walls covered with Victorian pictures in ornate frames. Half were of scenes from the Old Testament and half were pin-sharp daguerreotypes of naked women with long hair and plump thighs. He turned on the light. The ceiling lampshade was made of yellow glass with nymphs and fronds painted on it and the light it gave out was yellow and strange.

The phone was on a little table and was modern, green and curvy. He sat on the stool beside it, extracted the Basildon Bond sheet from his matchbox and dialled.

'Yes.' It was Betty. He recognised her voice.

'This is Ralph,' he said.

'Oh hello, Ralph. Yes, I know who you are and I passed on the message. Has Tom not been in touch?'

He wouldn't reply to that.

'Is Veronica home?'

'You'll have to wait while I fetch her.'

'I can wait,' he said.

He heard the clunk of the handset going down at the other end. He heard a strange singing noise. Quite a long time passed. Then he heard footsteps.

'Yes.'

'This is Ralph.'

'I know who you are,' said Veronica from the other end. 'You don't have to tell me. We got your last message. What do you want now?'

'Well …' he began.

'You really have some cheek, young man,' she said. 'You take the biscuit, you know that?'

'I'm not being cheeky,' he said quickly.

There was a long pause. The line whispered and chirped.

'What are you ringing about?'

He could feel his heart thumping.

'Do you think Tom could come back?' he asked.

'Come back?'

'Just to visit and say hello to Doreen,' he said quickly.

'You want Tom to come and visit Doreen?'

'Yes,' he said.

'After what she's done?'

'Yes,' he said, though he had no idea what he was agreeing to.

'Do you have any idea what you're asking? She's a horror, Doreen. She's done the worst thing a woman could do to a man. You do know that, don't you?'

'No,' he said.

'Well that makes it even worse. You're asking what you're asking and you don't even know what's going on.'

'Doreen's sick and Tom said I was to tell him if she got sick,' he said quickly.

'Oh I bet she's bloody sick. Of course she's bloody sick. Stupid bloody woman. Of course she's bloody sick. It's called morning bloody sickness.'

'Tom said to tell him if she got sick,' he said again.

'Well he would,' said Veronica, 'because my brother is a soft-hearted eejit. But I'm here to tell you that I am not and, I can assure you, I have enough of a hard heart to do for the both of us. So let me make myself perfectly clear. After everything she's done, her lies, her carrying on behind his back, Tom will not be having anything to do with her ever again, do you understand? And while I have you, you can do something for me. You can go and tell her my brother never wants to see her again. Got that? And you can add, from me, I think she's gutless. She should be doing this, and that she put you, a child, up to this, well, that tells you everything you need to know about her.'

'She didn't ask me to ring,' said Ralph.

'Pull the other one. Of course she did.'

'She didn't. I'm doing this myself.'

'I don't believe you.'

His throat hurt. This was the feeling he always got before he cried.

'I'm only twelve,' said Ralph, 'and I'm useless at lying. I'm no good at it.'

Silence.

'Can you at least tell Tom I phoned?'

'I'll tell him,' she said, 'and I'll tell him to avoid Doreen like the plague. Got that? Don't ring again.'

The phone went dead.

He returned the handset to the cradle and stared at the button in the middle of the dialling ring with Ginny's number and the message, 'For Ambulance, Fire, Police, ring

999'. His thighs were trembling. His stomach was churning. He'd sort of known all along, hadn't he, without admitting it to himself, what this was about? Yes, he'd sort of known. But also he hadn't known. But now he'd heard Veronica, it wasn't possible to both know and not know anymore. There was only one possibility. The trouble was, he wasn't sure he was ready for that.

It was some minutes before he was able to return to the kitchen.

'Everything all right?' asked Ginny when he did.

'Yeah.'

'He told me.' She pointed at Benedict, who was sitting sipping a mug of Horlicks. 'We don't have to pretend I don't know. Did you get Tom?'

'No, but I left a message.'

'I'm not going to press you but you do understand, any problems, worries, anything, you can come to me.'

She stared at him and he looked down at the floor.

'Do I hear yes?'

He nodded, 'Yes.'

As soon as he got home he hid the sheet with the number in his H. Upmann box and then he hid the box under his socks.

December

Dear Ralph,

It's turned, the weather. Oh. My. Lord. We don't know how lucky we are in England. We grumble a lot. Why is it always raining? Why are there always gloomy grey skies hanging over us? Why doesn't the sun shine more? We should try living with the sort of snow they get here. One season here and we wouldn't be nearly so ready to complain about our weather, I'd hazard. We might even start to be a bit grateful for it.

We've had two falls so far. Heavy ones, and I mean heavy ones. And this snow isn't like the warm slushy stuff that lies around for a few days and then melts away like we usually get. Oh no, this snow is thick, heavy, deep, and well-nigh impenetrable. Our first fall was a few inches: it wasn't nice but one could cope. The second – completely different. When I opened the door of my cabin the morning after the second fall, what I saw was snow several feet deep stretching in every direction. Oh yes, lovely and white and pristine, but absolutely impossible to move about in until the snow plough had been up and cleared a pathway. Oh yes, the snow plough. That's right. My employers have their own private plough. For their estate. So it can continue to function, no matter the weather. Can you imagine having your own private plough? The rich are definitely different to us.

Obviously, this second fall held things up for a while but in a surprisingly short space of time, the snow had been cleared and we were back at work. The Americans really do not hang about. (That's another regard in which they put us to shame.) Within a day or two our construction programme was back on track. I've also got two huge heated glasshouses where I'm cultivating a mass of things which will be planted out in the spring and I've no end of re-potting and general faffing about to do and whilst we waited for the snow ploughs, et cetera, I was in there doing what had to be done. So, rest assured, your mother is busy. Very.

I'm always droning on about work but there are so many other things to report on. I don't have much direct experience of what I'm about to say – I get what I know from watching their terrible television programmes, and talking to the men who are doing the construction work – but even from these limited sources I'm discovering a lot about the US that isn't pretty. The whole country is simmering with discontent, anger, and frustration. There may be a lot of rich people here but there are also a lot of very poor people, and like their weather, which is so very extreme, when they are unhappy the poor people are *really* unhappy – the colour bar, police brutality, segregation, the war in Vietnam, these are just some of the causes of their unhappiness. Now in England we have some of the same problems but like our weather we don't seem to do 'extreme' in the same way as they do in America. In fact, we don't do extreme at all, full stop, and that, as I am beginning to discover, is a blessing. I feel a need to deliver a sermon coming over me, its title 'The Superiority of English Moderation over American Excess' but that would just be too tedious. So I'll stop now before I start.

Love, Mum xx

★

He lay in his bed, half-awake. Saturday morning. No school. Bliss. He could hear the frames of his bay windows moving as the wind blew and what sounded like tiny stones being flung, handful after handful, against the glass.

Footfalls in the hallway and then Doreen beside him.

'Wakey wakey.'

He opened an eye and looked up. It looked like she had a helmet on but it was the curlers she had in and the way her hair was arranged around them.

'Ralph,' she said. 'I've got to go to the hospital this morning. I'd forgotten all about it. I'm away with fairies at the moment.'

He rubbed his face, yawned, sat up.

'Are you sick?' he asked.

'No,' she said. 'I'm not. It's just a check-up.'

He wondered where this was going.

'Can I ask you a favour?'

'You're not going to make me hoover again?'

Over the proceeding weeks she'd complained of back pain and he'd had to hoover the stairs for her, several times, and do all sorts of other chores as well.

'I can leave you with Ginny,' she said. 'Or, if you like, you can come with me instead.'

So that was where this was going.

'To the hospital?'

'Yes.'

'Will I be let off hoovering again if I come?'

'We'll see.'

He shrugged his assent. 'All right, might as well.'

She made him two soft-boiled eggs for breakfast and advised him to bring something to read. He decided he'd bring his *Lord of the Flies*. In class they were still working their way through the novel and he decided he'd re-read those pages that he knew they'd cover in English on Monday.

Doreen opened the front door. They peered out. Water was sheeting from the gutter of the little porch in front of them while in their garden thick spears of rain were thudding into the flagstones.

'Today of all days,' said Doreen, 'I have my bloody hospital appointment.'

Doreen stuck the umbrella out and opened it. Water dinning on the stretched material.

'Hold my arm,' said Doreen, 'and keep dry.'

He banged the door behind. They moved forward as one and crossed the garden. Through the gate and out to Falkland Road. A membrane of water covered the pavement. Their shoes splashing as they walked. Rainwater surging in the gutter. A ferocious wind gust wrenched the umbrella's struts upward. The rain drove at him and stung his face. Doreen lunged the umbrella forward. The struts snapped back into position. The umbrella over their heads again, they passed the Boscombes'. Both his socks, where they touched the toes of his leather shoes, were already damp. They passed under the railway bridge then hurried on to the end of Falkland Road and turned right onto Putney Bridge Road, heading for the High Street. A parade of shops – greengrocer, barber, butcher, the hardware shop where they bought their paraffin. Every shop window streaming with condensation. Two old women in capes with matching oilskin hats fixed under their chins by cords, their garments slick with wet and dripping. The wet in his shoes had spread along the soles of his socks and crept up his heels. He imagined blotting paper soaking up ink.

They got to the High Street and crossed at the Belisha beacon. On the other side their local Wimpy Bar and another streaming window with a message in big loopy writing that was supposed to look like snow written inside so it could be read from outside in the street and that seemed to Ralph to be floating in wet: 'We wish all our patrons a very Happy Xmas and a prosperous New Year'.

They turned in the direction of the river. His shoes completely flooded now and with each step he felt water was being pressed out of his socks' wool and then, a moment later, reabsorbed. Squelch, squelch, squelch.

They turned left just before the bridge. The river was to their right, its surface ruffled by the wind and slashed by the rain. The Spencer Arms loomed ahead. Its windows had messages written inside them in white too like the Wimpy, including, Ralph noticed, '1965 is going to be brilliant'. There were a couple of Mods in the Arms' doorway. They were waiting for the bus, he guessed. The stop was just a few feet away at the kerb.

They reached the pub's doorway. One of the boys spat out into the rain while the other stared gloomily at the river.

'Room for two more?' asked Doreen.

The Mods' hair was plastered to their heads and the shoulders of their mohair suits were so saturated they were dark, like wet cardboard.

'Yeah, all right,' said the one who'd just spat.

Doreen collapsed the umbrella and she and Ralph squeezed in. Both youths had Woolworths bags, the small kind for holding singles. They'd been shopping for records in Woolies, Ralph guessed, on the High Street.

'Where's your coats, boys?' Doreen asked.

'You what?' asked the one who'd spat.

'Why aren't you wearing your coats?' she asked. 'You know – raincoats. People wear them in the rain. Haven't you heard?'

'Didn't feel like it.'

'But look at that rain,' said Doreen. 'You can't go out in this without a coat.'

'It's only water.'

This was the other one. The one who'd been staring at the river.

'When you get home, you hang those jackets to dry on a good hanger, or they'll lose their shape,' said Doreen.

'You're worse than our Mum,' they both said together.

'Oh, you're brothers?' asked Doreen.

'Twins actually but not identical,' said the spitter.

He and his brother then laughed together, though Ralph had no idea why.

The bus appeared round the corner and came towards them, water flying up from under its wheels. The twins waved their arms at the driver, although it wasn't a request stop. The bus pulled up. The twins jumped on and bolted up the stairs to the upper deck.

'Going to Queen Mary's?' Doreen called in to the conductor who was standing in front of the luggage hold.

'Course,' he called back.

They got on and sat on the banquette seat just inside on the left. A single passenger sat on the banquette opposite. It was a man in a wet coat, a sodden scarf wrapped round his mouth and a damp hat pulled down over his forehead. His eyes were bright blue, like gas jets. The window behind the man was smeared and spattered with rain. Ralph could only just make out the river beyond.

The conductor pressed the button in the wall of the luggage hold. The bell pinged in the driver's cab. The bus pulled away. The conductor approached them.

'One and a half,' Doreen said to the conductor, proffering a half-crown. 'Queen Mary's.'

The conductor twisted the handle. Their tickets shot out of his machine. He tore them off. They were white oblongs with smudged blue writing. He handed them to her with the change.

'Will you give us a shout when we're there?'

'Course,' he said.

The conductor went to the stairs and climbed to the upper deck.

'What a day,' said Doreen. 'Aren't you very good to come?'

'I'm not doing anything,' Ralph said.

The image of Steed came fleetingly to mind. Wasn't that the sort of thing he'd say? He thought so.

The bus trundled on. He could hear the tyres splashing through the water in the road as it moved along. He wriggled his toes. Not only were both socks quite wet but there was water inside his shoes sloshing about. There was also a drip on the end of his nose but it was too much of an effort to get his handkerchief out of his pocket. He wiped his nose on the sleeve of his duffle coat.

'Ralph,' said Doreen. 'Don't do that. Have some manners. You're being watched.'

She nodded across the aisle. Then she opened her handbag, pulled out a tissue and gave it to him.

He looked across and saw the man on the opposite banquette with the bright blue eyes staring. He touched his nose with the tissue, then turned his head and leant into Doreen.

'Why's he staring?' he whispered.

'No idea but he's giving me the heebie-jeebies. Distract me. Talk to me.'

'What about?'

'Anything.'

'Like what?'

'Tell me about this book you're doing in school.'

'*Lord of the Flies*?'

'Yes.'

'It's about these boys marooned on a desert island, and it starts off with them together, and the leaders are Ralph and Piggy, but then all the other boys turn against Ralph and Piggy, and they pretend their friend Simon, who's a hermit …'

'Whose friend?'

'Ralph and Piggy's. They pretend he's a pig and they kill him but they know he isn't a pig and then later they kill Piggy and Miss Loudon says what the book says is we need dialogue and balance and consensus and democracy and the rule of law to stop us behaving like animals.'

'That sounds very interesting,' said Doreen.

Ralph didn't believe she meant it. He also knew he hadn't explained it very well. It was much better than he'd explained it. He thought it was a brilliant book.

'When I was a girl,' said Doreen, 'growing up, the house was so crowded, I used to go out into the fields and imagine what it would be like to be alone. I thought that would be just glorious. But now I've reached the ripe old age that I am, nothing frightens me more than being alone. Lord, listen to me, what am I like? It's him across there staring who's making me blather like this.'

Ralph put his head down but lifted his eyes and looked across again. The eyes were still staring but he wondered if they were seeing him and Doreen. The man wasn't looking out, he decided, he was looking in.

★

A corridor, Queen Mary's hospital. Polished dark wooden floor. Pools of rainwater. Where they lay, the wood was black not brown. Smell of bleach and hot dust. And stretching for as far as he was able to see, hanging from the ceiling and jutting from the walls like road markers, square varnished boards with, written in red, mysterious acronyms and long, unfamiliar Latin words that meant nothing to Ralph.

'Maternity,' said Doreen quietly, 'that's what we're looking for.'

That was a word he did know. He looked and yes, there was a board sticking down from the ceiling with 'Maternity' on it, bold and red, plus an arrow pointing the way.

'There it is,' he said.

Doreen saw it too. They went forward. He heard his shoes squelch. His thoughts were surging. Over the proceeding months all sorts of things had happened that he knew must fit together only he hadn't been able to see how: then, when he was on the phone to Veronica, though he'd no intention of ever sharing this with Doreen, it had begun to dawn on him what might be happening because of the quip about morning sickness. Only he hadn't been sure. Not one hundred percent sure. Now, at last, he was. Only now, he also realised, it wasn't enough.

A nurse in uniform heading towards them.

Yes, he had a fact and yes, it was a big fact but facts weren't what mattered.

The nurse's uniform made a scratchy sound as she moved.

It was what flowed from the facts that mattered.

A waft of starch from the nurse's uniform as she passed.

What was his mother going to say about this?

Double doors swung open for them.

And was Doreen going to stay and look after him?

Double doors swung shut behind them, the edges clicking and banging as they ticked backwards and forwards.

Or would she have to go away before his mother came home in the summer?

The floor underfoot had changed.

And if that happened, if Doreen went, where would he go?

From wood to polished concrete.

To Ginny's? Or to his mother's sister?

Speckles in the mix, flashing.

But his aunt lived in Reigate, miles from London.

Strong smell of baked radiator paint.

He'd have to change schools, so that wasn't going to work.

Faraway, so faint, a human cry. And what about Tom? A ringing phone. No one answering. Was Tom now gone for ever?

While his thoughts churned and the sensation of the place flooded over him, he and Doreen followed the signs, going left, going right, passing through swing door after swing door, until finally they reached an open door with 'Maternity' on it and went through.

On the far side Ralph found himself in a vast waiting room. Rows of chairs, the curved wooden stacking kind like they had at school and on the chairs only women, some pregnant, sitting, waiting, some with children. Low voices, everyone on their best behaviour. There was a smell of hot nylon, scorched cotton and the special dog pee smell that he knew came from wet tweed when it was in contact with heat. Every cast-iron radiator in the room had something drying on it. Doreen handed him the umbrella.

'Over there.'

She pointed at two seats.

'And hang the brolly and your coat on the hook.'

While she went away to the counter he trotted over to the selected spot. He hung the umbrella and took off his coat. As he stretched up to put the hood over a hook, he felt his shoulder blades and his back were damp. He fished his book out of his pocket. It was soaking and had expanded like a concertina.

He sat and began separating the pages one by one and blowing on them. Doreen returned, hung her wet coat near his and sat beside him.

'I suppose the penny's dropped?' she said.

'Yes,' he said.

Oh he understood. He knew for sure. Now what he needed were his questions answered. But he must be careful. He mustn't show how anxious he was. He must look calm. He remembered his hero, Steed – there was his model. Every sentence before it was spoken needed to be submitted to the Steed test and checked to see if he could have spoken it and, if not, then the sentence would have to be rejected. So what first? A general inquiry. He tried it out in his head. It would do.

'How will you manage?' he asked.

'Oh I will, I'll have to, won't I?'

Now something grown-up.

'I don't think my mum will mind.'

He was impressed by that.

'She doesn't,' Doreen said.

'You've told her?' he asked.

It was out before he could vet it. It sounded like a criticism of her, which was wrong.

'When you were at school I phoned her one day. Took hours. She thought I was ringing about you and once I told her why I was calling, she was more relieved than anything. To be honest I wasn't sure she really followed what I said. Then, a few days after the call, I got a telegram telling me all was good and not to worry.'

He much enjoyed hearing this piece of information.

'You're not leaving then?'

'No.'

'Is it a secret?'

'What?'

'This.'

'From who?'

'Benedict.'

'I wouldn't think so.'

'Are you pleased?'

'I don't know. I'm frightened of the pain. And the future. And how I'll manage. I live in your house. I can go on working there and mind my baby. But if I have to leave, it'll be a different story.'

'But you don't think that's going to happen do you?'

'No.'

He paused. It came to him. What to ask next.

'What will they say at home?'

'In Waterford you mean?'

'Yes.'

'My mother will probably kill me.'

'Will she?'

'No, not really kill me. You know what people are like when they're raging, they come out with, "Oh I could kill you." Well that's what she'll be like.'

'Because you're having a baby?'

'Yes.'

'But won't your baby be her grandchild?'

'Yes.'

'So she should be happy then, not raging. Shouldn't she?'

Doreen took off her glasses, pressed both eyes with the heels of her hands, and put her glasses back on.

'Not under these circumstances.'

'But you're married,' he said.

He was delighted by this. It was true. She was. All she had to do was call Tom home and these circumstances would go away. That's how he saw it. It was so simple.

'Tom isn't the daddy.'

Of course he'd known this as well but up until now he'd hoped that this wouldn't matter. All right, so it did, in which case, obviously there was only one answer then.

'Marry the daddy.'

'It's not as simple as that.'

'My mum got a divorce. You can.'

A tear rolled out of Doreen's left eye and meandered down her cheek, leaving a wet streak behind.

'He wouldn't marry me,' she said. 'I'm sure he wouldn't.'

'Have you asked him?'

'No, but I know the answer.'

'MacGraw,' a nurse shouted, reading the name from the manila folder she held.

'Don't like doctors,' said Doreen. 'They're always poking.'

She stood up and walked across.

'MacGraw?'

'Yes.'

'Mr Humphries will see you now.'

The nurse indicated a small room with a man in a white coat inside at a desk and an examining table behind.

Doreen stepped forward. The nurse followed and closed the door.

At the far end of the room Ralph noticed a woman with bare feet. Well, if she had, why shouldn't he? He unlaced his shoes and pulled off his wet socks. He laid his socks lengthwise along the hot pipe behind his seat that connected two radiators. Then he stuck his legs out, wiggled his wet toes, sat back and opened his damp paperback.

By the time he read the last line of chapter nine, which described Simon's dead body after his murder being borne by the swell out towards the open sea, he was tingling and trembling in the space behind the stomach and near the spine where such sensations registered. The story of Simon's killing was so shocking it was inevitable he would feel what he was feeling and the fact he'd already read the material didn't matter. He could read the story of Simon's death ten times and it would always disturb him. But there was a puzzle here. He had read all C. S. Forester's Hornblower novels which, set at sea during the Napoleonic wars, were also full of people dying. Yet none of the deaths in those Hornblower books affected him in the way Simon's death did. Forester's dead sailors didn't seem real. He couldn't see them. On the other hand, he saw the whole of Simon's end as clearly with his mind's eye as he saw anything with his actual eye. So how did he explain the difference? It occurred to him now that maybe this was to do with the way the words were laid down. Forester's words just described, whereas the words used to describe Simon's end didn't just describe what happened, they *were* what happened. When the boys were spearing Simon, the sentences were like spears, they were sharp hurting killing things, and at the end, when Simon's body was carried away to sea, the sentences rolled like the waves that bore him away.

He draped the damp book over the hot pipe near his socks and sat back to think further about this. In the past he had never had any trouble telling those books that did and did not work apart. His feelings had done that job for him. But now, he realised, instead of relying on his feelings he might actually be able to explain why. Some authors didn't make you believe, and theirs were the books that didn't work. But other authors, because they made their words seem like the things they were describing – spears, waves, whatever – they made you believe completely, that's how the magic was done, and theirs were the books that did work. He would talk to Miss Loudon about this in Monday's class, he decided.

*

The next day was Sunday. When she came back from Mass in her black dress, he thought Doreen looked stouter. She also seemed different in another way.

*

Morning. Cold, dark, wet fog, frost smeared over every surface. He peered ahead down Falkland Road through the gloom. Ginny standing by the gate of 56 with Benedict beside her. Perhaps she was going to offer to drive them to school. He hoped so.

'Hello, Ralph,' she said when he came up.

'Hello.'

'Have you got any plans on Sunday?'

'I don't think so.'

'Why don't you come for lunch then? Say one-thirty.'

'Righto.'

'Righto, till Sunday,' said Ginny. 'Have a good day at school.'

'Oh right, thanks,' said Benedict.

The boys trudged to the railway steps and began to climb in synch. Neither spoke.

Once at the top they saw all the grey surfaces of the footbridge were white with frost. They began to walk.

'Why did your mum invite me to lunch?' asked Ralph.

'What?'

'On Sunday.'

'Obviously she's heard you're not being fed.'

'But I am being fed.'

'Not what she's heard.'

'Do you know something?'

'Two and two make four?'

'You do know something.'

'Two and two is four. You do too.'

Ralph reached up and snapped Benedict's cap off.

'See your cap?'

He danced away to the parapet and put his arm over the top. It was a long way down to the river.

'Tell me or I'll let go. I'll drop your hat in.'

'Oh don't be such a baby,' said Benedict.

'I will. And it's Friday.'

On Friday mornings everyone's uniform was checked when they entered school. Without his school cap Benedict might get fifty lines.

'I'll denounce you,' said Benedict. 'I'll say you threw my cap in the river deliberately to get me into trouble. They'll probably send you home you know.'

Ralph hadn't imagined it would go like this. He'd thought Benedict would just tell him what he knew straightaway and that would be the end of it. But it wasn't to be.

'Oh here,' said Ralph,' have your sordid cap.'

He held the hat by the peak and swiped it back in place on Benedict's head.

'Oh good, we've calmed down,' said Benedict. 'Now, say sorry.'

'I didn't do anything,' said Ralph.

'You were going to throw my cap in the Thames and that cap cost a guinea.'

'No it didn't.'

'Oh dearie me, she's still smarting.'

'You do know. I can tell.'

'I don't know what she's going on about.'

'One day I'll know something you'll want to know and I'll remember this and I won't tell you.'

Benedict didn't offer a reply to this. They walked on. In the cold silence Ralph heard the tiny noise of frost compressing underfoot with each step he took.

'You'll have to swear,' said Benedict eventually. 'if I tell you.'

'What?'

'To keep it a secret. I'm not supposed to tell you. It's supposed to be a surprise.'

'Of course I'll swear.'

'Go on then.'

'I swear. Cross my heart and hope to die.'

'And you won't let on I've told you. When the time comes, you act like it's a surprise. You know nothing.'

'What do you think I am? An idiot? Of course.'

'Your mum's ringing our house on Sunday to speak to you.'

'Oh.'

Then a second later he came out with it without thinking.

'Why would she do that?'

'As a surprise.'

'She could surprise me at home just the same.'

'She could, but she's going to surprise you at our house.'

'But wouldn't it make more sense to surprise me at home?'

'How would I know?' said Benedict. 'This is something she and my mum cooked up. Ask her yourself on Sunday when she rings.'

For the rest of the journey to school and indeed for the rest of the day, a little throb of anxiety kept pulsing. His mother had something to say that she didn't want Doreen to know about. That's why he was having to go to Ginny's to take her call.

★

On Sunday he traipsed along Falkland Road to the Boscombes'. Through the side door and in. Douglas sitting at the table and Ginny standing close by him. His hand was on the back of her knees, just where the hem of her dress was. As Ralph came forward he let his hand drop.

'Hello,' Ginny said. 'There's a roast chicken for lunch but first you've a surprise.'

'Really,' said Ralph, taking care to sound excited.

'Your mum's ringing. At two. Isn't that a nice surprise?'

'Really,' he said.

He thought he didn't seem very excited but he didn't think she noticed.

Ralph sat at the table. Ginny gave him a mug of tea. Douglas talked about the underwater telephone cable between Britain and America and the unnerving noises users frequently reported hearing during calls.

'Ignore them if you can,' he said. 'Blank them out.'

The phone rang in the front room. Ginny went to answer. A few moments later she summoned him.

He went to the front room. The electric light was on. The bulb gave off a low whine. Ginny stood holding the green handset.

'Sit down,' she said.

She pointed at the little table. He sat. She handed him the handset.

'She'll be through in a tick.'

He put the earpiece against his head. He heard the echoing thrum Douglas had spoken about. Ginny left, closing the door behind.

'Hello,' he heard, the voice far away, rather faint.

The noise of the cable was bigger than the voice it carried to him.

'Yes.'

'This is your mother, Ralph.'

He wondered why she said that. Who else would it be?

'Yes,' he said, 'this is me.'

'Can you hear me?'

She didn't sound like she sounded in life. She sounded like a recording of herself.

'I can,' he said.

A tiny delay before she had his words.

'I'm so pleased to hear your voice. Are you pleased to hear my voice?'

On top of her words, the echo of her words.

'Yes,' he said.

'Are you well? Is school all right? Working hard?'

'Yes.'

'Everything at home okay?'

149

'Yes.'

'We don't have long,' she said.

Fizzing then a pop.

'How is Doreen?'

'Fine.'

'I'm very worried.'

'She's all right.'

'How can that be? Tom's gone. She's having a baby. It isn't his. She must be in a terrible state.'

Noises. Oceanic.

'She's. All. Right.'

'You're not just saying that so I won't worry?'

Too emphatic, she'd think he was lying. Row back.

'No,' he said. 'She's soldiering on.'

'Soldiering on,' his mother said. 'Right. Good.'

He'd picked the right phrase.

'And looking after you all right is she?'

'It's better than that,' he said. 'She's absolutely brilliant. I haven't one bad thing to say about her.'

'Really, she's coping and everything's fine?'

'Yeah,' he said.

'Well, I *am* pleased. That is a relief. I was very worried when I heard. What an ordeal for her. I can scarcely imagine what she's feeling.'

Now he could move safely to what he really wanted to know.

'Are you going to throw her out?' he asked.

'What?'

'Throw her out?'

'Why on earth would I do that?'

'Because of what's happened.'

'That's precisely why I wouldn't throw her out.'

Clicks and bangs like hammering heard in a distant room.

'You don't do that to a woman in her condition. She needs to be cared for, not punished.'

'Ma'am?' The voice was American. The operator. 'One minute.'

'We haven't long, Ralph. I'll have to be quick. Doreen has to go home for a few days at Christmas. She wrote and asked if she could bring you but I've decided you'll go to Wales with Ginny instead. I've already written to Doreen. She knows.'

'But you said. In your letter. You couldn't get back here for Christmas, so I could go with Doreen.'

'I didn't promise, Ralph, I just floated the idea, and now I'm telling you – no.'

He felt the hot tremble of disappointment.

'Please let me go.'

'I know you want to, darling, but I have to say no. Doreen's got a lot to sort out with her folks and she won't be able to do that with you in tow.'

'But I know she won't mind having me,' he said. He was sure this was true.

'Ralph,' his mother said, 'there's nothing more to discuss. You'll go next year, once I'm back.'

'But that's ages away.'

'Ten seconds,' said the operator.

'Don't worry, it'll come round soon enough. Big kisses my darling boy. I'm missing you madly. And I can't wait till I get back home and see you again.'

'Time,' said the US operator.

The line went dead. There was just the underwater susurrus in his right ear and the high-pitched noise from the electric light in the other.

'You can replace the handset how.' This was an English voice.

He put the handset on the cradle. The phone clicked mysteriously a couple of times. He thought of an animal settling itself after exertion.

He got up and went back down to the kitchen. Ginny was sitting at the table drinking a glass of cider.

'So,' she said. 'Nice chat? And you're coming to Wales for Christmas. Isn't that brilliant?'

★

Doreen packed a big suitcase with his Wellington boots, heavy jumpers, other clothes and Christmas presents to put under the Boscombes' Christmas tree in Wales. He lugged the case to the Boscombes' one evening and Douglas put it in the boot of Ginny's red Saab. He and Ginny were going down early to light the fires and get the farmhouse aired and would take the case with them. Ralph, Benedict and Jeannie would follow by train. Clive was also making his own way to Wales and bringing his new girlfriend, Yvonne, with him. They would not be staying in the farmhouse but in a tiny labourer's cottage beside it that had once been home to the shepherds who'd worked on the farm. It was Benedict who had told him about these arrangements.

★

Friday night. He would leave for Wales in the morning. Doreen gave him fish pie for supper, his favourite meal. Once they'd eaten they went to the River room. The fire was lit, coals of red anthracite smouldering in the grate. He turned the television on. It hummed as it warmed. He sat on the armchair. Doreen sank down on the sofa and swung up her feet. She was stouter about the middle.

'That's better,' she said.

A soft crumpled noise from the set and the sound of studio laughter and the image of Eric Morecombe and Ernie Wise in dinner jackets on the screen.

'I'm going to miss you. Are you going to miss me?'

'Yes,' said Ralph.

'That didn't sound very convincing.'

She picked up her knitting. She was making a blanket for the baby. He heard the needles clacking.

Ralph sat watching the screen but not paying attention. He felt miserable.

'I don't really want to go to Wales,' he said.

'We can't have what we want just because we wish it,' said Doreen.

This was something she'd recently said quite often, 'But it isn't for long. Blink and you'll miss it,' she continued.

Doreen put her knitting down, heaved herself up and went out. A few minutes later she called him to the kitchen.

He went through and found her at the table.

'I've made you a timetable.'

She waved a bit of paper covered with rectangles drawn using the bread knife as a ruler inside which he could see what she'd written.

Sat 19 Dec 1964 Leave for Wales	Sun 20 Dec 1964	Mon 21 Dec 1964	Tues 22 Dec 1964	Wed 23 Dec 1964	Thur 24 Dec 1964 Christmas Eve
Fri 25 Dec 1964 Christmas Day	Sat 26 Dec 1964	Sun 27 Dec 1964	Mon 28 Dec 1964	Tues 29 Dec 1964	Wed 30 Dec 1964
Thurs 31 Dec 1964 New Year's Eve	Fri 1 Jan 1965 New Year's Day	Sat 2 Jan 1965 Home from Wales	Sun 3 Jan 1965 Get ready for school	Mon 4 Jan 1965 Back to school	

'It's just fourteen days you're in Wales,' said Doreen, 'and they'll fly and before you know it we'll both be back.'

It still seemed like a long time whatever she said.

As he lay waiting for sleep later, the back of his throat felt sore. When he was sad he always got this feeling at the back of his throat.

In the morning the soreness wasn't there but after breakfast, when he knew the time to go was looming, it came back.

'Come on, Buster,' said Doreen. 'You've a train to catch.'

She had her coat on. He pulled on his duffle coat and stowed *The Day of the Triffids* in his pocket with her time-table tucked inside. They went out by the side door and into the street. Mrs Moody's next door had a holly wreath on the knocker and inside her front room stood a tree decorated with coloured electric lights that were turning on and off.

They walked to the Boscombes' gate.

'I won't come in,' said Doreen. 'I've got to go back and get everything tidied up and give a key to Mrs Moody.'

She put her arms round him and kissed him on the top of his head. He could feel her bulge through her coat.

'Be a good boy and I'll see you soon unless you see me first.'

He went through the gate. She turned and went home.

Paddington Station. They were on the platform. The Carmarthen train was there.

'There it is,' said Benedict.

He pointed at the number 4 on the grimy carriage that matched the one on Jeannie's booking sheet.

'Do I get a prize?' Benedict hooted.

Benedict opened the carriage door and went in. Jeannie next. Ralph last. The corridor smelt of stewed tea, hot metal and stale tobacco.

'Found it,' he heard Benedict shout, meaning their compartment.

He saw his friend vanishing sideways, Jeannie following. He came up and looked through the glass into their second-class compartment. He saw three dockets attached by buttons that indicated their reserved seats.

'This is us,' said Jeannie.

He went in and put his coat on the narrow rack below the wider higher one, which was for suitcases, and sat as Jeannie instructed in the seat by the window facing the front of the train. He felt its coarse itchy material through his trousers. The window on his right was smeared with watermarks and spotted with little black smuts. Benedict sat opposite. Jeannie sat beside him, her picnic bag beside her to the left. It was leather, cream with black trim. Two dented Thermos flasks with tea and soup stuck out of it – Ralph imagined them as a pair of lighthouses – with food for the journey packed between.

A woman in a heavy fur coat stalked along the platform outside, followed by a porter pushing a handcart. As he stared he imagined Doreen at home, turning off the gas at the wall, tightening the taps in the sink, sliding the bolts on the side door home, pulling on her black coat and her black gloves that she wore to Mass, opening the front door, lifting her suitcase out, pulling the front door closed behind, handing Mrs Moody the key to hold in case of emergencies and leaving Falkland Road.

'I'm hungry,' he heard Benedict say. 'Can I have something now?'

A man passed the window with a dachshund in a box, its head sticking out.

'No,' said Jeannie. 'We haven't left the station.'

Benedict tapped his toe with his foot.

'Biscuit, fatso?'

His throat was sore: the sadness ache.

'Suppose so,' Ralph said.

It might help him ignore his throat and the feelings that went with it.

'Please, Jeannie,' said Benedict. 'We're dying of hunger.'

She prised the lid off a Quality Street tin and extracted two shortbread fantails, one for each of them.

'Not another word about food till we're out of London,' she said and snapped the lid back on.

The sounds of metal shod wheels rumbling on concrete; a guard's whistle; an engine pulling away; a man coughing in a nearby compartment; carriage doors slamming; a baby wailing. Ralph took his first bite. Grains of sugar from the shortbread sprinkled the carriage floor. With his mind's eye he saw Doreen again but now he reversed the pictures he had just seen. He saw Doreen coming down Falkland Road, knocking on Mrs Moody's door, retrieving the key, opening the front door, lifting her suitcase in, going through to the kitchen, pulling off her gloves and her black coat, sliding the bolts on the side door, untwisting the taps to fill the kettle, turning the gas back on at the wall, lighting one of the burners and setting the kettle on the flame. For the next few moments as he chewed, this image was his whole world and for as long as it lasted he forgot the soreness in his throat.

★

It was getting dark. The train was slowing. Outside, a board bearing the word 'Carmarthen' loomed up, then vanished.

They pulled on their coats and went down the corridor to the door at the end of the carriage.

'Clive said he'd get a platform ticket,' Benedict said, 'and be on the platform waiting.'

There was a noise of metal grating on metal below their feet. The train lurched and stopped. Doors could be heard flying open. Benedict dropped the window, turned the handle on the outside, and threw the door back. They all got out and down onto the platform.

It was raining. The platform was long. There were lamps at regular intervals. Their light was yellow.

'Clive said he'd be here,' said Benedict.

They were near one end and they saw that everyone who had alighted was heading toward the other end where the exit was. Clive was nowhere to be seen.

'But he said he'd be waiting,' said Benedict.

'I'm sure he's out front,' said Jeannie.

They began to walk. At the top of the platform a man in uniform swung a green light. A whistle as the train began to slide forward, moving in the same direction as them. Lighted carriages flickered by, with people inside, like mannequins, looking out. He imagined being seen by these people and getting smaller in their eyes as the train accelerated away. The guard's compartment passed and now it was the train's rear he was seeing, the discs of the buffers, a swaying chain, coloured lights. The lamps got tinier and tinier and then they were gone, swallowed by the darkness. From the rails came a whispering, strange and mysterious, which gradually became fainter until finally it too disappeared.

'Clive must have forgotten,' said Benedict. 'Mum does say he's got a head like a sieve.'

They came to the end of the platform. A door opening on a waiting area to their left. A ticket collector in British Rail livery sprawled on a bench. He saw them. Stood.

'Tickets, please.'

The accent was musical and unfamiliar to Ralph.

Jeannie proffered their tickets.

The ticket collector punched a hole in each ticket and three little discs fluttered to the floor where they joined, Ralph noticed, hundreds more little rounds from all the other tickets punched earlier.

They went through the doorway behind the ticket collector and found themselves in a waiting area with benches and a steel cigarette vending machine with smash-proof glass in the front with wire inside. There was another doorway opposite the one they'd come through from the platform. On the far side of this the car park and set-down area.

They sidled through and found themselves in a yard enclosed by a high stone wall and lit by more yellow lamps. Metal gates in the corner. The gates were open. A few parked cars here and there. It was not quite dark yet but almost.

'There.'

Benedict pointed at a Land Rover. The driver's door opened. Clive curled out and drew himself to his full height.

'Me boy,' he shouted.

He opened his arms. Benedict ran forward and threw himself against his father's torso. Clive threw his arms round his son, then bent his enormous frame forward and kissed him on the top of his head.

Clive and Benedict parted. Ralph came up. He saw that Clive was wearing a battered trilby, a huge spotted handkerchief tied round his neck, and a muddy trench coat. It was how Morecombe or Wise might dress in a sketch about farmers, he thought.

'Greetings, young Ralph.'

They shook hands. Clive's hand was huge, warm and filthy.

'Good journey?'

'Yes, thank you.'

Ralph glanced behind. The Land Rover looked ancient. It was splattered with mud. He noticed a woman he didn't recognise in the front passenger seat. That was the famous Yvonne he presumed. Jeannie came up, breathing heavily, carrying her picnic bag.

'Hello, Jeannie.' Clive kissed her loudly on each cheek. 'Let me introduce you to someone.'

Clive turned and waved at the woman. She got out and came over. She wore a long coat made of squares of brightly coloured wool sewn together and a felt cloche cap.

'Can I introduce Yvonne.'

So it was her. Ralph stared and recalled the first description Clive had given of Yvonne with its emphasis on her long blonde hair. On account of that he'd got it into his head that she was like Ursula Andress whom he knew from photographs he'd seen in the cinema foyer of their Odeon which showed the actress in a white bikini walking out of the sea in the James Bond film *Dr. No*. In person, however, Yvonne was nothing like Ursula Andress. She was small and round with an enormous head and if she did have blonde hair it was hidden under her cloche cap. She also didn't look happy, which was something else he would never have said about Ursula Andress.

'Hello, how do you do everybody?' Yvonne said.

Her voice was high and squeaky.

'You know Benedict of course,' said Clive. 'This is his friend Ralph. And this is Jeannie, our rock, without whom we simply would not be able to manage. And this, everybody, is my good friend Yvonne. Right, let's get this show on the road. Fferm ar Bryn, here we come.' He moved everyone in the Land Rover's direction. 'I was thinking, Jeannie, you could go in the front with me given your seniority, and everyone else can go in the back. Is that all right, Yvonne?'

'If I must, I must,' she said.

Clive led Ralph, Benedict and Yvonne round to the rear and opened the door to reveal a windowless space fitted with slatted benches and lit by a wavering bulb. Its smell, carried out to them by a fug of hot air, was a mix of engine oil, twine, straw and mutton. Clive folded down a set of steps.

'Just mind the floor,' said Clive. 'The action of the axle banging and thumping below heats it up something rotten. It can give you a nasty burn if you're not careful.'

As he clambered in, Ralph could feel the heat coming off it. It was like stepping onto one of the hotplates at school. He took himself down to the driver's side corner. Benedict took the corner opposite. Yvonne sat on the same side as Benedict, but stayed up by the door as far from them as she could get. Ralph decided she wanted to have nothing to do with them.

'If you need to stop, bang on the partition,' said Clive. 'And please, whatever you do, do not be sick in here. Vomit on the hot floor cooks hard in seconds and the smell is disgusting.'

He folded away the steps and closed the door. The interior light cut out. It was dark, hot and smelly.

Ralph heard the driver's door slam and the engine start and then he felt the Land Rover moving across the car park, nosing through the gate, and going on along the road. Under the floor he heard thumping and banging as the axle turned. Outside the little window in the back door, occasional car headlamps. Then darkness. For a while they were on the level and going fast. Then they slowed and started to climb. Underfoot now – heat. He could feel it through the soles of his shoes. He swung his feet onto the bench so they wouldn't have to touch the floor. Outside the rear window, lights again.

'Abergorlech,' said Benedict.

They passed out of Abergorlech. Clive was now driving slowly. There was less thumping. Ralph could hear Yvonne in the corner. She was making a strange groaning noise.

A few minutes later the Land Rover stopped. The engine cut. Yvonne fell silent. Through the rear window Ralph saw a house with its lights on. They had arrived, he guessed. The Land Rover's rear door creaked back and there was Clive.

'Everyone alive?' he asked.

'Barely,' said Yvonne.

Clive folded the steps down. Yvonne put her hand out and Clive took it.

'I need a fucking drink,' Ralph heard Yvonne mutter as she clambered out.

'Are you sure that'll help you?'

'Of course I am,' said Yvonne. 'I'm an adult. I know what I want.'

'I've some cider in the farmhouse,' said Clive.

'Absolutely not,' said Yvonne. 'I want spirits.'

'Go in and ask Ginny,' said Clive. 'She should have some whisky. And if not, I'm sure I've seen some rum in Shepherds Cottage.'

'*Show me the way to the next whisky bar,*' Yvonne sang as she stamped of.

'Ralph,' said Clive, beaming through the door. 'Welcome to Fferm ar Bryn.'

★

On Tuesday Clive suggested a walk to the tunnels from where coal was mined at the beginning of the Industrial Revolution.

These lay halfway up the mountain that rose behind Fferm ar Bryn. Because they were eighteenth century, he said, these workings ran into the mountain rather than going downward like later mines. Everyone agreed to go.

Ralph went to the tack room to get his Wellington boots. As he was looking, he remembered the story of Theseus – it was in another of his Roger Lancelyn Green books, *Tales of the Greek Heroes.* When Theseus entered the Minotaur's Labyrinth in Crete, he remembered, he had unravelled a ball of thread so he could find his way out later. Since they were going into a set of tunnels, Ralph thought, they should do the same.

He found his boots and carried them to the farmhouse kitchen.

'Jeannie?' he said.

She sat at the table drinking tea from a chipped mug.

'Have you a ball of twine?'

'What do you want that for?'

'So we don't get lost in the tunnels up the mountain.'

She found him a large hairy white ball.

They set off, Douglas and Ginny, Clive and Yvonne, Benedict and himself, following the path on which rails had once run that carried coal-filled trolleys from the mine above to the valley below. Finally, after a good hour and a long and often steep climb, they reached a level area, quite high up. There was a line of square entrances cut into the side of the mountain with old machinery and slag piled outside. Clive issued torches. Ralph took his ball of twine out of his pocket.

'What are you doing with that?' asked Benedict.

Ralph explained without mentioning Theseus.

'Good idea,' said Clive.

Ralph tied the end of the ball to the wheel of an upturned hopper.

'Dark enclosed spaces – never my thing,' said Yvonne.

'Don't worry,' said Ginny. 'You'll never be in the dark.'

'Won't I?'

'We never go in so far that we lose sight of daylight, do we Clive?'

'No, never.'

Douglas had lit a roll-up and as he smoked he moved the switch of his torch backward and forward and a pale light in the torch head pulsed accordingly.

'Not much in these batteries,' he said.

'Take mine,' Ginny said and they swapped.

'Line secured, Ralph?' asked Clive.

Ralph yanked the twine. His knot was good.

'Yes.'

'We are ready to go.'

They filed in through the main entrance, the beams of their torches probing ahead to show rails, hawsers, tools, props, Ralph turning the ball as he went so the twine played out behind.

It had been chilly on the mountainside but inside the gallery the atmosphere was icy as well as unusually still. As they ventured farther in, it became colder and stiller again. The air tasted of old stone and damp. The noises they made as they progressed sounded bigger, clearer and somehow farther away. Ralph found the experience of this new place exciting.

'It's a bit spooky isn't it,' said Douglas, 'or am I alone in thinking this?'

'I agree,' said Yvonne. 'It's creepy.'

'Really – do you think so?' asked Clive. 'I don't think there's anything malevolent in here.'

'The ghosts of dead miners?' Douglas asked.

'The old stories I've heard don't mention any.' Ginny said this quietly.

'But I tell you what the stories do mention,' said Clive, 'and we can do a little experiment ourselves and see if they're right.'

'Not the mine spirits,' said Ginny.

'Yes,' said Clive, 'the mine spirits.'

'I've forgotten what they are,' said Benedict. 'What are mine spirits?'

Ralph didn't believe his friend had forgotten, but pretending he had was an excellent ploy, he thought. He was also very keen himself to know what they were.

'Well, the old miners," said Clive, 'they weren't full time miners like we're used to. They were farm labourers who came up here and did a bit of mining in their spare time. They were very much in touch with the old ideas of the earth as a bountiful mother filled with magical, supernatural beings, and they believed that if you closed your eyes, and waited, the mine spirits who lived down here would come to them, and if they liked you they would kiss your cheek and stroke your hair and then you would know you were bound to prosper in whatever you did, because they, the mine spirits, would help you.'

'Please can we have a go?' asked Benedict.

'Is that such a good idea?' Yvonne asked.

'What harm can it do?' asked Clive. 'Lights out, torches away. This has to be done in darkness. The spirits don't like the light.'

Ralph stuffed the ball of twine in his pocket. Everyone turned their torches off and put them away.

'Form a circle,' said Clive, 'facing outward, and all hold hands.'

Ralph felt Ginny take his left hand and Benedict his right. The entrance was a tiny point of light far away.

'Eyes shut,' said Clive.

Ralph closed his eyes.

'Now we wait. The thing is not to move, not to look, not to speak. Stay absolutely quiet, and calm.'

Ralph listened to the sounds round him. He heard water moving and strange rustles and groans. His feet were numb and his nose was wet. Now and again he turned his face from side to side in the dark to make it easier for the mine spirit if it were there to touch him. But nothing happened. None came.

Then he heard a cry and the sound of running. His heart raced. Ralph opened his eyes. He heard the sound of running and a strange echoing clattering as objects flew about. Yvonne had bolted, he realised. He found the small point of light at the entrance. It seemed a long way off.

'Yvonne.' This was Clive. He sounded mostly angry and certainly not sympathetic. 'What the fuck are you doing?'

'She's had a panic attack, Clive.' This was Ginny, speaking very quietly. 'Don't raise your voice. It'll only make things worse, for her and for us.'

The sound of Yvonne running and then another cry, this one horrible and frightening, followed by the sound of something heavy falling.

'Jesus H Christ,' said Clive.

Somewhere far out in the darkness Ralph heard Yvonne whimpering. He tried to gauge from which direction the noises were coming. As far as he could tell she'd run deeper into the mine, towards the darkness, rather than the other way, towards the entrance and the light.

'Yvonne, where the fuck are you?' shouted Clive.

'That's not going to work,' said Ginny. 'Be gentle.'

'Yvonne,' said Clive quietly. 'Can you hear me?'

'Yes,' came Yvonne's voice, small and faraway.

Torch beams shot out into the black as they all attempted to locate Yvonne but all the beams picked out were tiny slivers of wall or roof.

'Have you fallen?' shouted Clive.

'Yes. I think I've fallen down something. I'm all wet. I'm bleeding.'

She sounded terrified. Ralph had never heard anyone sound like this before.

'I think I've got a fix on her.' This was Clive. 'Where's the twine, Ralph?'

'In my pocket.'

'Right, give it to me.'

Clive and Douglas moved into the darkness, Clive turning the ball, paying the line out behind as they went.

'Keep your torches focused on them, boys,' Ginny said.

Ralph and Benedict did as she told them. Their torch beams played on their backs and for a while they followed their progress. Then the darkness swallowed them and they were gone and only the sounds they made betrayed their presence.

'Okay, Yvonne,' said Clive. 'Give us a shout.'

'Here,' Yvonne called back.

Ralph heard Clive and Douglas moving farther and deeper into the mine and then their voices calling out and Yvonne's calling back.

'They must have gone a long way in,' said Benedict.

'I don't think they've really gone all that far you know,' said Ginny. 'In pitch black everything just seems farther away than it actually is because you can't judge distances when you can't see.'

'What happened to Yvonne?' asked Benedict.

'She just didn't like it in here,' said Ginny. 'It's not to everyone's taste you know.'

Out in the blackness the voices gradually clarified. They shone their torches round. More bits of wall and ceiling and then they were there, Clive, Yvonne – she was hanging onto Clive's arm – and Douglas.

They followed the twine back to the entrance and stepped out into the air. It had started to rain lightly.

'I don't know what happened to me,' said Yvonne. 'I'm so sorry.'

She started to weep and pulled the end of her scarf out from under her coat – not the coat of bright woollen squares but a man's Crombie which she'd obviously borrowed from Clive for the expedition – and wiped her face on the end of the scarf. Her coat was filthy after her fall. Her ear and chin were both cut and bleeding.

'Don't you worry about a thing,' said Ginny. She rubbed Yvonne's back. 'You felt whatever it was you felt. What happened was what happened. You have nothing to apologise for.'

While he listened to Yvonne sobbing and Ginny talking, Ralph wound up the twine. It was muddy in some places and swollen and wet in others but he got it all rolled up.

They started their descent.

'Jolly good you brought the twine,' said Douglas.

The other adults, including Yvonne, agreed.

'What made you do it?' he asked.

Ralph felt he could risk telling the truth. He told them about Roger Lancelyn Green's Theseus story and the writer's strange reference to Theseus taking a clue of thread with him into the Labyrinth.

'That's an old word for a ball of yarn,' said Ginny.

He was delighted with this piece of information. There was so much Ginny knew. She seemed to know almost everything.

★

When they got back they planted the Christmas tree in a bucket filled with sand and stones in the front parlour of Fferm ar Bryn. Under Ginny's supervision, the boys decorated the branches with sugared almonds, barley twists, ribbons and candles in silver candle-holders. She did not allow electric lights and other kinds of commercial Christmas decoration.

As it got dark Douglas lit the fire. As the room warmed up the old Victorian furniture began to give off a damp smell. Once the fire really got going and everyone left, Ralph stretched on the button-down sofa and lay staring at the logs in the grate spitting and whistling as they burned. He loved the crackling sound the wood made as it burnt, the delicate shapes made by the pale grey woodsmoke curling and drifting up the chimney and the warmth of the fire drenching him.

Ralph heard someone come in. He was in a sort of trance, so he didn't look. He heard the pedals of the old harmonium at the far end of the room clanking up and down as they were depressed and then a tune starting, a hymn. It was Clive. He came across from Shepherds Cottage for a while every evening and played the harmonium and drank cider.

Ralph lay still, following the slow, grave tune while staring at the dancing flames, which besides yellow and orange, colours he expected to see, also included blues and greens. When one thought about it, there was so much one didn't see unless one looked.

More footfalls. Benedict, he assumed. His friend regularly joined his father at the harmonium and when this happened Clive would stop the hymns and play popular songs from the radio and the Hit Parade that Benedict knew. One of their current favourites was 'The House of the Rising Sun', which had been in the charts in the summer.

'Clive?' he heard.

The voice wasn't Benedict's as he expected. It was Ginny's.

'That's me,' said Clive.

The breathy music of the harmonium didn't stop. Ralph realised neither adult knew he was there. He also knew it was too late to do anything about that now. Far too late. He would just have to stay where he was and hope he wasn't noticed. He pressed himself down into the sofa so there was less chance he might be seen. He closed his eyes. He would pretend to be asleep.

'What was all that about today in the tunnel?' Ginny asked. 'Yvonne's a fucking lunatic. What the fuck are you doing with her?'

Clive played three heavy chords, wha, wha, wha, like in a film.

'It's just sex,' he said.

'If it's just sex,' said Ginny, 'you know where to come.'

Ginny went out. Clive played on for a few minutes and then left. Ralph heard the front door open and bang shut and then Clive stamping across the yard toward Shepherds Cottage.

★

The Long Room, where Ralph and Benedict slept, was on the ground floor of Fferm ar Bryn and at one end its windows overlooked the yard at the front and at the other the orchard and the fields at the back that ran to the mountain. Like the rest of the farmhouse, its furnishings were Victorian – a battered old wardrobe with a worn spotted mirror, a heavy chest of drawers and a marble-topped table with a pitcher and ewer.

Ralph woke. He was on the bottom tier of the bunk bed Clive had made with pine planks salvaged from the same chapel the harmonium had come from. The mattress under him was a square of hard foam covered with a fitted sheet made from old curtains that Ginny had run up on her Singer sewing machine.

He opened his eyes. The bolster under his head smelt of lavender, his sleeping bag smelt of grass and tent canvas. The boards above – the bottom of the tier Benedict was sleeping on – were a mix of the painted and the varnished. Doreen's timetable was directly above, fixed with drawing pins. He'd scored off five days – Saturday, Sunday, Monday, Tuesday, and Wednesday. Today was Thursday, so he hadn't crossed it out yet.

Benedict's even breathing drifted down but at the same time he could also hear something else – a sort of faint, just perceptible whisper. He also noticed the light this morning wasn't the usual sombre grey but had a pearly luminescence. He sat up and shrugged off the sleeping bag. He put his feet down onto a slightly pillowed, enormous, dusty cold flag and stood.

He looked first at the back window and then at the front. Both windows had muslin curtains and there was no doubt the light bleeding through them was different this morning.

He went to the front window, looked out and saw the whole yard was filled with dazzling, wondrous, pristine snow.

He heard Benedict stirring behind.

'You won't believe what's happened,' Ralph said.

'What?' asked Benedict. He was sleepy, not yet awake.

'It's snowed.'

Benedict jumped down and bolted across.

'Oh wow.'

'Do you think we're snowed in?' asked Ralph.

'Probably. I hope so.'

Shepherds Cottage was just over to their left. There was snow on its roof and piled up along the front. The door of Shepherds Cottage was moving as someone inside tugged it away from the snow banked up against it. It took considerable effort from behind but finally – triumph. The wood swung back and there was Clive in a full-length flannel nightshirt and an old-fashioned nightcap with a bobble on the end.

The boys waved. Clive saw them.

'Snow,' they shouted.

'I can see,' Clive shouted back.

He gazed round, his eyes wide, his mouth open. He looked back at the boys and shrugged as if to suggest exaggerated, bewildered, delighted surprise.

'Why did no one tell me this was coming?' Clive shouted at them. 'I left my snow shoes in London.'

'Look at Mum's Saab, Ralph,' said Benedict. It was parked by the wall on the far side of the yard near the gate. 'It's completely covered. You can't see any red at all.'

Ralph nodded. He was filled with a kind of ecstasy.

★

Ralph and Benedict got dressed. Went out to the yard. The snow at least a foot deep. Every step had to be a high one. Hard going. Clive came and joined them. They went to the gate and looked along the track in the direction of the Abergorlech Road. Nothing but snow, deep snow, deep, full and flawless for as far as the eye could see.

'Yes, I'd say we won't be seeing anyone for a few days,' said Clive. 'We're snowed in, boys.'

'Breakfast boys,' Jeannie called from the front door.

Ralph went in and through to the tack room to take his things off. Benedict stayed out for a few moments talking to Clive. Then he followed Ralph inside.

'Yvonne's not going to like this snow,' said Benedict.

With the wooden bootjack Ralph tugged his right Wellington boot off.

'What do you mean?'

It seemed highly unlikely to him that anyone wouldn't like the snow.

'She doesn't like it here,' he said. 'She's already told Clive she wants to go back to London and when she discovers she's stuck here and can't leave, she'll probably go mad.'

'How do you know this?'

'Clive just told me.'

His friend's father told him things like this all the time. Ralph wished he had someone who'd tell him things too but he didn't. He felt a stab of envy. Into his mind swept fleeting thoughts. First of his mother. Then Doreen. He did not welcome their appearance now. But if he went through to the kitchen and lost himself in conversation with Jeannie – the best thing to do when threatened by his feelings – he might with luck keep the sore feeling of sadness out of the back of his throat.

Christmas Eve. Snowflakes outside the kitchen window, floating and turning, and appearing not to be moving downward. Ralph at the table cutting the rind off a slice of bacon, dark and wiry like a piece of cooked string. Benedict beside him eating porridge with so much Golden Syrup added it was yellow.

Clive stamped in. He had snowflakes in his hair and on his shoulders.

'Seen Yvonne anyone?'

'I saw her going off for a walk,' said Jeannie.

She was at the sink washing earth off big knobbly carrots.

'What time was that, Jeannie?' Clive didn't sound happy.

'I don't know. Maybe half an hour ago. I was in the front room getting the place ship-shape for tomorrow and I saw her come out of the cottage and I waved and she waved, and she went out the yard gate and up the track.'

'Did she have a bag?'

'I think so.'

'Jesus Christ,' said Clive.

He announced she must have set off for Abergorlech. Hoping to catch the bus to Carmarthen and then the train to London. If they were running, that was, and this he very much doubted. He would have to go after her and find her and bring her back. Benedict asked if he and Ralph could come too.

'Why not?' said Clive.

They abandoned their breakfasts, got togged up and set out. Small flakes swirling, their touch on Ralph's face like the points of cold pins pricking him. The landscape, white and silent with nothing in it except Yvonne's neat footsteps which they followed up the track towards the Abergorlech road. They hadn't gone far when they saw her, sitting in the snow with her Gladstone on her lap.

'Wait here,' said Clive. 'I'll go and have a word with her.'

Clive went over and crouched down on his hunkers beside her. The boys waited. Yvonne and Clive talked for a long time. Then Clive called the boys over.

'We're going back.' Clive stood and pulled Yvonne to her feet. 'I'll take your bag,' he said.

'No thank you,' she said.

They retraced their steps. No one spoke. Not a word through the whole short trek. They arrived in the yard.

The door of the farmhouse ahead of them, the door of Shepherds Cottage on their right.

'What about coming in and I'll ask Jeannie to rustle you up a nice cup of tea and something to eat?' asked Clive.

'I don't want a cup of tea,' said Yvonne. 'I don't want anything to eat. I want a fucking drink. Ginny has whisky. I want a whisky.'

'Right,' said Clive.

Ralph stared down at the snow around his feet as if he were fascinated by what he was seeing and wasn't hearing what the adults were saying. Out of the corner of his eye he saw that Benedict, a few feet away, was doing the same thing.

'And when I've had my first,' Yvonne said, 'I want a second, and when I've had my second, I want my third, and when I've had my third, I want my fourth. Do you understand? And then I want to go to sleep and I don't want to wake up until this fucking so-called holiday is over.'

'Is that such a good idea?' asked Clive.

'It's the best idea I've had today,' said Yvonne, 'and I'm sticking with it.'

She opened the door, went into the farmhouse.

'Ginny?' Ralph heard her call. 'Ginny?'

Christmas Day was on the Friday and Yvonne was pale and complained of a headache and ate almost nothing but drank wine steadily all day and talked incessantly, mostly about politics. At the end of the afternoon, when they were all in the parlour, sitting in front of the fire, and Jeannie was in the kitchen washing up, the Cluedo board came out. Yvonne asked to be excused, saying she wasn't feeling well, and went back to the cottage to lie down. Two minutes after she left,

Clive announced he'd go across and see how she was. He might have to make a hot water bottle for her, he added, because she had complained that their bed was damp.

'That Yvonne,' said Ginny, as soon as Clive was gone, 'she isn't ill. She's just had too much to drink. She's a bloody alky. And speaking of sick, I'll tell you what is making me sick, it's the way she drones on about the poor and the dispossessed in that awful, thin, reedy little voice of hers. That makes me sick. Christ, she says she cares but you know what?'

'What?' asked Douglas, with what sounded to Ralph like very little enthusiasm.

'She doesn't care about anyone or anything except herself. She is one selfish cow.'

Douglas rolled a cigarette and lit up.

'Are we going to play Cluedo?' asked Benedict.

'Let's wait a bit,' she said. 'Your dad might come back.'

Ginny stared at the fire.

'Do you know who Yvonne reminds me of?' asked Ginny.

'Who?'

'Florence Nightingale. You know the type. Appears to care, kindly, tolerant, wears their bloody bleeding heart on their sleeve. Bollocks. In actual fact they're nasty, cruel, inflexible, dogmatic, dangerous and phoney.'

'Who is?' asked Ralph. He was confused.

'Both of them.'

'Really?'

'Yes, really.'

'Even Florence Nightingale?'

'Awful woman, contemptible, truly ghastly.'

There was a small lull.

'Ginny,' said Ralph.

'Yes.'

'Can I ask you a question?'

'Go on.'

'About Florence Nightingale?'

'Yes.'

'We did her in history and the teacher said we wouldn't have hospitals or nursing as we have now without her and nothing about her being ghastly. The teacher said she was a saint.'

'Well Ralph, you have put your finger right on the nub of *the* problem,' said Ginny. 'Florence is one of our icons, the emblem of human beings at their best, the kindly lady with the lamp who nursed the suffering wounded in the Crimea.

'And nurse them she did, that's true, but the rest, this idea that she was a paragon, a perfect woman, it's a lie. Not true. She wasn't. She was a vicious, controlling, obstructive, self-regarding, egotistical piece of work. Yes I know this will come as a shock because it wasn't what they told you in school but it's true. Trust me. And my point? Obviously human beings are not paragons. They're never paragons. Human beings are always a confused mishmash of desires and needs and sometimes they're kind and thoughtful and sometimes quite frankly they're selfish little shits. As was she. And so what? And so what? You don't have to be perfect to do good. But our masters are not comfortable with that. They like Florence up there on her pedestal. And why is that? Easy. It's so that they can tell us women this: Florence is what we're supposed to be like. We're all supposed to be little Florences, not as she actually was, but as they tell us she was and for one simple reason, Ralph: control.

'You see, the person who suppresses their truth, their desires, their appetites, their human energy, and lives like a paragon, like her, which essentially is what's being asked of us, that's the core of our social contract, these paragons will cause the state no trouble, ever. They will just go to work and draw their wages and never put their head above the parapet and do the caring and the nurturing and the child rearing and the rest without which society can't function, and they will never challenge or question anything. They will just blindly, obediently follow the rules and hallelujah, when we all follow the rules, society functions just fine and dandy, because everyone knows their place and nothing changes, ever.

'However, when you refuse to model yourself on whatever the icon is and you start to acknowledge what you are really like as a human being, then the trouble starts, at least as far as the state is concerned. You see, once you acknowledge your own wants and needs, it isn't very long before you find you have to acknowledge that other human beings also have wants and needs, and as soon as you accept that truth, the next step, inevitably, because everyone, all of us, every one of us should have their needs and wants met, has to be revolution. Because to meet everyone's wants and needs we need a revolution. And one day we will have our revolution, once we've dumped our icons. Do you understand?'

'Clive isn't coming back, is he?' asked Benedict.

'No, I don't think so,' said Ginny carefully.

'So can we play Cluedo then?'

In bed later Ralph thought about what Ginny had said. He could certainly see there was often a difference between how someone appeared and what they were really like. It was the next step in her argument that he found difficult. The world she wanted, it seemed to him, would be like the island in *Lord of the Flies*. It would have no controls. Everyone would just do what they pleased. Living in such a world would be absolutely terrible, he thought.

★

By the following Monday the roads were open to vehicles and the trains were back to normal as well.

★

On Tuesday morning, after breakfast, Clive got the Land Rover going, and scraped the ice from the windscreen and lights. Clive was driving Yvonne to the railway station and the plan was that Benedict would go with Clive to keep him company on the way back.

The Land Rover's horn beeped. The party was about to leave. Ralph and Jeannie followed Ginny and Douglas outside. Yvonne was standing by the Land Rover in her knitted patchwork woollen coat and cloche hat. Jeannie gave her a quick kiss and went back inside. Ginny gave Yvonne a hug. Douglas kissed her on both cheeks. Ralph stepped forward. He took a close look at her face but he was unable to tell whether she was happy to be leaving or not. She leaned down and kissed him briefly on the cheek.

'Right, let's go,' said Clive.

Benedict clambered into the back of the Land Rover and his father closed the door. Yvonne got into the front passenger seat.

'See you all later,' said Clive.

He got behind the steering wheel, grinned at Ginny and held up his right thumb.

'Look at him smiling,' said Ginny. 'He's never been more relieved. The lunatic is going. He's getting shot of the moody cow at last.'

Clive released the brake and drove slowly forward across the yard and out through the gate. The snow was deep but it was dry and hard. Two clean tracks made by the vehicle's wheels opened behind. Ralph thought of the

Land Rover as a boat on a white sea and the lines as two ropes trailing behind from the stern.

'Can you explain why the BBC lets that lunatic make programmes?' asked Ginny.

'Only radio talks, not programmes,' said Douglas. 'And I can't imagine she gets big audiences.'

'I still find it incredible.'

The Land Rover was on the track climbing slowly toward the summit of a low hill.

'Maybe she's rather good at talks and gets the best out of people,' said Douglas.

'Don't be ridiculous,' said Ginny. 'Did you hear the one on public laundries in the East End? Beyond belief. Dreary, uninteresting, pointless. I really can't see what Clive sees in her.'

'She might have a wonderful side we just haven't seen.'

'Don't make me sick.'

The Land Rover reached the crest of the hill and then slipped from sight.

'Are you jealous?' asked Douglas.

'Of her. Are you joking?' Ginny let out a long, terrible laugh.

They adults went inside. Ralph hung round the yard. A rat appeared in front of the buildings across from Shepherds Cottage. It was black and had a long wavy pink tail. It moved carefully over the snow's hardened surface. Then it disappeared into a hole in the wall of an outbuilding. A few moments later one of the cats that lived in the yard appeared. The cat was black, bony and sleek. The cat went to the hole the rat had disappeared into and sank onto its haunches. Ralph waited to see what would happen. But nothing happened and after a bit he got bored and went inside.

★

On Wednesday Ralph and Benedict made a snowman. Once the body was done they added blue buttons for eyes, a big knobbly parsnip for a nose and a silver zip attached to some stretchy black fabric for a mouth, after which they tied a green chiffon scarf round the neck and set a huge battered old riding hat on top of the fat round head.

They stepped back to appraise their creation.

'Know what we need?' said Benedict.

'What?'

'A pipe. Wouldn't that be brilliant? And I know who has one.'

He walked to the door to Shepherds Cottage. Ralph followed.

He took the handle and turned it. The door was locked. This was strange. The door was always open.

'Clive?' Benedict shouted.

'Hang on,' Clive called from inside.

Ralph heard first one and then a second bolt being slid back. The door swung open and there was Clive in an old workman's shirt without a collar, the cottage's small parlour-cum-kitchen behind him, an iron range on one side, a huge old cupboard on the other, and a table in the middle at which Ginny sat on a hard, upright chair dressed in a blue kaftan, her knees tucked up under her chin and her feet bare.

'Hello boys,' said Ginny.

Ralph was surprised to find her there.

'Come to pay your parents a surprise visit?' Clive asked.

Ralph looked down at the floor to avoid making eye contact with Ginny. Clive, he saw, was wearing thick woollen socks and there were wisps of straw stuck in the wool.

'What are you up to?' he heard Ginny ask.

'Ah, making a snowman,' he heard Benedict say. 'We thought a pipe would finish him off, look really good you know. So, ah, could you spare one of your clay pipes?'

'Can I spare one of my clay pipes, Ginny?' Ralph heard Clive ask.

Ralph looked up and saw that Ginny was thinking.

'Why not?' Ginny said eventually. 'It's not as if it's forever. You'll get it back when the snow melts.'

Clive waved the boys forward. They sidled in and shut the door behind them. Clive went to the cupboard and began to search the shelves.

'Now, where did I put them?' Clive said.

'Oh yes, here we are.'

He set a long cardboard box on the table and lifted the lid off. Inside, on a bed of crumpled tissue paper, a clutch of pale white clay pipes, little bowls with flowers and leaves in relief, curving stems and flattened crimped mouthpieces.

'It never ceases to amaze me,' said Clive, 'how something once so common, as these pipes were, can vanish, just like that, almost overnight.'

'What happened?' asked Ralph.

'These beauties, they're fragile, they snap easily, and a smoker would only get one or two smokes out of them. Then along came the mass-produced wooden ones, expensive, yes, but, they lasted a lifetime, and hey presto, the clay pipe was rendered obsolete overnight and that was that. Gone. But they are beautiful things, wouldn't you agree?'

Clive lifted a pipe out of the box and a fine chalky dust floated down off it and formed a white patch on the table top.

'Yes,' Ralph nodded. They were.

The boys went back to the yard with a pipe and Benedict carefully rammed the stem in at the side of the silver teeth and black lips that were the snowman's mouth. The pipe was an excellent addition, they both thought.

'Now all that's missing are these.' Ralph waved his hands. 'He can't smoke if he doesn't have hands, can he?'

'Yeah, good point. Let's look in the orchard.'

They went round to the apple trees behind their bed-room. They were low and small, their branches bare, dense, tangled, their knobbly barks encrusted white with ice. The boys began to search for snowman limbs, tree by tree, branch by branch.

'See you later, boys,' they heard Ginny call. She and Clive walked past. 'Just going for a walk if anyone asks.'

'All right,' Benedict yelled back.

The adults trudged off, heading for the old narrow gauge railway bed that tracked up the mountain. The boys went on looking for arms for their snowman and it was not until the adults were dots disappearing into the white landscape that they found two branches with finger-like twigs on the end. When they snapped them off some of the ice fell away but some remained, stuck fast to the bark.

They carried their finds back to the yard and pushed the end of each limb deep inside the snowman's body. Then they rotated the branches to get the extended fingers in the optimum position, with the thumbs upward.

'Boys, have you seen Ginny?'

It was Douglas. At the door of the farmhouse.

'Gone for a walk,' said Benedict.

Douglas went back inside and closed the front door.

'Don't know if he and Mum are going to last,' said Benedict.

The boys stepped back to look at their creation.

'What do you think?' asked Benedict.

The battered riding hat, the huge eyes, the pointed parsnip nose, the silver teeth, the pipe, the unlikely scarf and the outstretched arms – none of it was typical of any snowman either had ever seen before.

'Bit sinister,' said Ralph.

'More scarecrow than snowman,' said Benedict.

They both heard whooshing and turned together. On the far side of the yard the bony cat was pursuing the black rat, both of whom Ralph had seen the day before. The rat was light and scampered on top of the snow's hard crust but the cat kept sinking through.

The rat reached the mouth of a downpipe on one of the outbuildings and bolted inside. The cat stopped and sat and stared at the pipe end.

The boys walked slowly across the yard. The cat dropped down and stretched out flat: it was utterly still though its tail fanned slowly on the snow. For a long time nothing happened. Then the nose of the rat appeared at the mouth of the pipe. The cat shrank into itself and became smaller. The rat's pink nose ventured farther out, followed by the mouth and then the whole head. The cat stayed down. Ralph watched, his breath shallow and still.

The rat put its two front feet on the snow and looked round. Then slowly it moved itself forward and pulled the back half of its body out of the pipe and got its rear legs onto the snow. Ralph's hands were hot and his mouth was dry. He felt anxious. If what he expected didn't happen, he would feel let down but he also knew that he would be relieved if it didn't happen. He was exhilarated and he was frightened.

The rat moved off sideways hugging the wall. It's intention was obviously to run along the edge of the building and on to the hole Ralph had already seen it run inside and once it was inside it would be safe.

The cat sprang up high and flew forward, front paws stretched ahead, tail arching behind. A javelin winging lethally forward. A sound, muffled, indistinct as the javelin point buried itself in the snow. A second later the rat flew up into the air and a second later again it was on its back, the cat's claws on its belly and its teeth at its neck. The rat was alive. The rat was wriggling. The rat's tail coiled and whipped. The rat's feet frantically pedalled as it sought to find the cat's head and push it away.

The cat lifted the rat by its neck and agitated it like a rag, then put it down for a moment before picking it up and resuming. This went on for a long time and Ralph knew that all the time this was going on the rat was alive and he did not want to go on watching and yet he could not stop.

Eventually, there was a low squeaky shriek. Then stillness. The rat lying on its back, its legs splayed, its mouth open, its long front white teeth, even from a distance, clearly visible to Ralph. The cat looking down. Then the cat turned the rat on its front, nipped the flesh of the shoulders between its teeth and lifted the rat up. The rat's legs and tail hung down. Drops of blood spattered the snow. Ralph was reminded of the little cardboard rounds punched from the tickets lying on the platform at Carmarthen Station. The cat, the rat in its teeth, walked across the yard, sidled out of the gate and vanished from sight.

Ralph had nothing to say. What he had seen had emptied everything out of him. He was sure Benedict was the same. The boys went inside and took themselves to the front room where they sat for half an hour in front of the fire gazing at the flames.

★

It was night now. Ralph, enclosed in his sleeping bag, lay on the bottom bunk looking up at Doreen's timetable. The following day, not crossed out yet, was New Year's Eve.

Benedict was in his bunk above.

'You know what?' said Benedict.

'What?'

'When we went to get the clay pipe today.'

'Yeah,' said Ralph.

'I bet Mum and Clive were doing kissy kissy before we arrived.'

'Really?'

Ralph had wondered about this but then rejected the idea.

'Oh yeah.'

'Ugh,' said Ralph, 'that's too sordid for words.'

'I agree.' Benedict said this quietly.

After a moment Ralph heard his friend turn a page of his book. It was the Beano Christmas annual. One of his presents.

'Going to read for long?' asked Ralph. He wanted to close his eyes in the dark and go to sleep.

'Give us a minute,' said Benedict.

★

Morning, New Year's Eve. Benedict still asleep in the top bunk in the Long Room. Ralph at the table in the kitchen. Jeannie, a mixing bowl wedged in the crook of her left elbow, turning flour, eggs, butter and sugar with a wooden spoon. Her bare white arms vast and incredibly strong. From inside the bowl the sound of the spoon thumping and the sliding and slurping as it blended everything inside into a tacky doughy sticky whole.

Ralph poured condensed milk over the cardboard-coloured Weetabixes in his cereal bowl. The milk smelt of confectionery and though it looked white there was yellow in it. Outside in the yard the noise of an engine and then a banging at the front door.

'Go and see will you?' asked Jeannie.

He went out to the hall and through to the porch. The floor was tiled and glistened with damp. A smell of damp plaster. A veil of spider's web across the side window. He pulled the front door back and found himself facing an adolescent telegram delivery boy in uniform whose motorcycle was propped up on its kickstand behind with its engine idling. The motorcycle was red and 'GPO' was written on the shin guards.

'Boscombe?' asked the delivery boy.

'Yes.'

He offered a buff envelope.

'Telegram.'

Ralph took the envelope. The initial before the surname was 'C'. It was for Clive.

'I'll see he gets it.'

The delivery boy went to his motorcycle and in one sleek fluid movement he dropped it off the kickstand, swung his leg and sank down onto the seat.

'Thanks,' Ralph called.

The telegram delivery boy waved and moved carefully across the yard and out the gate. Ralph crunched over the hardened snow to the cottage door. He knocked. The sound of the motorcycle growing fainter as it moved up the track in the direction of the road.

'Yes,' from inside.

'It's me, Ralph.'

'Come in.'

He opened the door and stepped in. Clive was sitting in front of the range, gazing through the open door of the firebox at the wood and coal burning inside.

'Telegram,' said Ralph.

'I thought I heard a motorcycle just now.'

Clive took the envelope carefully with one of his huge hands. He hadn't shaved.

'But I was so caught up with my own miserable thoughts I couldn't be bothered to get up and open the door.'

There was a bottle of Scotch and a tumbler with half an inch of drink in it on the table. The room smelt of the whisky.

'Does that ever happen to you?' mumbled Clive.

'I suppose,' Ralph said automatically.

Clive tore the envelope open, pulled out the telegram, unfolded it, began to read.

The fire sighing. Ralph wanted to go but he thought it would be awkward if he just turned and walked away now. He should have gone earlier when he'd handed the envelope over.

'Well I never. Hip hip hooray.' Clive looked up. He smiled brightly. 'I've got to go to London,' Clive made a face. 'Christ, that means I'll miss New Year's Eve at Fferm ar Bryn. Oh well, can't be helped. If I tell Benedict I'll make it up to him, will you back me up, Ralph?'

'Yes,' said Ralph, who didn't see what else he could say.

Clive took the glass from the table and threw the contents into his mouth. He swallowed. He shuddered.

'Lovely,' he put the glass on the table. 'Frankly I'm relieved. I didn't want to see in the new year with the lovebirds but don't you ever say to Ginny that I said that.'

'No,' said Ralph.

A small hiccup came out of his mouth. He looked at the telegram again. '"Darling. Stop. All forgiven. Stop. Come now. Stop. See in New Year with me. Stop. Love always. Stop. Yvonne. Stop." That's a turn up for the books, I can tell you.'

He tipped a finger of whisky into the empty glass and drank it back and then poured again.

'Ever been in love?'

Ralph felt his face redden.

'No.'

'Well keep it that way. You'll be better off. Trust me. Yvonne snaps her fingers and I tear back to her. It's pathetic, it really is. But I can't help it. I have to.'

He emptied the glass again.

'Right. I'm going to have to go and beg Ginny to drive me to the station. Or Douglas. Are they up yet?'

'No.'

'Of course they aren't.'

He got to his feet. He really was too big for the room.

'The thought of being stuck in the front of the Land Rover with him all the way to Carmarthen and him droning on in that dreary Scottish voice of his is absolutely appalling.'

He looked at Ralph.

'What were you doing when you answered the door?'

'Having breakfast.'

'Well go and finish. And thank you for bringing the glad tidings by the way. I'll pack and come over later when the lovebirds are up.'

Ralph left and closed the door behind. He went back to the kitchen and sat at his place. While he'd been away his Weetabixes had softened and he broke them up with his spoon. The white sticky dough was out of the bowl and on the table. Jeannie was pummelling it.

'Who was at the door?'

'Telegram. For Clive.'

'Oh,' said Jeannie. 'I bet I know who it's from. Yvonne. Am I right?'

Ralph nodded and took a mouthful of Weetabix and condensed milk.

'And I bet he'll go haring back to London now and into her arms,' said Jeannie. 'Oh yes, I know how love goes. You just wait and see.'

She gave a short bitter laugh. Ralph nodded but said nothing. He took a second spoonful. Jeannie kneaded the dough. He thought about the grown-ups. In their different ways, and to different degrees of course, none of them were really happy.

January

Jeannie, Benedict and Ralph got a taxi from Paddington to Falkland Road. The cab dropped Ralph off right outside number 88. At the sight of the garden with its flaking terracotta pots and the narrow redbrick house behind, Ralph felt a surge of joy. He ran down the passage and threw open the door.

'Well. Miss me did you?'

Doreen sat side on to the kitchen table, her legs stretched in front and resting on another chair.

'Miss me, miss me, now you gotta kiss me,' she chanted.

Ralph closed the door. She was definitely larger.

'Certainly not,' he said.

'Oh you nasty boy. Sling on the kettle and come and sit down and tell me everything, especially the filth.'

'There wasn't any filth,' he said.

He went to the stove, jiggled the kettle and heard water slopping within. He lit the gas and put the kettle over the flames.

'Really, no filth?' asked Doreen. 'None whatsoever. I'm surprised.'

He sat at the table beside her.

'We had snow.'

'Good.'

'Saw a rat killed by a cat. Watched the whole thing, the chasing, waiting, pouncing, killing.'

'Ugh, that's terrible. What did you want to watch that for?'

'I was making a snowman in the yard and it just happened there.'

'You didn't have to look, though.'

'I had to. Couldn't stop.'

'Well, I wouldn't have looked. Rats!' She shuddered. 'When I was a girl they used to get into the meal bags at home and then they'd swim down into the meal like it was water and you wouldn't know they were in there until you put your dipper in and they'd spring up like a monster out of the sea. It gives me goosebumps just thinking about it. So – what else?'

'What do you mean?'

'You've got to sharpen up. Ginny was there with Douglas and wasn't Clive with his one Yvonne?'

'Yes.'

'So, how did they all get on?'

'Ginny didn't like Yvonne and I don't think Clive likes Douglas much.'

'That doesn't surprise me.'

He described the day in the mine when Yvonne panicked and the other day Yvonne set off for Abergorlech, hoping to catch the bus there to Carmarthen Station, but didn't get far because the snow was so deep, and how they fetched her home and not a word said on the trudge back, and then the altercation at the door.

'That sounds terrible,' said Doreen when he finished, though she didn't sound to him as if she meant it. He felt she was rather enjoying what she'd heard.

'What about Ginny and Clive?'

'Benedict says they're still friends.'

He described going for the pipe for their snowman and how they found Clive and Ginny inside the cottage.

The whistle went.

'Go on, make the tea like a good lad,' Doreen said. 'My feet are killing me. My back is killing me. My bones are killing me. You have to help me.'

She kicked off her shoes and wriggled her toes.

He made a pot of tea and carried the pot to the table along with two mugs and a bottle of milk from the fridge. The glass had condensation all over. He sat again.

'Did you miss me?'

'I suppose,' he said.

'I suppose!'

Doreen drove a stockinged heel at his elbow and hit him with such force he nearly toppled backward off his seat.

'You disgusting boy, how could you not miss me? I missed you. Woke up Christmas morning and thought, Oh, I wish I was with Ralph, he'd be more fun than this lot.'

He took the lid off the pot and peered in to see if the leaves had settled. They hadn't. He put the lid back.

'What was Christmas Day itself like?'

'Yvonne got so drunk she couldn't play Cluedo.'

'You didn't have a good time, did you?'

'It was fine.'

'Pour the tea.'

He filled the mugs and added milk, taking care to make hers a bit milkier than his because that was how she liked it. He passed her mug across. She peered at it.

'Glad you haven't forgotten how I like it,' she said. She put the mug to her mouth and blew across the tea.

'Did you get any nice presents?' he asked.

'Special scissors for cutting fabric,' said Doreen. 'From my mother.'

'Oh.'

'They'll come in handy, making things, as I will, for the baby.'

Ralph moved his own tea closer.

'Somebody from here had carried news of my condition back home,' said Doreen.

'Oh,' said Ralph again.

'No matter how far from home you think you are, you're not,' she said.

'Oh,' said Ralph for the third time.

'They weren't very pleased, I can tell you. My mother said I'd made my bed so now I could lie in it. Well that put me in my box, didn't it?'

Ralph thought hard about what he could say next and then he had it. 'Were they cordial at least?'

Doreen snorted. 'Cordial. Where did that come from?'

'I don't know. It just means …'

'I know what it means,' she said. 'And the answer's no. Seething they were.'

'Seething,' he said.

'There's another word for your dictionary. You can pull that out one day and impress someone.'

'So ah?' He wasn't sure how to ask what she planned to do now so in lieu of words he just rotated his hand in the air.

'What now? said Doreen. 'Battle on is what, and you know, all things considered, I'm all right. I'm here. I have a roof over my head. I have you.'

Her eyes looking back at him seemed peculiarly intense.

'I really missed you,' she said. 'Thought about you most days, wondered what you were up to, whether you were happy, having a fine time and so on. Ah Jesus, Doreen, Slop Central, the boy doesn't want to know.'

Her eyes looked wet to him now. His only experience of tears was with his mother. When she'd wept, he'd had to stay with her and say soothing things over and over again. It had numbed his mind at the time and then after his mother's tears were over, he'd always felt shaky because he'd glimpsed her misery and that was terrifying. Doreen was not his mother but if she cried it would be the same story so he hoped she wouldn't.

At the same time, far out at the very edge of his thoughts, only just perceptible because of its distance from his centre, he was aware of another idea. He wanted her to know that he was sorry for what her mother had said. He was sorry that her family were seething. He had missed her too and now that he was back in her presence he was glad. But what words would he use to say such things and how would he find them? He'd never before articulated anything as strange and complex and difficult as what he had to say now.

'You know your timetable?' he asked.

'Yes,' said Doreen.

'I had to sleep on the bottom bunk and so I pinned it on the underneath of Benedict's bunk above me. Every night I scored the day off, and every morning it was the first thing I saw.'

'That's marvellous,' said Doreen.

She wiped her eyes and gave his hand a squeeze. Her hand was hot and small.

★

Dear Ralph,

On Christmas Eve I had drinks with the MSJs and then drove myself home in my Ford station wagon. I fell asleep quickly but then the dreams started up. Was that the two martinis? These mostly involved myself with a lot of unnecessary luggage trekking through forests, wading through swamps, and struggling across dusty plains. I woke in the dark very early Christmas morning and lay for a long time hoping (believing) I'd nod off again but I didn't: so I got up and had a long bath (the steam and hot water didn't put me to sleep either) and then abandoned all thought of sleep and drank a cup of coffee. Then I drove myself back to the MSJ residence for the traditional Christmas day festivities: the MSJs' two grown-up daughters were there, with their husbands (both Wall Street financiers) and their children. We all went to a little American clapboard jewel of a church; then we came back to the mansion for pancakes and freshly squeezed orange juice, the opening of presents under the enormous and exquisite Christmas tree in the hall, lunch (turkey, ham, the full works) and party games. By four o'clock the little ones were worn out with the excitement and inevitably the tears started to flow. I sat in the library and stared through the enormous windows at the darkening sky while they were pacified by an army of staff. At six neighbours' for cocktails, at eight a supper party, at ten I fled home and … I had thought, bed. But as soon as I got inside the cabin it hit me.

I had been with people all day. They had all been sweet. Whatever else they might be, Americans are always warm and friendly and enthusiastic. The MSJs, their children, their grandchildren, their friends, they all knew I was away from home, and away from you. And I knew they knew from the way they acted toward me. And I was grateful for that. Hugely. But the horrible fact remained: no matter how kind people are, the pain that comes from being separated from where you want to be, though it can be postponed, cannot be dodged. Your feelings, your real feelings will always out, and in my case that moment came when I entered the cabin. I was overwhelmed with sadness and loneliness and I knew I wouldn't sleep. I would have to sit with my feelings awhile. So I lit the fire (which I'd taken care to lay before I left) and sat staring at the flames, thinking of you and having a quiet little weep. After a while I did feel slightly better, well enough to sleep at any rate. I went to bed; no dreams disturbed me as on the previous night. But again I woke early in the dark and knew I was properly awake. So I went through to the fire, raked the embers, got the fire going (the sound of the pine logs crackling as they caught was marvellous) sat down and wrote this. So think of me as you read this, in my nightdress and dressing gown and thick bed socks, firelight reflecting off my face, scribbling away and writing these very words that you're reading now.

Tons of love, Mum xx

★

Ginny was waiting outside St David's at the end of the school day. She was going to see Maud and taking them with her.

They drove to Barnes. Maud opened the door to them. She was thinner, smaller and paler, thought Ralph, than when he'd seen her on Guy Fawkes night.

'Hello,' she said, her voice sounding similarly diminished.

They trooped through to the kitchen. Maud made coffee in old mugs with pictures of the Queen Mother on them for herself and Ginny, and crumpets and hot Ribena for the boys. They all sat at the big scrubbed pine table. The coffee and Ribena steamed. The butter on the crumpets melted and pooled on the plates.

'Well, Saturday morning,' Maud began, 'Arnold told me he had to go to his supplier on Mile End Road, needed my car, said cheerio and left. I haven't seen him since. This morning, to the bank. As expected, account emptied, Friday last. So this little flit of his was planned.'

'Had he his passport?' asked Ginny.

'No! He had to hand that in when he got bail. But you can buy them easy enough, or so says my bloody father who's become a bloody world expert on the criminal underworld, and yes, since you're asking, these fakes ones they're good enough to get you out through Harwich and into Europe.'

'Oh Maud,' said Ginny. 'I don't suppose any of his friends might know anything?'

'No,' said Maud. 'No one's heard a peep. Not his sisters, his parents, the gallery, his children, even his bloody wife. He's gone, not a word of warning and left not a trace behind.'

Ralph stared at his Ribena. The liquid was purple and the table seen through it was purple too. The women sipped their coffee.

'What happens about the bail?' asked Ginny quietly.

Maud laughed. An angry miserable laugh. 'Well, after the bank I went to see his solicitor didn't I? Had the happiest half-hour of my life. His bail was set at ten, which I don't have, obviously. The house was the surety.' She waved wildly round the kitchen. 'So he doesn't show up at the trial? Simple: they take the house. Obviously. I'm going to be homeless. I'll have to live with my daughter. In Bootle. In fucking Bootle.'

'Oh my God,' said Ginny. 'How could he?'

'Oh, that's easy. They caught him red-handed. He was guilty. His solicitor told him he was going to prison. Non-negotiable, a certainty. Five, six, seven years. He couldn't face it. So he scarpered.'

Ralph looked at his crumpet. He had been looking forward to it but now he no longer wanted it.

★

His mother's message on the back of the postcard:

Dear Ralph,
Though they pretend otherwise Americans want to be like us. If they could they'd have a Queen and hereditary peers but as they don't they have their ceremonies, like the swearing in of the new President, instead (see over). If you point this out they get shirty, so on this subject Mum keeps mum.
    Love, Mum xx

The caption explained the man in the picture overleaf with his hand on the Bible was Lyndon B. Johnson and he was being sworn in as the 36th President of the United States and the woman in the hat and coat alongside him was his wife, Claudia Alta 'Lady Bird' Johnson, the new First Lady.

★

Sir Winston Churchill died.

'His funeral's going to be on telly. We'll watch,' Doreen announced.

Ralph would never have thought to watch. 'Why?' he asked.

'Historic occasion,' she said with a finality that settled the matter.

★

Saturday, the day of the funeral. Clouds, heavy, dark, oppressive, lidded the sky; the river below, treacle black, sullen, swollen. They turned the electric lights on when they got up and they didn't turn them off all morning. That was the sort of day it was.

★

Later. Ralph on the floor of the River room, ankles crossed, Doreen on the sofa, breathing heavily, massaging her belly with both hands.

On the television a grainy black and white picture of Churchill's flag-covered coffin on a gun carriage trundling slowly through a London street. Then shots of the pavements crowded with people standing watching, many with transistor radios to their ears so they could listen to the BBC coverage as they paid their respects. All in dark clothes, all solemn, all the men bareheaded. Then, surprise – a man, hat on, smoking, the mourners round him standing slightly apart.

The mobile camera stopped to stare.

'Oh-oh,' said Doreen. 'Someone hates Churchill's guts.'

One mourner at least was doing his own thing, observed the commentator.

'Jesus. Everyone knows not to smoke at a funeral,' said Doreen. 'And you take your hat off when the coffin passes. I mean, even if you hate someone, you still behave.'

The camera left the man in the hat. Another angle on the trundling carriage. Further shots of pavements crowded with silent, grieving mourners. One image after the next, all different yet all showing the same thing, the coffin, the crowds, while over it the commentator in his slow sad voice spoke of the nation mourning the passing of its wartime saviour. All this went on for quite a time.

Finally, the gun carriage stopping at the bottom of a great set of steps. St Paul's Cathedral. Soldiers hoisting the coffin onto their shoulders. Soldiers carrying the coffin up the steps and through vast doors.

The picture changed from outside to inside the Cathedral. The camera high up, looking down. Seen from above, a sea of heads. Gliding up the nave, far away, a gold crucifix, the coffin and figures in black behind. Sir Winston's relatives, the commentator explained. A choir singing. Finally, the altar. The coffin set down. The relatives slipping away, sitting. A strange emptiness once the choir stopped singing. A man coming to the front. The Dean, said the commentator. The Dean speaking. His voice echoing, giving Ralph a sense of the vastness of the place.

The Dean talking of God and death, sacrifice and service. Boring. Ralph stopping listening. At last the Dean finishing and the whole congregation singing 'The Battle Hymn of the Republic'. That was stirring. Then a soldier playing 'The Last Post' on a single trumpet. The music made Ralph quiver inside. After the trumpeter finished, a long moment of silence in the cathedral and nobody moving. The sensation of everyone holding their breath.

Then the commentator again. The BBC would now close down for thirty minutes as a mark of respect, he explained, and resume a little after midday when it would follow the coffin's passage to Tower Hill from where a boat would take it down the Thames to Waterloo Station.

'Turn over,' said Doreen.

Ralph went over to the television and pressed the buttons for the two other stations. There were no pictures, just music.

'I don't know why they're not showing pictures for half an hour as a mark of respect,' said Doreen. 'Do you understand?'

'No,' said Ralph.

'Well turn it off for now,' said Doreen. 'We'll put it back on later. I want to see the boat with the coffin on the river.'

Ralph pressed the button. A fizzing noise, a white dot momentarily and then the screen went black.

'Well, did you enjoy that?' asked Doreen.

Ralph moved his hand over the convex screen and felt static prickle his palm.

'Well, not enjoy, but you know what, you'll never forget that you know. For the rest of your life you'll know where you were and what you were doing the day Churchill was buried,' she said.

'Does that matter?'

'Oh, it will.'

Ralph sat on the floor again. He wasn't certain she was right. But he wasn't going to say anything. No point, he thought.

'I found it very interesting,' she said.

'Really?' He had the feeling she was only saying this because she felt she had to. 'Do people always speak in funny voices at funerals?' he asked.

'Yes.'

'Why?'

'To show respect.'

Ralph considered this.

'And if you didn't, I suppose you'd get in trouble?'

'Yes. But the thing is, *you* wouldn't. You'd know how to conduct yourself. So you wouldn't.'

'How do you know that?'

'Because I do. As you're growing up, you learn these things, they become second nature. So you do them without thinking. I mean, if you'd been in the street outside St Paul's today, you'd have known how to behave, wouldn't you? Course you would. You wouldn't have been telling jokes or singing or running about, would you?'

'No. But what about the man who kept his hat on and was smoking?'

'Ah, but he knew the rules. He hadn't forgotten. He knew. He was just making a point.'

'I see.'

And he did. But at the edge of his thoughts another idea was forming. When people were together, like they were in the streets and in St Paul's, it was not only that the rules were obeyed because everybody knew what they were, they were obeyed because everybody *made* everybody else obey them. The group made sure. It was like in *Lord of the Flies*. Once Jack and all the boys were together, their rules were *the* rules and Ralph and Piggy were supposed to do as they said. But they hadn't, same as the man who kept smoking as the coffin passed hadn't. But from where did it come, the ability to refuse, to say no? Did you just feel it? As often as not he didn't know what he felt, or it took him ages to work it out, so how would he know whether he agreed or disagreed? And then, assuming he'd worked out what he felt and he had realised he didn't want to follow the rest, did he know for sure he could stand against them? On the island, would he have stuck with Ralph and Piggy, or gone over to the other side, the wrong side?

'Hot buttered toast?' asked Doreen. 'What do you think?'

'Yeah,' he said.

"Go and put some on then."

He went through to the kitchen, took the loaf out of the bread bin and began to slice it.

February

After he got home and had changed Ralph remembered Benedict had the biology textbook he needed. He went back to the Boscombes' and slipped in through the side door.

'Hello?' he called.

'Here.'

It was Ginny. She was on the far side of the partition, in the back. He went through. She was bent over the top of the washing machine, pulling out wet clothes that were all knotted and tangled from being spun together and dropping these into a basket. There was no sign of Jeannie.

'Benedict about?'

'Hope so,' she said, looking round at him. She wasn't smiling.

Ralph pointed at the ceiling. Benedict's room was at the top of the house.

'Yeah,' she said. 'Go you on up.'

She seemed muted, flat. He sloped off, got the book, returned. The drying horse was up, some clothes already hung over the bars, Ginny draping a sock.

'I got it.' Ralph waved the textbook.

'I've been doing laundry my whole bloody life,' she said. 'Well, since I got married anyway. And I hate it. Do you ever do it?'

His answer was only going to make a bad situation worse. He knew that. But he had to answer.

'Ah, no,' he said quietly.

Ginny took a second sock, stretched it and hung it.

'Thought so.'

She picked up one of Benedict's school shirts and flapped it ferociously to remove the creases.

'I'll be going then,' said Ralph.

She stopped flapping the shirt and looked at him.

'Not myself today,' she said.

'Oh don't worry,' he said.

That was what one was supposed to say in these situations, wasn't it?

'Malcolm X was shot,' she said. 'They killed him. Did you hear?'

He shook his head. 'No.'

'Really knocked the stuffing out of me. As a species we just don't seem able to resist doing whatever's bound to make a bad situation worse.'

He nodded and fled.

★

The front of the postcard showed Stan Laurel, dressed in an ill-fitting suit and battered bowler, with the figures '1891–1965' underneath.

Dear Ralph,

The fat one Oliver Hardy went in '57, now the thin one is gone. I saw Laurel & Hardy in the Horsham fleapit every Saturday when I was a girl. They showed some of their old films on television after Laurel's death. They have stood the test of time. Our first treat when I return will be a trip to the Waterloo Station cinema. They still show Laurel & Hardy films.

Love, Mum xx

March

The end of the day. Ralph and Benedict meandering. The open air swimming pool, empty of water, the bottom strewn with leaves and twigs. The gravel on the path crunching below their polished shoes. Stands of oak, chestnut and elm, and in the spaces between the trees, great wild clumps of daffodils with intense yellow blooms. A smell of earth, leaf mould and rotten tree.

The boys sallied out into Lark Hill. Petrol fumes, rubber and burnt oil. Their bus rolled up to their stop. They boarded and climbed to the upper deck. The front seats were taken so they sat halfway down on the left. Ralph got the window. On the pavement below a man was carrying a goldfish bowl with an eel swimming in it. The bus lurched away.

'We're going to Wales for Easter,' said Benedict.

'Oh.'

Ralph wondered was he about to be invited. He hoped not.

'Just me, Mum, Douglas,' said Benedict. 'Then Easter Monday, I go to Clive at his parents'. Yvonne'll be there, groan, groan. Mum and Clive, not getting on.'

Benedict stopped speaking. Ralph knew to say nothing, just wait. It would come.

'Started a week ago. No, further back than that. Mum gave Douglas, who's living with us now, she gave him Clive's hut, as a study.'

'Did she?'

'Yeah. When she told Clive they had a huge row. He was shouting that he still wrote in it and they'd agreed he could go on using it when he moved out and she was screaming back, "You don't live here anymore. You've got another bloody life. You've got bloody Yvonne. You can bloody well f-u-c-k off."'

The bus stopped. Benedict stopped. The sound of passengers getting on and off. The bell. The bus pulling away. Background noise. Benedict could speak again.

'Mum hates Yvonne. Says she's a drunk and a lunatic and unhinged. And you know what she called her the other day?'

'What?'

'A c-u-n-t. Clive can't stand Douglas. Says he's a great fat useless slug who sits round his house drinking his cider and talking rubbish about politics. And the new thing is the key. Clive has a house key and Mum doesn't want him to have it anymore. She doesn't want him coming in willy-nilly she says. It's not his house. He lives in White City.'

Benedict blew out his cheeks and exhaled.

'But Clive is refusing to give up the key. So now Mum's talking about changing the locks and Clive having to phone before he comes to be sure someone's in. I said to Mum I liked that Clive could come whenever he wanted and she said that was the problem, that he could come whenever he wanted and she wanted to put a stop to it.'

'Oh.'

Ralph sat trying to think of something else to say but all he could think was how happy he was not to have been invited to Fferm ar Bryn for Easter.

The bus stopped near the big school and the maroon uniforms swarmed on. They made such a racket conversation was impossible and that was a relief.

★

Dear Ralph,

It's all happening here. They jailed Martin Luther King, the civil rights man. In Selma a mob attacked clergymen who supported him, a demonstration about this led by nuns (nuns!) was stopped. In Montgomery a protest march by college students was attacked by state troopers, and they found bombs in Selma and the President had to send 3,000 troops to protect the civil rights people there.

Everyone in America is on tenterhooks regarding these events, even here in Rye which is white and rich. But of the actual violence, that you may have seen on television or read about in the newspapers, no, there's none of that here. You can therefore rest assured that nothing will happen to your dear old mother.

I also have to say these events have opened my eyes (though I keep this to myself). I am so relieved I come from a country with a long tradition of tolerance and generosity toward outsiders. Crikey – is that the time? (I'm looking at the clock.) Can't go on – have to stop – have to phone a supplier before the end of the working day whose stuff was dud and get the whole order re-sent. I am expecting fireworks.

Love, Mum xx

April

Pale sky, milky sun, spring heat. Ralph wore his satchel crossways – it was bulging with books and Common Entrance practice papers to do over the Easter holidays – and his coat with his cap stuffed deep in one of the pockets was draped over the top. He wanted to take his blazer off too but his pockets were so full of stuff that he hadn't managed to squeeze into his satchel, he couldn't risk taking it off in case it all fell out.

Beside him a bed of tulips, sagging stems, heavy heads. He stopped to peer. They reminded him of the Mekon, the evil genius with the giant brain and tiny body who floated about on a saucer in the Dan Dare comic strip in the *Eagle*. At the junction where the stems met the flowers he noticed little yellowy-brown collars, their texture like enamel paint. He'd never noticed these before.

He went on. Cherry trees ahead. Flaking puce trunks and frothy blossom. He stared. White one moment, pink the next, and white again the moment after. The way the colour pulsed made his eyes fizz.

He went down the dimpled crumbling brick steps and along the gravel path. In the distance he could hear an engine thumping and water gushing. The pool was being refilled. Swimming resumed after Easter. On either side of him on the trees a fierce fur of green – the young leaves showing.

When he got to the stop he found his bus was parked there. The nice conductress with the red face was on the platform.

'Oh hello,' she said. 'Aren't you supposed to be on holiday?'

'The school is,' he said, 'but if you're doing Common Entrance you get an extra day today – exam practice.'

'What's Common Entrance? Like the Eleven-Plus?'

'No, you do it when you're thirteen. I'll be going in November, or next March.'

'And where's your mate?'

'He got an exemption. He's in Wales.'

The day before, while Douglas and Ginny drove with the luggage, Benedict had gone on the train with Jeannie.

'Doing anything nice for Easter yourself?'

'Dunno. Doreen might take me to Battersea Fun Fair.'

'Who's that?' asked the conductress. 'Your mum?'

'No. She's in America working. Doreen looks after me.'

'Oh.' She looked at him.

'And she's having a baby.'

'Oh lovely,' said the conductress. 'A little brother or sister for you. You must be over the moon.'

'No. Not Mum. Doreen.'

She looked at him again, more closely. 'Doreen, who looks after you?'

'Yeah. But Tom's gone.'

'Who?' asked the conductress. 'I'm confused.'

'Her husband.'

'Tom?'

'Yeah. So it's just me and Doreen at the house now.'

The conductress looked at him a third time. Her expression was much more complicated than the previous times.

'Step aboard my chariot,' she said. She winked.

As he stepped aboard he heard his compass rattling inside the tin protractor box in his blazer pocket. He glanced down the aisle. The empty lower deck. Why not sit here for a change? He meandered up to the end and sat on the left. He could see straight ahead through the window. Good spot.

The bell pinged. The bus moved off. He paid his fare. The streets slid past but his attention was inward, on the tulip heads in their enamel collars, the vibrating cherry blossoms, the green burr on the trees.

★

The footbridge stretching ahead, the gun metal railway tracks glinting through the girders. Down below, the black river at low tide, banks of bare silt like wet liquorice.

Ralph walked forward, scanning the faraway Falkland Road gardens. He found the Boscombes' ladder, a thin black smear at this distance, and farther leftward, their own garden and their tall thin house. He imagined Doreen inside, in the kitchen, shoes off, stockinged feet resting on one of the high-backed Danish chairs and then himself bursting though the side door and her crying, 'Ah Ralph, how are you?'

He was in sight of the steps leading down to Falkland Road. Two figures swaggering toward him who had just come up. Both wore parkas. Older than him. Bigger. Did he turn and go back? Trouble was they'd see him turn and he didn't think he could make it across to the other side ahead of them.

They were closer now. He heard their voices. Be well out of their way when they passed. That was the thing. The trouble was, the footbridge was narrow, only six foot wide. He'd just have to do his best, do what he could. He shrunk closer to the girders between the footbridge and the railway tracks. He dropped his head. He would avoid eye contact too.

Looking down. Only seeing the asphalt surface, grey and pulpy, lumpy and bumpy. Then into view they came, from the hems of their parkas down. One wearing desert boots, sandy-coloured and corded; the other oxblood monkey boots.

The shoes coming, the shoes passing. Then empty asphalt. They'd passed. He'd done it. Safe.

'Sorry mate.' A voice behind. 'I think you dropped something.'

Turning, he saw a fist. Flying at him. Knuckles catching him, his cheek, the side of his nose, the bone rim under his eye. Thunking of bone on bone. Falling back. Shock, pain, wetness, blurring, instantly. Fist vanishing and then barrelling back. Turning away. Fist hitting his ear. Hot feeling. Roaring in his head. Another jab. Other eye this time. The second youth swiping him with his open hand. Banging his head.

Someone walking past. Speaking uncertainly. 'Going a bit hard boys.'

'Fuck off.'

Hands patting his pockets. Cuts inside his cheeks where the flesh had been mashed against his teeth.

'Where's your fucking wallet?'

Shouting. 'Don't have one.' Blood on his tongue.

Hand rummaging. Where his wallet would be. If he had one. Homework book in there. Coming out, flying away.

Shouting. 'No money.' His nose, dribbling.

His satchel. Undoing clasps. Contents spilling out.

'Let's chuck him.'

Dragging him to the river side. Lifting him up. Seeing through swollen lids the shining silt far below. Faraway voices. 'What are you doing?' And heels. Women's. Scuff, scuff, click, click. Running. Coming from the same side he'd come from.

'If you don't give us your fucking money, we're going to throw you over, you little cunt.'

Inching him higher. Sticking his foot forward. Finding a gap in the lattice. Jamming it in.

'Where's your fucking money?'

Right hand snaking into his blazer pocket. Prising the protractor box open. Fumbling. His compass. Wrapping his fingers round the stem. Pulling his hand out. Jabbing. Feeling something hard. Bone. Teeth. At the end of the compass point. Back and up, back and up.

'What the fuck … the little cunt.'

Letting him go. Yanking his foot out of the lattice. Jumping back. Feeling footbridge. Under his feet. The one he'd jabbed. Blood on his hands. His face. Spots only. Pillar box red.

Women coming up. Parkas turning. Desert boots and monkey boots speeding off. Passing the two women. Head scarves, light coats, bare knees. In his mouth, metal taste of blood. Lip torn too, bottom one.

'You okay?'

'Jesus!'

Putting something in his left hand. Hanky of some sort.

'That'll keep the worst off your shirt.'

Steering his hand to his face. Hanky to his nose. Flow interrupted.

'Pull his shoe out, Annie.'

Right foot no shoe. Yes. Just his sock on the asphalt. Only noticing now. The other he'd left behind stuck in the lattice.

'Come on, darling. Your shoe's in front of you.'

Hand guiding his foot into the leather. Pressing down. His foot wriggling and squiggling.

'Give it a stamp.'

Stamping weakly.

Shoe on.

'Good boy.'

Hanky sodden already. So much blood.

Women gently unhitching satchel from shoulder. Sensing them moving round. Picking up. Textbooks. Exercise books. Papers. His homework book.

'Get his coat.'

Smeary picture. Woman in headscarf peering at the name tag in his coat's collar.

'Goswell, R. What's the R for?' she asked.

''alph.' Lips so big, mangled, he couldn't say it.

'Come again.'

''alph.'

'Ralph. You called Ralph?'

Nodding. Hearing sobbing. Didn't realise where the sound was coming from for a moment or two. Then realising. Himself.

'It's the shock, Nancy.'

'Where do you live, Ralph?'

''alkland Road.'

Grasping his arms. Pulling him gently along. Feet moving automatically. Hot tears. Flowing hard. Salty too. Over his cheekbones. Down his face. Lips wet. Sticky. Blood gluing them shut. Snot on his chin. Everything blurring. The girders. The tracks. The asphalt. The sky.

'We're at the steps, Ralph. One at a time now.'

Going slowly step by step by step, down they went and then finally feeling pavement through his shoes.

'Which way, darling?'

Pointing. Walking. Mouth really hurting now. Not just the inside cheeks but the gums. Probing gently, tongue pushing. Every tooth sore, bruised, throbbing.

'What number's your house?'

''ighty-'ight.'

'What'd he say?'

'Eighty-eight I think.'

Parked cars, front gardens, redbrick houses, all indistinct. Closing on the Boscombes'. Clive's scooter at the kerb. The front wheel on the pavement. Fixing a puncture. Clive's voice. 'Ralph? Jesus!'

'Two of them. On the footbridge.'

'Tried to throw him off.'

'I'll take him home,' said Clive.

'Here's his coat and satchel.'

Patting his shoulders.

'Bye, Ralph.'

Clicking away. Clive holding his arm. Clive asking. Explaining what happened as best as he was able. Turning through their gate. Passing the bulky terracotta pots. In the side door. Doreen shouting, crying. Sinking down on one of the high-backed chairs. Clive going upstairs to his mother's office to phone the doctor.

Doreen speaking. 'Drop your hand.'

Lowering the hand with the hanky that had been covering his mouth and nose. Doreen taking the hanky. Then she opened his other hand. Compass still there. Took it away. She put it on the table. Easing his school tie off.

Opening his collar. Warm flannel on his face. Softly, carefully rubbing. Congealed sticky blood and saliva wiping clean. Flannel cooling. Rinsing and squeezing sounds. Flannel back, warm again. More careful rubbing, cleaning. Doreen breathing. Doreen muttering 'Oh God' over and over. Clive coming back. 'Doctor's coming.'

Later. The doorbell ringing. Clive answering.

A third presence in the kitchen. Male. Elderly. Dr O'Dwyer. Smelling of tobacco and sherry.

Warm hands touching face.

'Open your mouth.'

Torch clicking on. Wooden spatula. Probing in his mouth. Slowly, carefully. Upward and outward.

'No missing teeth,' said the doctor. 'Lot of tearing and scraping inside the mouth. He'll not enjoy eating for a few days. Lip's split. If it hasn't closed by tomorrow, I'll stitch it. Nose might be broken but nothing we can do about that. Certainly bruised. Badly. Likewise the eyes. But the eyes themselves, well let's see. Right, Ralph. See my finger.'

Nodding.

'Follow the finger as I move it. Follow the finger.'

Following the finger tip from side to side, up and down, far to near.

'Right, open and close your jaw.'

Moving his jaw. Aching hurt.

'Just chew for me.'

Touching his teeth shut.

'That hurts?'

Nodding.

'Thought it would.'

Fingers feeling round his ears, the top of his head, his neck, his shoulders.

'Some trauma but nothing's broken or worse. Put him to bed. He needs rest and plenty of water. Soft foods.

Poached fish. Soft-boiled egg. Rice pudding. That sort of thing. I'll be back tomorrow morning at ten.'

Dr O'Dwyer leaving. Clive leaving. In his bedroom, Doreen undressing him and putting him into his pyjamas. He didn't care. No shame. Just bed. The quicker, the better. That's all he wanted. Covers lifting back. Getting in, sliding down. Pain. Neck, shoulders, head, mouth, teeth. Cool sheets. Laying head on pillow. Opening mouth. Can't bear his teeth touching. Closing his eyes. Swishing sound of curtains closing. Half-darkness.

Later. Covers lifting away at the bottom of the bed. Hot water bottle slipping in. Bottle too hot to touch with his bare feet. Heat radiating up. Tucking the covers in again. Doreen kissing him. The top of his head.

'There's a jug of water here. I'll leave the light on in the hall. And I've brought everything else through, your school bag and everything.'

'My compass?' he asked.

'Your compass.' She stopped. 'It's beside your bed.' She was thinking something. He could tell. She was wanting to ask what he was thinking but then decided not to. He was sure of it. 'I cleaned it,' she said.

Doreen clicking way. His mind slowing, closing down. Thoughts receding. Needing to pee. Too sore to move. Too tired to move too. Never had he been so tired. Never. Slowly, slowly, breathing slowing. So tired. Never so tired before. It was exhaustion the like of which ... Quietening. Slowing. Slipping, slipping into ...

★

He woke the next morning, Saturday. Through his open bedroom door the electric light in the hall showing palely in the dawn light. Right hand hurting. Cramping. Pulling hand out from under the covers. Opening his fingers and expecting to find the compass there – silver, lethal, slim. But no, it wasn't. He felt as if he'd been holding it all night but it was gone. It wasn't there. Stumbling upstairs. Peeing. His pee thick and yellow and dark. Brackish. Running back to his room. Ah, yes, there it was. The compass. His compass. Beside the bed. He'd forgotten. Falling into bed, sleeping until ten. Woken by Dr O'Dwyer. Needing stitches. In his lip. The pain of the needle going through, the thread being pulled behind. After the doctor left, back to sleep. Woken at lunchtime by Doreen. Curtains opening. Light flooding in. Doreen looking at him, her upper teeth showing. Thinking she was going to cry. Looking like it. Didn't though. She has a soft-boiled egg for him. Cut up with small bits of soft white toast. Trying to chew a mouthful. Can't. Lips and teeth hurting too much.

'I'll make you rice pudding,' said Doreen taking, it away. 'I've got a vanilla pod and I'll get some cream.'

Lying back, staring up at ceiling. Churning roiling thoughts. The whole scene on the bridge again, speeded up, slowed down, sometimes in colour, garish, sometimes colourless, over and over, and then he was flying, falling, hurtling toward the liquorice black silt. And the liquorice black silt was hurtling to meet him. Knowing what was coming and not being able to stop. Unbearable idea. He wouldn't have survived. No. Terrifying thought. As it was registering, a sensation, like congealing, right in his centre. He could be dead. His legs began to shake. Terror, pure terror. Gradually the world outside reasserting itself. Doreen clattering in the kitchen. A car driving past outside. The long slow mournful hoot of a tug passing on the river.

★

Ralph got up on Sunday morning and ran a bath. He sank
into the water and lay still. The steam rose around him.
Black hairs showing below. In his armpits too. Not many.
Only a few. But showing. Wiry. His head was throbbing. So
were his gums, lips, cheeks, nose and teeth. New pains as
well, not noticed before. Knuckles and fingers, shoulders,
armpits, his right foot, which had been stuck in the lattice and kept him tethered like an anchor every time the
two assailants tried to haul him upward to throw him over
the rail and onto the mud flats below. Church bells, light,
tinkling. From St Mary's at the bottom of the High Street
beside the road bridge over the Thames. Ginny had once
told him Parliamentary Army officers held councils inside
St Mary's in the middle of the Civil War while their horses
waited outside in the graveyard. Had they heard those same
bells? He was enjoying this when, unbidden, the memory.
Jabbing with the compass. Hitting something hard. Bone.
Teeth. No picture, just the feeling of colliding, his compass
with he didn't know what. The sensation sickening, terrifying, exhilarating.

The water cooled. Ralph sat up. There was a rubber
hand shower that ran off the taps. He fiddled with the hot
and cold to get the temperature right, then washed his hair,
taking care not to get his lips or his stitches too wet as the
doctor had advised.

He pulled the plug and looped the chain that attached
it to the overflow around the cold water tap. He stood and
lifted first one and then the other leg over the side of the
bath and onto the floor mat and as he did he felt all his
new pains again.

He took a big towel off the rail and wrapped it gingerly around his middle. From beside him came the sound
of his bathwater draining down the plughole. He noticed
the taste inside his mouth, like old rubber. He put a pearl

of Colgate on his toothbrush and then carefully began to stroke the bristles over his teeth. He had to go gently. The whole procedure took ages. Rinsing with lukewarm water hurt almost as much as brushing had. He bent forward and spat. White toothpaste froth with threads of brown splattering on the porcelain. He ran his tongue round his mouth. His gums were bleeding.

He found a hand towel and used it to wipe the steam off the mirror over the sink. The action made a squeaking sound. Once the glass was clear he bent forward. It was a second or two before he understood what was staring back at him – himself, but as he had never seen himself before.

His head and face were bruised and swollen. His nose was warped and bent. The split in his lip had already produced a nasty toffee-coloured scab and the stitches, tightly drawn and neatly tied, were like small flies that had alighted on his mouth. His eyeballs were badly bloodshot and his eyelids – they reminded him vaguely of a bicycle inner tube – were hugely inflated and dark black. He was looking at himself through two tiny slits.

The last of the bathwater glugging down the plughole and rushing along the pipe under his feet. He pulled his pyjamas and dressing gown back on and went down to the kitchen. Doreen was there, dressed for the day, her belly showing.

'Any better after your bath?'

'I don't know,' he said.

'Happy Easter.'

She waved at the chocolate eggs and the envelope with his name on the front on the table.

'I don't think I'm ready for Easter,' he said.

'Course you aren't. It'll wait.'

She put a small bowl of cornflakes with hot milk in front of him. The milky steam drifted up. She sat opposite him.

'Fine pair of shiners you have there.'

'Will I still have them when I go back to school?'

'You might. Don't know. Bruises take time.'

He looked into the bowl, the bubbles round the edge, the bits of soggy flake poking above the surface.

'What's worrying you? The questions? People asking, wanting to know?'

He nodded without looking up.

'People are nosy. It's human nature. They hear something, they see something, they're curious. When I was home for Christmas, everyone in the parish was talking about me. Now nobody came and asked me directly, but if they had, you know what I'd have said? "Yeah, you heard right." They wouldn't have liked it, that would have been brazen, but it would have been true. And that's all you can do – be true. Anyone asks, "Where'd you get your black eyes?" you just tell them. You were jumped by two yobbos. And that's it. Let them make of it what they will. You've told the truth. There's nothing they can do with the truth.'

He nodded, though he wasn't sure it would work.

'Now you know Benedict will ask. Clive will have told him. Ginny too. You prepared for that?'

This hadn't crossed his mind.

'We'll worry about the future later. In the meantime, you focus on getting better. You need to get your strength up. Try a mouthful. Go on.'

He sniffed the steam coming up but caught nothing.

'My teeth hurt.'

'I know but you don't have to chew,' said Doreen.

He scooped a small bit of cereal into his mouth. It was hot, sweet. He let it sit, then swallowed.

'You going to tell my mum?' Ralph asked.

'Tell her what? You met a couple of highwaymen? Why would I? No, we don't want to worry her, do we?'

Ralph agreed.

'One more thing. From now on, you're alone, you take the road bridge. I know it's longer but never mind.'

He pushed the bowl away.

'Don't want it?'

He shook his head. 'Not hungry really.'

'When you've had a shock you often aren't. But your body will let you know soon enough when it's hungry. So what are you going to do? Back to bed?'

He shook his head and pointed at the River room.

'Go in then.'

He went and turned the old armchair covered in bottle-green velvet to face the window. He sank down and looked out through the glass wall at their garden falling away, the wall at the end and the river beyond.

A police launch appeared on his right, small, snug, compact, with white buoys lashed to its bulwarks, wake lines fanning from its stern that got longer and longer as it pushed upriver.

In the sky overhead the lower clouds were bulky, dense, solid, while the higher ones gave the appearance of having been torn up, teased out, pulled apart. The sky between the tears was washed blue. The sun, halfway up the sky and over on his right, a soft, creamy disk radiating a rich lemony light. A spring morning, Ralph thought. Or did he only think this because he knew the date? He wasn't sure.

The doorbell rang at the front of the house. He heard Doreen shouting, 'I'll go.'

Indistinct noises, which he assumed were Doreen opening the door, speaking to the caller and the caller speaking back. Then footsteps down the hall and into the kitchen and across to the archway into the River room.

'Ralph,' said Doreen, 'you've got a visitor.'

'Morning, squire. Happy Easter. If you believe in it.'

234

He knew the voice. At the same time it didn't make sense. He turned and saw Timothy moving toward him, a brown paper bag under the arm with the claw at the end.

'Christ,' he said. 'Clive said you got a hiding but he didn't say how bad.'

Doreen offered tea. Timothy accepted. Milk, no sugar. Doreen went away. Timothy pulled a hard chair from the refectory table, dragged it across and sat stiffly. He put the paper bag on the floor.

'What happened?'

Ralph told the whole story.

'Sweet Jesus,' said Timothy once he'd finished. 'Let's bring back conscription if it's come to this. A bit of square-bashing might put manners on these yahoos and I speak as one who hated square-bashing and everything else to do with the army.'

On the river the police launch was gone, though its wake remained, lines of white cord floating on the polished surface of the water. Doreen returned.

'Oh, a cup and saucer,' said Timothy.

'Nothing but the best,' said Doreen.

'It's a relief to know standards aren't slipping,' said Timothy as he took his cup of tea.

He looked at her intently. 'How are you?'

'You mean?' She reached her arms round and cupped the belly that stuck forward and stretched her dress. 'It's hard to sleep sometimes. What am I saying? It's hard to sleep all the time. I have to sleep on my back, which is purgatory. I've always slept on my front. My feet are killing me. I'm permanently exhausted and I've still two more months of this torture to go. But other than that, I'm fine and dandy.'

'When is the happy day, by the way?'

'June fifteenth.'

'Good time to have your birthday,' said Timothy. 'I'm late December, which is awful. Endless joint Christmas and birthday presents when I was a kid. But yours won't have any of that malarkey.'

'Hadn't thought of that,' said Doreen. 'Well, I'll leave you to it.'

'Nice to see you,' said Timothy. 'And you are looking tremendously well incidentally. Fettle never finer, as my father liked to say to anyone in bloom. He was a clergyman and that's the sort of thing clergymen used to say. Thought it was funny. It wasn't. He didn't get that though. Well, of course he didn't. He was a clergyman. Didn't get anything really.'

'Bye, then,' Doreen said.

She slipped off.

'Well, she's a tonic,' said Timothy. 'I wouldn't mind being looked after by her.'

Timothy blew on his tea. Sipped. Nodded at the window.

'You'd never get tired looking out at that. "Sweet Thames, run softly, till I end my song."'

He put his cup and saucer on the floor and picked up the bag.

'I've brought you something.'

He opened the bag and pulled out two books. One was a large red hardback. The other a thin, creased paperback.

'When I heard from Clive what happened, I thought, someone goes through the shit you went through, you got to do something that will help them. But what? And then I thought, I know. I was miserable as a boy. But there was one book I could always rely upon. I just had to open it and start turning the pages and I was away, transported from the vicarage out into the world and once I was out in the world I was happy. I was free. So I thought, I'll get him one of them.'

He opened the large red book. *The Faber Atlas* was printed on the title page, over which was drawn, in crayon, boldly, brightly and almost childishly, stars, a moon and a sun.

'So I did. Popped in to John Sandoe and picked this beauty up yesterday.'

Timothy flicked forward. Continents and countries flashed past and more crayon drawings, many more – page after page of flowers, birds, animals and trees.

'Went to see poor old Maud last night,' Timothy said. 'Got her to add the pictures. They're to assist the escaping.'

Timothy closed the atlas and handed it to Ralph.

'And this is a book of stories, by a Russian. They're brilliant. There's a great story in here about an old man, he drives a horse-drawn cab in St Petersburg, sixty years ago which isn't very long ago. My old man was studying divinity when this was published. And he's so lonely, not my dad, the character in the story, he ends up talking to his horse because there's no else who will listen. But the one to read is "The Lady with the Dog". When you read it you'll think, Ah, yuck, it's a love story. It is, but persevere because what it's really about is that we hide what we really care about, and we show the world what we don't care about. Everyone has a secret centre, you included, and the story says that's what counts. Guard it well.'

He handed the book to Ralph. Ralph looked at the cover. *The Lady with the Dog and Other Stories*. The author's name above the title – Anton Chekhov.

'Thank you,' he said.

★

It was a plain white airmail card with his address on the front.

On the back his mother had written:

Dear Ralph,
Spring has sprung. Literally. I am full of the joys.
Love, Mum xx

Underneath she'd drawn a sunflower and the sun above.

May

Ginny said, 'Maud's having a terrible time. And today may well prove the worst day ever. So remember, boys, be agreeable, do as you're asked, and don't forget we're here to help.'

He was in Ginny's car, in the back. Benedict had the front seat. Through the window he saw Maud's road, elms on either side with bright new leaves and behind the green trees, one large detached redbrick house after another, every one in its own substantial garden.

'So is that clear?' asked Ginny. 'You are to be nice.'

'Yes,' said Ralph.

'Benedict?' asked Ginny. 'Did you hear what I said?'

'Yes.'

'Try and sound enthusiastic, Benedict,' said Ginny.

'How long are we staying?' he asked.

'All day. I'd say it'll take that long.'

Ralph saw Maud's house. A pantechnicon was parked outside, deep blue with 'Bentall's Furniture Depository' on the side in gold writing.

'Saturday's supposed to be my day of rest,' said Benedict. 'This is child cruelty. I'm going to report you.'

'Actually Sunday is the official day of rest,' said Ginny, 'but please do report me. Maybe the NSPCC will take you off my hands.'

'Hilarious,' said Benedict.

'You sound exactly like your father.'

In the rear, Ralph shrank down. The sooner they got inside Maud's, the better.

Ginny parked and they walked back. The pantechnicon was open at the rear. They stopped and stared into the huge cavernous back. It was strewn with tea chests and piles of old blankets and grubby curtains and smelt vaguely of rotting fish.

'You know, for ages,' said Ginny, 'the little voice in my head's been saying, It can't be true. Maud can't be made to sell her home to pay the bloody bail. It won't happen. But now, seeing this, I think, Ginny, how could you be so stupid, so pathetically deluded?'

She untied the scarf round her head and retied it. She straightened her sheepskin waistcoat. She smoothed the front of her dress.

'It was always going to happen, of course it was, and now it is happening. But when we don't want to face the truth, if it's bad, we just blank it out, don't we?'

They turned to the house. Part of the front hedge had been dug up and was piled beside the front path. This was to allow access to the garden. A large flatbed lorry, with a crane on the back and planks under the wheels to protect the grass, was parked by Arnold's fibreglass worm casts. Two men were at work disassembling one of the sculptures into the separate lengths that made it up.

Ralph and Benedict followed Ginny down the path to the front door. The door was ajar. Ginny pushed it open.

'Hello,' Ginny shouted.

Ralph followed Ginny and his friend into the hall. The pictures had been taken down and were stacked against the wall. All the drawers had been taken out of the shallow hall table and piled on top. From upstairs came the sound of men talking loudly and banging. Maud clumped out of the kitchen. She wore a coloured scarf wrapped round her head and a housecoat with buttons up the front. Her legs were bare.

'Remind you of anything?'

She turned on the spot in front of Ginny.

'Ah, no.'

'One of those German women who cleaned away the rubble after the war? Remember the newsreels?'

'Oh, yeah,' said Ginny. 'So you do. And how are you today? Or is that question banned?'

'Of course it's fucking banned,' said Maud.

'Of course,' said Ginny. 'I must remember to keep my mouth shut.'

'Morning boys,' said Maud. 'All right?'

Ralph and Benedict nodded and mumbled simultaneously, 'Yes thanks, Maud.'

'So you can both speak, well that's excellent. Working with deaf mutes would have been very difficult today. Anyway, before I get completely carried away with my own sarcasm, I'm very grateful. Spending a Saturday helping your mother's friend clear her house, that's quite something.'

'Oh don't worry about it,' said Benedict. 'We wouldn't have been doing anything anyhow.'

'And you, Ralph, how are those wounds?'

Maud stepped up and stared at his face.

'Better,' said Ralph, 'but not completely healed yet.'

'No,' said Maud, screwing her eyes up and leaning closer. 'I can see.'

She turned to Ginny.

'Christ,' said Maud. 'It takes so long to recover, doesn't it? And that's just the body. Think of the heart.'

She shook her head.

'We'd better knuckle down.'

★

'Right, Ralph,' said Maud.

They were alone in the kitchen. Benedict and Ginny were elsewhere in the house. Through the French doors Ralph could see out to the garden, and the workmen using the crane to lift a section of fibreglass tubing onto the back of the flatbed.

'Tea chests.' She pointed. 'Newspapers.' She pointed. 'Crockery.' She indicated the whole kitchen. 'Each piece to be wrapped really well, like this.'

She took a plate from the dresser and wrapped it in several sheets.

'Then stacked like so and the wood shavings and saw-dust packed round it.'

She put the paper-wrapped plate in the bottom of a tea chest and heaped the shavings already in the bottom around it.

'Once the chest is full you then chalk on the side what's inside and where it came from.'

She took a long white chalk stick from the table.

'So, in the case of this tea chest you write, "Plates. Dresser. Kitchen." Got that?'

Ralph set to work. Now and again he looked out the French doors and saw the sculptures shrinking and the pile of fibreglass pieces on the back of the flatbed growing. Then he heard the lorry's engine starting. He looked up. The sculptures were down. Everything was on the flatbed. The lorry crawled over the grass and went through the gap in the hedge. Then it was gone. Shortly after, he ran out of newspaper. He was about to go and look for Maud when he saw she was in the garden. He would go and ask her. He opened the French doors and went out. Maud was standing in the middle of where the sculptures had stood.

He walked forward. Maud had her back toward him. At first he thought she was doing nothing except standing but when he got closer he saw that she had her head down, her hand over her eyes and that she was crying. He turned round. He'd go back in and find one of the removal men. They'd have newspaper.

'Don't run away,' she said without turning round. 'I'm not fucking contagious, Ralph.'

Ralph stopped, turned.

'Look, they're gone, Arnold's worm casts, and I've been living with them for almost as long as I've lived here.'

She waved at the concrete squares ringed round her on which the pieces had rested.

'End of an era. End of a life. End of everything.'

She seemed calmer but he hadn't forgotten her vehemence of a few moments before. What he needed to do now was to say something and then he could slip away because that would be their conversation finished and she couldn't accuse him of being rude. The trouble was, he couldn't think what. All he had in his head was one idea. Run. Then into his thoughts, unbidden and unexpected, a thought. Yes, no reason not to.

'Thank you for the atlas,' he said.

Maud turned and looked directly at him. A sheen of tears covered her face. Her eyes had shrunk.

'What?'

'You drew on an atlas for me, birds and stars …'

'Oh yeah, I remember. That's right. Thought it was a bit weird myself, drawing all over a perfectly good book, and a reference book if you don't mind, but Timothy insisted.'

'They're very colourful,' he said.

'Should be. I was using the best crayons on the market.'

'And they make the book more …'

He stopped.

'Interesting?'

'Valuable,' he said.

'I don't think anyone will pay for my scribbles,' she said.

'Valuable to me I meant,' he said. 'I know I'll keep it. I'll have it for ever.'

'Well thank you, Ralph. That's nice to know. I'll remember that when I'm sitting in my daughter's house in Bootle.'

He nodded. Her daughter was married to a lecturer at the University of Liverpool and had a baby.

'I'd better get on with my packing,' he said.

Maud nodded.

'Oh, I need newspaper.'

'The room with the washing machine. Tons in there.'

He went inside and got more old newspapers and carried these back to the kitchen. Outside he saw Maud was where he'd left her, holding her head in her hands and probably, he guessed, weeping.

★

They all went out to watch the pantechnicon drive off with the furniture. It was going into storage. Then they went back inside. The house had a different sound with nothing in it. They ate bread and cheese off sheets of news-paper sitting on the living room floor. All over the walls there were squares where the paint was lighter than on the surrounding wall because pictures had hung there. Maud burnt everything left over from their meal in the hearth. Buckets of hot soapy water, cloths and mops were then issued to Ralph and Benedict. They washed the floors, the doors, the wainscoting, the windows and any other wood-work downstairs while Maud and Ginny did the same upstairs. Every fifteen minutes the mop water was so black it had to be tipped away and fresh clean hot water drawn. Ralph frequently wondered as he worked when the task would end but eventually it did and then the whole house smelt of damp and soapy water and was ready to be handed over to the new owners. Maud was staying the night on a camp bed in a sleeping bag. On Sunday a gardener was coming to put the hedge back and tidy up the garden and on Sunday afternoon Maud's son-in-law was driving down from Bootle to collect Maud and take her and the few things left in the house up north.

It was dusk when they left Maud's. The sky was mauve but the trees in the road below were black shapes, their vivid green leaves no longer showing. Ginny unlocked the car. Ralph didn't wrangle with Benedict about it being his turn to sit in the front as by rights it was. He hap-pily scooted into the back. The front seat was tipped down. Benedict and his mother climbed in. Doors clunked shut. The interior smelt of Ginny's sheepskin waistcoat and the plastic covers on the copies of *Great Expectations* on the back ledge, which had heated through the day while the car had sat in Maud's road. The familiar smells of a familiar space.

Ginny started the engine and turned the car around slowly. She drove up the road. He saw Maud's house with some of its lights on, the hole in the hedge used by the lorry that had taken away Arnold's sculptures. It was just a brief glimpse and then Maud's house was gone and he was seeing her neighbours' houses in between the dark trees.

In the front of the Saab no one spoke. He was grateful for that. He didn't want to struggle to put anything into words and he didn't want to listen. He just wanted to sit quietly and wait while the complicated feelings pulsing away inside wore themselves out.

Ginny braked and stopped at the end of the road. The waterworks was opposite with its brick walls and vast stretches of water, shining squares of mirror in the evening light. When a gap appeared in the traffic, Ginny eased the car out, turned right and drove on. The cars streaming toward them all had their headlamps on, white and bright but not dazzling because it wasn't dark enough yet. On the left, playing fields, spectral football nets, signs for Old Barnes and Putney Cemeteries, a woman and a dog walking. They passed Barnes Railway Station and turned onto the Upper Richmond Road.

'I want a cigarette,' said Ginny. 'I haven't wanted a fag for years.'

'Disgusting,' said Benedict.

'That's what you say now. Wait till you start smoking. You'll love them, like I did, till I had to renounce them.'

Ginny drove on through the gathering spring dusk. The taillights of the car ahead glimmered and cast a red glow over its bumper and boot. Ralph wondered how Ginny looked when she smoked. He tried to imagine a cigarette on the edge of her wide mouth. He couldn't. The next moment he realised he had started to recover from the day because for the few seconds he was trying to imagine Ginny with a cigarette, he had forgotten Maud.

When he got home, he found Doreen in the River room lying on the chaise lounge with her feet up and staring out at the dark river and the lights on the far bank.

'Feeling virtuous?' she asked.

'How do you mean?'

'After your day helping?'

'Oh, I don't know. I felt a bit sad really, for Maud.'

'When you grow up, you won't do something like that husband of hers, will you?'

Ralph shrugged. A pointless question not worth answering. Of course he wouldn't.

'I'm feeling things,' she said. 'Kicks.'

'Kicks?'

'I can feel the heel. Here.'

She motioned him over.

'Put your hand there.'

He was reluctant to do this. He didn't like touching. Especially her stomach. He didn't move. She took his hand and put it on the side of her distended belly. It was surprisingly hard, which he hadn't expected.

At first nothing and then two prods from below in the centre of his palm.

'Oh yes,' Ralph said.

He withdrew his hand. It was a relief not to be touching, not to be embarrassed by touching her.

'It's been like that for the last half hour. Crazy.'

She closed her eyes. He heard her breath going in and out. He heard a train on the bridge, clattering.

'I cannot wait for this baby to be born,' she murmured.

June

Doreen went on the bus to the hospital to have her baby and Ralph walked up the road to the Boscombes' to stay there while she was away. A few days later, when he got back from school with Benedict, Ginny told him, 'You can go home.'

He carried his case back and found Doreen in the kitchen breastfeeding a baby girl whom she introduced to him as Catherine. He was scandalized by what she was doing and didn't know where to look but he stayed with her and made her a cup of tea. Later he fried some eggs for tea and served them to Doreen, heavily salted, on rounds of buttered toast. Doreen cried quietly and told him she didn't know what she'd do without him. He was simultaneously appalled and elated by what she'd said.

★

Dear Ralph,

Doreen's had a little girl. Is she sweet? I asked Doreen for info but the letter she sent was rather short, more a telegram really. Perhaps she's just so tired she can't actually face writing anything more complicated than something short and gnomic. It is absolutely exhausting having a baby. I remember only too well. But I'd still love some more news. Perhaps you can jog her. You know, say to her, 'My mum would love to hear from you.' That might work. And I do know she's an indefatigable letter writer. I mean, she writes long screeds home every week, doesn't she? So, something to me, here in the USA, would be brilliant. Might get my mind off things too. I'm okay but you've heard me before on this topic: working for people. It's great. And to be paid to do what you love. What's not to like? But now growth has started and the garden has started taking shape, the requests are flooding in from the MSJs. 'Could you change this? Could you alter that?' When they ask I want to shout back at them, 'It was all in the drawings. You should have studied the drawings. Why didn't you study the drawings? The time to make changes was before the ground was turned, not now after it's been done.' Of course I don't. I just listen and smile and try to accommodate their requests. Going demented.

    Love, Mum xx

July

Ralph sat at the kitchen table reading 'The Lady with the Dog' in the book Timothy had given him. It was about a married man and a married woman falling in love. It was slow. Not a lot happened and nothing happened at the end. But he'd been told it was important and he was determined to persist until he had grasped its secret. This was his third reading and he was at the part where the hero, Gurov, and the heroine, Anna, go and look at a waterfall.

As he read he could hear two sets of breath – Doreen's slow and deep; the baby's faster and shallower.

'I'd a peek outside earlier,' said Doreen.

Ralph looked up. Doreen was opposite, in her nightie and a cardigan, her newborn daughter asleep on her lap.

'Going to be a scorcher,' she said.

Catherine was swaddled in a blanket with only a bit of her head and face showing. Her thin fine hair was tawny.

Her nose and mouth were tiny. Her stretched eyelids had tiny veins showing blue in them. She reminded Ralph of a shell – smooth, compact, perfect.

'Be a lovey,' Doreen said. 'Get the deckchairs out.'

'What, now?'

'I'd like to get some sun before it gets too hot. Yes, please.'

He got up.

'There'll be a reward in heaven for you, Ralph.'

'I know.'

He went to the River room, slid the door open and went out. The sky above, blue and empty, clean and clear except for the vapour trail of an aeroplane, high up. Down the steps and over to Mr Cameron, the gardener's hut beside the stub of brick wall separating their garden from Mrs Moody's. He opened the door, went in. Inside, a smell of fertiliser, twine and sack. Shelves with pots, gardening stuff and a red butterfly batting against the glass of the small cobwebbed window. Ralph cupped his hands over it, felt a tiny tickle on his palms and carefully closed his hands completely.

Outside, he threw up his hands and opened them and watched his prize flutter away.

He carried the deckchairs out, swept them with one of Mr Cameron's stiff brushes and set them up. Then he dropped down into one. The canvas felt slightly damp as it firmed and tightened. The air was chilly but there was heat from the sun on the side of his face. He looked down. Low tide. The river shrunken, the mud flats huge. The stretches of silt were glistening and silvered, the river a dark polished wood, heavy, dense, inert. He remembered he'd left his book inside.

★

He sat on his deckchair and read some more of the story. He was at the part where Gurov walked his daughter to school before he went off to meet Anna secretly in a hotel and there was the long paragraph about the secret life inside every person that was the best of them. What was it Timothy had said? Everyone had a secret centre that they had to guard.

Beside him he heard Catherine's tiny cry as she nuzzled and the quiet sound of suck after she latched on.

He stood and put his book face down on the canvas.

'Just going to look at the river,' he said, speaking as he turned away from Doreen so he wouldn't see anything.

'Okey-doke,' said Doreen quietly.

She seemed not to notice his uneasiness.

He went down to the wall and leant over. The ooze smell rose up to him. Earlier when he'd looked the river hadn't been moving but now, as the tide had turned it was moving, and instead of being black it was now brown and under the brown it was green.

He thought about the passage he'd just read. He remembered two words in particular. One was 'sheath' and this was what Gurov showed the world and it was everything that was false about him. The other was 'kernel' and this was the best of him, his love for Anna, and it was hidden inside the sheath. Ralph had always understood secrets were wrong but now he was being told that, on the contrary, secrets were good.

His thoughts rolled on. In the past he had wondered how people like Ralph and Piggy went against the group on the island but now, having read this Russian story, he thought perhaps he had his answer. It was their secret centre, their kernel, where their beliefs and certainties were hidden that had enabled them to know what was right and to stand up against the others and to act the way they did.

He turned and looked up the sloping garden. In front of the glass back wall, Doreen pacing backward and forward with Catherine. The feeding was done. Safe to go up.

He climbed back to the top. Doreen had Catherine over her shoulder. Her hand was on the baby's back, caressing and kneading and she was pouring words into the tiny whorl of Catherine's perfect miniature ear.

'Tom,' he heard, 'this is Catherine.'

In a nearby garden someone was pushing a lawnmower, the metal drum that housed the cutters turning and clanging.

'Isn't she lovely?' he heard. 'Isn't Catherine lovely?'

He went to his deckchair, picked up his book and sat. Doreen's murmurs continued, as before. She was having a conversation she'd never had. One she wished to have. With Tom. He stared at the page and pretended to read. White paper, small black print. Doreen behind. Pacing. Backward. Forward. Her quiet voice spinning on. Growing fainter. Eventually, it became impossible to hear her but by this stage he didn't need to. No. Not anymore. Knew enough. Knew everything really. Then, into his thoughts. Out of where? On the strength of what he'd heard. It came. Yes. He had a plan. A great plan. Something he would do. Something only he could do. Yes. Only remained now that he act. Carry it through. But he wouldn't tell. He'd do it in secret. But that was all right. Secrets were all right. Hadn't it said so in the Russian story?

He got up, slipped inside. He went to his bedroom, got a pound in change from his H. Upmann box and put the money in the pocket that zipped up in his sports jacket hanging on the back of the door.

Then he took the sheet of Basildon Bond with Betty Mottram's number and went upstairs to his mother's office.

The room was square, the same size as his. There was a desk with the phone, a drawing board, shelves crowded with books and a vast cork board with papers pinned everywhere. A black and white photograph in the middle, of people at a race track in their best clothes, some shouting at the horses, some looking at their fellow racegoers, some talking, some smoking, two kissing. It was his mother's. She had taken it when she was eighteen, won a prize with it.

The four London telephone directories on the filing cabinet. He took volume three, sat in his mother's chair and turned the wafer thin pages until he found Mottram. There was half a page of Mottrams.

Starting from the top he read down the numbers column looking for the letters WIL and every time he hit a WIL number he checked it against the number on Tom's sheet – 3286. The fourth time – success! Correspondence. He had the Mottram address. He took a biro out of the jam jar by the phone and copied onto Tom's sheet the address by the number: 70 Furness Road, NW10. Betty Mottram's house.

He put the directory away and fetched his mother's battered *London A–Z*. He found Furness Road at the bottom of a page of spongy paper. He ringed it in Biro. The nearest Underground station was Willesden Junction. He stuck the Basildon Bond sheet in to mark the page and closed the book. He was ready.

★

'I'm going to see Benedict,' he said.

He and Doreen had just eaten lunch. Catherine was asleep in her pram parked behind the side door.

'I might go for a walk,' said Doreen. 'Take a front door key.'

The house keys were kept in an old Jacob's biscuit tin. Ralph fished out a house key attached to an ancient lead Beefeater figure with much of its red paint flaked off.

He put the key in his trouser pocket, pulled on his jacket, stowed the *A–Z* in the side pocket and went out by the front door. He walked up Falkland Road quickly. Until he was far enough away, there was always the danger that Doreen would come out and call him home, having worked out what he was about to do. But she didn't. She couldn't read his mind, so how could she know? And yet he couldn't shake off the idea that she might until he was beyond her recall.

Ralph reached the railway steps and began to hurry up. If he went by the road bridge it would add twenty minutes to the journey to the Underground station. He couldn't waste the time, he felt. Not today.

He stopped at the top and stared along the footbridge. Not one person, as far as he could see. He'd risk it, he thought. He began to walk. He went fast, anxiety and fear needles in his pelvis. The whole grey simmering length he met no one other than two women with a mob of young children in swimsuits and sandals, all carrying buckets and spades.

'Yes?' asked the man behind the glass in the ticket office of Putney Bridge Underground Station.

'Willesden Junction, please. And I want to come back.'

'Return?'

'Yes.'

'Well, say so then.'

He passed the money through the hole at the bottom of the glass. The ticket and his change came back.

'Know where you're going?'

'Not really,' said Ralph, 'but I can look at a map.'

'District line to Paddington, then the northbound Bakerloo line, terminating either Harrow or Wembley.

Willesden Junction is six stops from Paddington. Got that?'

Ralph nodded.

'And don't bother to say thank you. I'm just doing my miserable job.'

Ralph went up to the platform to wait for the whispering sound to flutter up from the rails and the District line train to follow.

★

Ralph came out of Willesden Junction and into a cobbled street with parked cars baking in the heat. He took the *A-Z* out of his pocket, checked his route and set off.

He skirted the railway lines, turned right onto a bridge that took him over the lines and then went right again. Tubbs Road was long and curved. He began to trudge up it, passing low redbrick houses. The air was still and hot. A man, bare-chested, his skin incredibly white, was sitting on a box on the pavement listening to a radio.

'All right?' asked the man.

Ralph nodded.

The man spat into the gutter and wiped his mouth on his forearm. He had blue tattoos.

He came to the T at the end and Harlesden High Street. Traffic grinding up and down even though it was Sunday. A spray of playing cards on the pavement, face down except one, the three of diamonds. A woman's stiletto in the gutter. A lorry with bales of hay piled on the back went past. He halted at the zebra crossing. Straw wisps from the hay lorry scattered all over the black and white stripes. A grey car stopped. The driver wore sunglasses. He moved his finger. Ralph crossed to the far side of the road and began to walk along. He had felt quite calm on the Underground train but now the encounter was looming, there were prickles in his hands and stomach. It wasn't Tom he feared. He might send Ralph home but he'd be civilised. Veronica, on the other hand, would very likely shout. He didn't relish that.

A dog was lying stretched out on the pavement, his head on his paws. Huge. Ralph didn't know what breed. He stepped round the animal and looked ahead. There was a road on his left. He looked at the sign attached to the wall, low down at the corner. Furness Road.

He turned in. The street ran away into the distance, long and straight. A school on his right but everywhere else, two-storey, semi-detached redbrick houses. The even numbers were on his left, starting low. He began to count. The prickles of anxiety were getting sharper.

Betty Mottram's house was number 70. And there it was. Joined to 68. He looked at it. Veronica lived in either 68 or 72. He went to 72 first. Through the gate and down the path to a small porch with the front door at the back. He rang the bell. He smelt onions. The door opened. A woman in a red and yellow sari and gold earrings.

'I'm looking for Tom MacGraw, staying with his sister, Veronica?'

The woman thought for a moment.

'You want Mrs Sharpe?' she asked.

'Yes, Mrs Sharpe.' That was Veronica's surname.

The woman nodded. Her earrings swayed. Ralph noticed they weighed down her lobes and the stretched holes they hung from showed as dark spaces. Doreen wore small gold studs that fitted snugly. Very different.

'Not this house, not next house, but next next house,' she said.

A small child appeared, ran forward and grabbed her sari. Without taking her eyes off Ralph, the woman whisked the child off the floor and onto her hip in a single fluid movement. Ralph shuffled backward down the path.

'Thank you,' he said.

The woman waved. Ralph backed out of the gate and turned. The door of 72 swung shut.

Ralph slipped passed Betty Mottram's house and turned in through the gate of 68. Short tiled path to the front door. A window with net curtains. Beside the window a plaque with the house number affixed to the brickwork. A front door with two panes of frosted glass, paint scuffed round the Yale lock and along the bottom. He rang the bell.

Farther down Furness Road, the tinkling chimes of an ice cream van. Another surge of anxiety. Eyes screwed, he stared at the frosted glass. A dark shape. It wasn't female. The door swung back. The bald, square, muscular figure of Ronnie.

'Oh fuck,' said Ronnie.

Ronnie's finger came straight up to his mouth. He slipped forward and part-pulled the door closed behind. Then he turned Ralph and propelled him back through the gate and along the pavement.

'What are you doing here?' asked Ronnie.

'Is Tom home?'

'You going to cause trouble? Is that why you've come?'

'No.'

'Why *are* you here then?'

'To see Tom.'

'You are here to cause trouble.'

'Doreen had a baby,' he said.

'Well, no surprise there.'

Ronnie toggled from one of his enormous feet to the other. Nothing was said for a few moments.

'Everything go all right?' he asked.

'Yeah.'

'What is it?'

'Girl. Catherine.'

'How's Doreen?'

His chance.

'She wants to see Tom.'

'I bet she does.'

'She doesn't know I'm here. I used my own money for the tube.'

Ronnie stared at him for a long time.

'Tom's inside listening to the match in Croke Park. Veronica's having a lie down. I'll tell him you're here. See if he'll talk to you. He might, he might not. Not up to me.'

Ronnie went inside number 68 and half-closed the door behind. Ralph looked down the road. He could see the ice cream van. He noticed the heat coming off the paving stones. He smelt a bin smell – a mix of anthracite ash and putrid rot. A man strolled past rolling a tyre.

The front door opened. Tom came out, engaged the snib and pulled the door closed. He was in a white shirt with his sleeves rolled up and he was smoking. He came out the gate and along the pavement. Nodded.

'You've come a long way.'

'Not really. I came on the tube. My own idea. Paid for my own ticket.' Ralph hoped he sounded bright.

'Ronnie told me. So. Catherine – what's she like?'

'She just eats and sleeps and vomits and you know what.'

'You haven't come all this way to tell me that. Why are you here? Spit it out.'

'She wants you to come back.'

This wasn't what he had come to say. Nor did he know where this came from. He didn't even know if it was true. But it was out before he knew, before he could stop it.

'Not going to happen.'

'Just to have a chat.'

Here was another idea that came without him willing it. It was adroit though, a good clarification.

'Why would I want to do that?'

'You'd like Catherine,' he said. 'It'd be worth doing just for that.'

Tom gave a long hard final pull on his cigarette, dropped the butt, ground it underfoot and slid it into the gutter. Smoke came out of Tom's nose, faint in the afternoon sunlight.

The chimes again, closer and closer and then the ice cream van stopped right opposite and all around them front doors banged open and children ran out clamouring.

They both looked over. The hatch was on the other side, so out of sight. They couldn't see the children but they could hear them. Then the first customer, a girl in a sundress with bare red sunburnt shoulders, a slice of vanilla between wafers in her hand which she was licking, slouched into view, and walked off.

'What are you going to say to Doreen when you get home? How will you explain where you've been all afternoon?'

'I won't have to. She thinks I'm at Benedict's.'

Ralph saw the door of 68 opening and a face lean out. Veronica. Tom, who had his back to the door, saw his expression and turned. Veronica shot down the path and out the gate and onto the pavement. She was in fur-trimmed slippers and wore a plain blue dress.

'When I heard the ice cream van, I got up from my bed to look out, and saw you two having your cosy little chat. What the hell's going on?'

'I think you should go back inside,' said Tom.

'No. You go. And I'll talk to him.' She pointed at Ralph.

'He doesn't mean any harm,' said Tom.

'Did I say he did?'

'You think it. I know you,' said Tom.

'No,' said Veronica, 'I know exactly what he is. He's just a boy she's sent up to wheedle and plead.'

'He came by himself. He wasn't sent.'

'Says who?'

'He's just a boy,' said Tom. 'Don't take it out on him.'

'Don't you see what she's doing? She's had her fun but now there's bills to pay, she needs her husband. Shameless, is what it is, shameless.'

'I think Doreen's a bit sad,' said Ralph.

'Oh I bet she is,' said Veronica. 'Bring out the violin.'

'I came here to see if Tom would like to see her and the baby …'

'What?' Veronica interrupted. 'Well, why don't you go home and tell her …'

'He's not going to tell her anything' said Tom. 'Didn't you hear. He's come of his own accord. She doesn't even know he's come.'

'You don't think she put him up to this? Sent him here to tug your heartstrings?'

'She didn't,' said Ralph. 'I promise.'

There was a long silence. Veronica folded her arms and stared up the street. The chimes again. The ice cream van drove off toward the high street.

'I suppose I'll go home then,' said Ralph.

'Do you need the toilet?' asked Tom.

'No,' said Ralph.

Veronica was still looking into the distance but Tom was staring at him. As he moved off, Tom winked at him, twice.

★

It was baking. The metal-framed classroom windows were all wide open. It was the end of the afternoon. Miss Loudon stood at the front, in the customary position she took when she dismissed the class.

'Before I send you on your way,' she said, 'I'd like to say something. I'm afraid I'm leaving at the end of this term.'

Every child went still.

'I would like you to know that though I taught, I was also taught, by you all. I learnt a lot from you. Thank you. See you tomorrow. Class dismissed.'

The children stood and began to file out. They were quiet, subdued. Ralph was not surprised. None would celebrate Miss Loudon's going.

★

The upper bus deck, sweltering, stinking of ash. Ralph and Benedict were talking about Miss Loudon.

'You know what Mum heard?' asked Benedict, ''bout Miss Loudon? The real reason she's going?'

'Go on.'

'She and Horrid Horace were seen holding hands and stuff.'

Horrid was Horace Hamilton, the PE teacher. When they had swimming at the school's open air pool, which wasn't heated, he would push reluctant swimmers into the freezing water. He was an awful man. His wife supervised the girls' netball and lacrosse games and was called Mrs Horrid.

'What stuff?' asked Ralph.

'Kissy-kissy.'

'Are you sure?' asked Ralph.

It seemed unlikely that Miss Loudon would have anything to do with Mr Hamilton.

'Oh yeah, Beady saw them,' said Benedict. 'In Richmond Park.'

This also seemed even more unlikely. Nearby Richmond Park was vast, as he knew from school nature rambles there.

'Are you sure?'

'Yeah. Beady saw them, reported them. And Miss Loudon was asked to go.'

'Is Horrid going?' Ralph asked.

'Mum never said.'

'Pity, that.'

The bus trundled on. He thought about the school secretary in the outer office that lunchtime he went to use the phone to ring Betty Mottram. She hadn't seemed then like a person who'd do what he'd just been told she'd done – tell on someone and cost them their job. But she had. On the island in *Lord of the Flies* Beady would have ended up in Jack's gang, he decided now, with those who wanted to have power and have everyone live the way they wanted and who were prepared to do terrible things to get their way. He, on the other hand, would be on the other side, of course. He'd have stuck with his namesake and Piggy. At least he hoped he would. He wasn't very brave. But he'd have tried.

★

Ralph crossed their boiling garden and went down the passage. He had taken off his tie, rolled it up and put it into his trouser pocket. He had his blazer off and was carrying it in his arms. His satchel strap was across his chest and his shirt underneath was wet with his sweat.

He came to the side door. No sounds from the other side. He turned the handle and pushed. The bolts were on. He sighed.

He went back to the garden and round to the front door. There was a heavy brown mat on the step under the porch. He lifted the right topside corner. The Yale key lay flat in the dust, bright and yellow like gold, which was where Doreen left it when she had to go out and she knew he hadn't a key. He picked it up. The key's outline remained in the dust. A many-legged insect scampered along nearby. He dropped the mat, inserted the key, pushed the door and went in. The hall was cool and still. Bliss after the heat outside. He pulled out the key and closed the door. He angled his head. The house had its familiar silent sound and smelt of the beeswax Doreen put on the banister.

He dumped his things on his bed and went down to the kitchen. He dropped the Yale into the old Jacob's biscuit tin the keys were kept in. He pulled the bolts at the top and bottom of the side door since this was where the pram came in and out. He went to the sink and ran the tap, his finger crooked under the spigot. Once the water was cold he filled a glass and drank. Then he wiped his head and face on a tea towel. Doreen would have been appalled if she'd seen but she wasn't there so he was safe.

He noticed a brown envelope on the table, cut open and with writing on it. The script was Doreen's, square and tiny.

He hung the tea towel and strode to the table and read Doreen's message:

Dear Ralph,
Good afternoon to you. It's 3 o'clock. Just popping up to Cullen's for one or two bits and bobs.
Sincerely, Doreen
PS: I ironed your good blue shirt and left it on the back of your door. Please put it on when you change out of your uniform. I want you to look your best for the Royal Visit.

He looked at the words 'Royal Visit'. What was that about? Unless of course?

★

Ralph was at his desk in his bedroom when he heard Doreen wheeling her pram across the garden and down the passage, followed a moment later by the sound of the side door opening and closing.

'Ralph,' Doreen shouted.

He could hear Catherine shrieking.

He went down to the kitchen. Doreen had her dress open. He looked away until Catherine's shrieking stopped and when he looked back she'd latched on.

'Veronica and Ronnie and Tom are coming over to see us about seven,' said Doreen.

She was sitting, feeding.

He noticed groceries heaped on the pram, which included brandy snaps in a cellophane-wrapped box. He loved brandy snaps.

'Put the white wine in the freezer box.'

He did, though he had a bit of a job ramming the bottle inside the ice-furred space.

'I got smoked salmon and that. Do the honours?'

He looked through the packages on the pram and took what he needed to the table.

'You want to hear this now,' she said.

The butter was wrapped in coarse crinkled yellowy paper, an anchor with rope looped round it on the front.

'Early this morning, you've gone to school, phone goes.'

He peeled off the wrapper but the butter, which had partly melted in the heat, stuck fast to it so hunks came away with the paper.

'Lucky to hear it in your mother's study. Guess who?'

'No idea' he said.

The butter was abnormally yellow too. That's what happened when it went soft.

'Veronica, Tom's sister. Who hates me.'

'Right,' he said.

He got the bread out of the brown bag. Smell of yeast. Flour residue on his fingertips from the crusts.

'Calling from a phone box.'

He smeared butter over the first slice. One pass with the knife and it was done. Easy work.

'"Don't have long to talk," she said.'

He sliced the crust off and proceeded to butter the next slice.

'I could hear she was a bit fluttery, a bit nervous. Wasn't on for a long chat. I could tell. Just wanted to get to the point and get off the line as quick as possible. Was I in tonight? Well, obviously, where else would I be? Yes. Would it be all right if Ronnie ran her and Tom down? After work. To see the baby. They didn't want to put me out. I wasn't to go to any trouble. They'd be in and out in next to no time. That's what she said. By which point the pips were going. "Yes," I said. "When?" "'Bout half six or seven?" I said. "Yes," she said. "Bye." Line cut out. And that was that. So what do you make of that?'

Ralph had quite a lot he could say but he wasn't going to say it.

'Why did she ring you from a phone box?' he asked. 'Don't they have a phone?'

An ingenious question, he thought, in response to Doreen's.

'No, they don't,' said Doreen. 'The neighbour has the phone. Betty, you call her. You ring her and she goes next door and fetches Tom or Veronica.'

'Oh, I didn't know that,' said Ralph.

The entire loaf was buttered. His first question had been cunning but then he had capped it with this lie. He was turning out to be as good at secrets as the man in the Russian story.

The salmon was in brown paper stained with fish wet. He unwrapped the parcel and laid the slices on the bread, using a combination of fork and finger. He didn't much like the touch of the salmon. It was damp, fishy and fleshy, none of which he liked. As soon as this job was done, he washed his hands fastidiously, and then, finding his fingers still smelt of fish, he washed them a second time for good measure.

'Put the salmon on the table next door.'

He carried the platters through. The sun was still high and its yellow light poured in through the back. The furnishings had been baked all day and there was a hot fabric smell.

When he came back to the kitchen, he found Doreen gingerly laying Catherine back in her pram. The feed had put her to sleep but she had a tendency to wake up when she was set down like this. He'd seen this happen. He hoped it didn't happen now.

'She's dying in the heat,' said Doreen. 'Like her mother.'

It didn't happen. She didn't wake. Doreen straightened up. She buttoned her front.

'Right,' said Doreen. 'What time is it?' She glanced at the small watch on her slim wrist. 'Oh no. I have to whip the cream. You, Buster, plates, serviettes, cutlery, on the table in the River room. Then put the cheeses on the wooden board for me.'

★

The doorbell rang.

'I'll go,' he said.

Ralph went down to the front door. He could make out three blurs through the glass panels. He opened the door.

'Ah, young Ralph,' said Ronnie.

Corduroy slacks, a blazer, a striped tie. A hint of after-shave. A green carrier bag in his right hand with 'Harrods' in gold on the side.

'All right?'

'Yes, thank you.'

'Hello, Ralph.'

Veronica. Wary tone. Blue jacket, matching skirt, pearl earrings, shiny black shoes and handbag. He thought of the racegoers in the photograph in his mother's study.

'Hello.' He thought he'd better add her name. 'Veronica.'

She acknowledged with a faint nod. Hard to know what it meant.

Tom stood beside his sister. He said nothing, just put up both thumbs and grinned. He also had a paper carrier bag.

'Um, come in,' said Ralph.

He stood back. They visitors filed past.

'Go on down to the back.'

He closed the door. A linoleum smell mixed with aftershave and perfume. Ralph sprinted after the visitors. Through the kitchen and into the River room beyond.

He found Doreen in front of the brick hearth in her black dress, the one she wore to Mass, the pram beside her, the hood down. Veronica was bent over, staring in.

'Something for the baby.' This was Ronnie.

He waved the Harrods carrier bag.

'More of the same,' said Tom, waving his bag.

'You shouldn't,' said Doreen.

Adults always said this.

'We'll leave them down here,' said Ronnie.

They set the bags on the table beside the food.

The men joined Veronica and peered down at Catherine sleeping in the pram. Questions and answers batted backward and forward by the grown-ups. Everyone stiff. Nobody at ease. Ralph felt they were all acting as they felt they ought to or as if they were being watched. He fetched the bottle of white. Opened it with the corkscrew. Poured. The wine was so cold it glugged out like paste. He handed the glasses round. Clinking and compliments and toasts.

'To the baby.'

'To the mother.'

'To the future.'

Catherine woke. She was fed, burped, passed from adult to adult, jiggled, kissed, admired. More questions. More answers. Catherine's mewling and gurgling had an impressive effect. Enabled the grown-ups to stop talking falsely like they had when they came in and to start talking properly, the way they always talked. It was still boring though.

Ralph counted the brandy snaps. There were twelve in total so with everyone getting two that left two over. Could he take three at the first pass? Probably not. He'd look greedy. He'd have to take two like everyone else. But then, would Doreen press a third on him? She knew he loved them. But Tom had a sweet tooth. Ronnie as well. The two left over might go to them. Might. He couldn't be sure. He hoped not. He was really hungry. When was Doreen going to give the signal to eat?

★

His chair faced the window. View of the Thames and the sky. Ronnie and Veronica opposite. Tom and Doreen by the hearth. His plate balanced on his lap. He ate a slice of bread and salmon. The butter was warm and runny, the fish slimy and peppery. He followed with a mouthful of blue-veined Stilton. As soon as it was in his mouth it felt like the surface was daubed with sweat. He took a grape, glistening with cold water. It had been run under the tap. He bit. The fruit parted. It was hard and jellied but it was cold too, which counteracted the clamminess of the Stilton.

As they ate, the visitors talked away. He half-listened. Got the general idea. The heat. News from Ireland. Work. He grew bored. Tuned out. Stared up. Out. Upward. Incredible evening sky.

On his left, the sinking sun, a round luscious disc, golden light streaming from it slantwise. The clouds lay all over the sky, looking like chopped-up bits of fabric. Hit by the sun's light, their undersides and edges showed plum and purple and violet. Between the clouds, smears of fiery pink and orange.

The wine was finished. They were on port. He was vaguely aware of glasses being topped up. Each adult in turn taking Catherine on their lap. Talking at her. Smiling at her. Jiggling her. Gooey words. Baby speak. Then a change in the sound texture. Ronnie and Veronica and Doreen talking. About someone they all knew. Meanwhile, Tom had Catherine. On his lap. Her head on his knees, her feet toward him. Looking up at him. Her little body wriggling. Gurgling too. Him bent over her. Looking down. Making little circles on her belly. Talking too.

Words not audible. Rapt. Totally absorbed. Never before had Ralph seen Tom like this.

'Time for dessert,' Doreen said. 'Ralph, would you be a love and throw on the kettle?'

He went to the kitchen, lit the gas and set the kettle on. He returned. The adults were gathered round the table, Catherine in Doreen's arms.

'There's an extra brandy snap for you, Tom, and you Ronnie. You get three each. I know you like them so much.'

He should have known, thought Ralph, who'd get the extra ones.

★

On Sunday morning Doreen came home from Mass with Catherine. She made a fry and called him. He went through. His plate on the table, bacon, sausage, blood pudding, egg, everything smeared with hot brown fat.

He sat and picked up his knife and fork.

'I've something to tell you,' she said.

'I'm adopted?'

'Try and listen. This is important.'

'And being adopted isn't?'

'Tom's coming back,' she said.

He looked at her.

'Today.'

★

That afternoon Ralph was in the kitchen when Tom appeared through the side door holding his suitcase, the one he had left with, followed by Ronnie. He greeted Ralph quietly and carried his suitcase away to the basement where Catherine and Doreen were having an afternoon nap.

'All right, young Ralph?' asked Ronnie, who'd remained in the kitchen.

'Yes, thank you,' said Ralph.

'What you doing?'

'Common Entrance paper.'

Ronnie pulled out a chair, settled down and looked across at him. Ralph stared back at Ronnie's bald, square head and his watery blue eyes and his red nose. His skin was smooth. He had shaved himself carefully that morning, obviously. There was a breath of soap.

'So what do you think?'

'About what?' he asked.

Ronnie laughed. He had a nice laugh, warm and chesty.

'The course of true love,' he said.

This was excruciating.

'I don't know,' he said.

'Well I can tell you what I know,' said Ronnie. 'Love is a mystery. I don't understand this myself. On the other hand, it's none of my bloody business. And all things considered, probably for the best. I think so. Do you agree?'

'I suppose,' said Ralph.

'You'd quite a lot to do with this,' said Ronnie. 'You know that?'

Ralph looked down at the paper.

'You should be proud of yourself. Any chance of a cup of tea?'

★

That afternoon he and Doreen and Tom and Catherine went out to Wandsworth Park.

On Sunday evening they ate together in the kitchen – lamb chops and mint jelly and peas and new potatoes.

On Monday morning, very early, Ralph heard Tom leaving the house and clambering into the van that had come to take him up to the site.

That evening Tom came home in his mud-caked work clothes. He washed and changed and began to play with Catherine in the River room. Ralph could hear them from the kitchen where he was doing his homework. Doreen was at the stove. Already it was as if Tom had never been gone.

★

He came into the classroom a good ten minutes before the roll. Miss Loudon was at her desk, her hair piled high on top of her head, a pencil stuck in the middle of the tangle. She wore a dress with yellow and red roses on it. She was with two girls. He watched them hand her little presents wrapped in paper and envelopes with, he presumed, cards inside. His present was in his satchel. It wasn't wrapped and he hadn't a card either. He went to his desk and sat. He got his maths book out and pretended to check something. The girls and Miss Loudon talking. He'd give his present later, when no one would see.

★

The day's end. All his classmates had filed out. He heard them shouting in the corridor outside.

'Not going home, Ralph?' asked Miss Loudon. 'The holidays just started you know. Time to get out of here as quick as you can.'

'I've got something for you,' said Ralph.

He opened his satchel and pulled out a long dark box encased in slippery cellophane.

'No card and it's not wrapped,' he said. 'Sorry about that.'

'Oh my,' said Miss Loudon.

She took his gift.

'After Eights. You do know how to please a girl. Thank you.'

'I'd better go and find Benedict,' he said. 'He's waiting for me. Got to get the bus.'

'Okey-doke,' said Miss Loudon.

He remembered he hadn't said it yet.

'Thank you very much. For everything.'

'Only did what I was supposed to do. As a teacher. Good luck next term.' She meant with his Common Entrance. 'Cheerio.'

He hefted his satchel and made his way between the desks to the far door. He turned. Miss Loudon was standing where he'd left her, holding his box of chocolates. She looked paler and smaller than normal.

'Bye,' he called. He turned again and went out.

★

Ralph and Benedict neared the Boscombes' gate. A black van at the kerb, 'Chubb's Locksmiths' written in red on it.

'The locks are being changed today,' said Benedict.

Ralph remembered their conversation on the bus about this.

'Come and see the blade me and Douglas found on the river,' said Benedict. 'It's lethal.'

He followed Benedict through his gate and across the garden. Clive's scooter wasn't there. There was a hollow in the hedge where it had stood. Ralph was sorry to see it gone.

The boys went down the passage. At the bottom the man from Chubb's was sitting on a box, a chisel in one hand, a mallet in the other, cutting a box shape into the edge of the side door. There were flakes of pale wood by his feet.

'All right, boys?' asked the Chubb's man.

They sidled into the kitchen and met Jeannie. She had a big white apron on.

'Your mum's gone up to the shops, Benedict. Don't imagine she'll be long.'

They dumped their satchels and blazers and ran down the garden to the hut. Douglas was working inside at the table below the shelves crowded with his collection of clockwork toys from Eastern Europe and the USSR, cars, aeroplanes, boats, trains, animals, circus performers, all displayed sitting on their boxes. Benedict pushed the door open.

'Can Ralph see the dagger?'

Douglas was still in the suit and tie he wore at work. This would be his last day of term as well, Ralph guessed.

'Sure.'

Ralph followed Benedict in. The inside of the hut smelt of the roll-up cigarettes Douglas smoked and creosote and roof felt.

Douglas took a bundle from the drawer of the table and set it by the papers he'd been reading. Ralph noticed 'Notes for Exam Markers' written in bold black letters at the top of the first sheet in the pile.

Douglas unfurled the cloth carefully to reveal a length of metal, much corroded, bulbous at one end and tapered at the other.

'It could be Viking,' said Benedict. Ralph had rarely heard him sound so excited. 'Or Anglo-Saxon.'

'Well, we don't know that yet,' said Douglas.

'But it's still a dagger,' said Benedict, 'whatever its age.'

Ralph could tell it was important to have this confirmed at least.

'Oh yes,' said Douglas. 'It's a dagger all right.'

'Go on, Ralph' said Benedict. 'Pick it up. Try it out.'

Ralph wiped his hot sweaty palm on his school trousers, grasped the handle and lifted it. Now he had it in his hand there could be no doubting it: this was an object that had been made for the purpose of stabbing and slashing. It was thrilling to be holding it.

'In my opinion it's a stiletto,' said Benedict, 'the assassin's favoured weapon.'

'Do you think it was ever used?' Ralph asked.

'Of course,' said Benedict. 'The assassin did his murder and then he threw it in the river. If you want to dispose of a weapon, there's no better place than old Father Thames, is there?'

Ralph agreed. There was no arguing with that. After a murder, where else would a stiletto go but in the river?

★

The boys were back in the kitchen. The locksmith was still working on the side door. Ginny was at the table. She lifted a long loaf wrapped in tissue paper and two bottles of milk from her shopping basket. She asked about their last day at school.

Benedict said it was boring and he was glad the holidays had come round. Ralph volunteered that he had given Miss Loudon a box of chocolates.

'That's nice,' said Ginny. She looked at her son. 'Why didn't we think of that?'

'I'm not in her form,' said Benedict. 'So of course I wouldn't give her a present today. Try and keep up, Mother.'

Ginny put the bottles away in the fridge and came back and looked at Ralph.

'I hope you made an effort. What kind did you give her?'

'After Eights.'

'Oh very sophisticated, Ralph. And was it your idea, or did Doreen put you up to it?'

'Both.'

Doreen had put the idea into his head but he'd taken the money from his H. Upmann box and gone to Pritchard's and bought them and then carried them home and put them in his satchel of his own accord and without telling her. Of course if he'd told her, Doreen would have wrapped them and made him buy a card. He wished he had told her now.

'Oh, Ralph,' said Ginny, 'I've something to show you. You'll like this.'

She went over to the Welsh dresser and took a postcard from one of the shelves and carried it back.

'I had this from Maud,' she said.

Ralph saw the card had a black-and-white picture of a ferry on a river with the words 'Ferry Cross the Mersey'.

Ginny turned the card over.

'Listen to this. "Please thank those two stalwarts, Benedict and Ralph, for their help packing me up. They're lovely young boys and a credit to their mothers. Love to all in Falkland Road, Maud." What about that?'

'Does she like it?' asked Ralph.

'What, Bootle?' said Ginny.

'Yes.'

'Have you been to Bootle?'

'No.'

'Maud's making the best of it, ploughing on regardless.'

Ginny returned the card to the dresser.

'Better run on,' said Ralph.

'Not long till your mum's back.'

'No.'

'My Lord, the time has flown since she went, hasn't it?'

No, it hadn't. It seemed to him that actually it was a very long time since she'd left and an awful lot had happened which made it seem even longer. But how did he explain this to Ginny? It was easier just to agree.

'I suppose,' he said.

He moved towards the side door. The locksmith had fitted a new brass lock inside the space he'd cut. The side door would no longer simply bolt. It was getting a proper lock.

'Tell your Mum I need to see her the moment she's back,' said Ginny.

'Will do,' he said.

He went round the locksmith and out to Falkland Road. He stopped beside the glossy Chubb's van. He looked back towards the railway steps and then the other way toward home.

August

A plain white airmail card, his name and address on the front.

On the reverse a pen and ink drawing: his mother in her check dress standing outside 88 Falkland Road with a speech bubble coming out of her mouth inside which was: 'Home At Last.'

★

The hot evening at the end of a baking day. Their kitchen. Ralph sitting in the middle of the floor, shirt off, a towel draped over his shoulders. Doreen behind dipping a comb in a bowl of warm water. Tom at the table knocking his gold dimpled lighter and his green and white Major packet together. He could never sit still when he smoked.

'Know how we cut hair in the army?' said Tom.

Doreen tugging the tines through his tangled hair, water drops splattering his neck as she did.

'Electric clippers,' said Tom.

Tom, inhaling, exhaling. The smoke from a Major cigarette was sharp and chemical and familiar.

Doreen working the scissors behind, testing the action, cutting nothing.

'No moving now,' she said. 'The hairdresser must not be distracted.'

'Any army barber could do any head in less than a minute,' said Tom.

The cold of the metal scissor arms on his neck, the blades closing, severing, opening. Feeling Doreen's fingers, hearing the blades rubbing against each other, he started to drift into a light trance. This always happened when she cut his hair.

'Come to think of it,' said Tom, 'I might have some clippers downstairs. Bought them when I came out of the army and thought I'd like to keep my locks shorn. Do you want me to get them?'

'No thank you,' said Doreen. 'When his mother gets home, I don't think she'll thank me if she finds he hasn't any hair. Wouldn't you agree, Buster?'

'Yes,' said Ralph dreamily.

She came round to the left side and began to run the tines through the hair over his ear.

'Excited,' she said, 'about tomorrow?'

Doreen had booked a taxi to take him and Catherine and the pram to Waterloo to meet his mother off the train from Southampton.

'Will I recognize Mum?'

'Course you will. A year's not that long.'

Snip, snip, snip. The tranced feeling folding him tighter.

'Think I'll just pop down to check on herself.'

Tom meant Catherine, who was in the cot at the bottom of the basement stairs. The sound of Tom grinding his cigarette in the ashtray.

'Don't wake her,' said Doreen. 'I only got her down half an hour ago.'

'Why would I wake her?' asked Tom.

'Because you do. You're always lifting her up to see if she's asleep and then she wakes up. I know you. You do it all the time.'

She didn't sound cross.

'Promise. I'll just check. That's all.'

Tom padding past, humming something, going out. His vague after-smell of engine grease and tobacco and London earth.

'Was it a good year?' Doreen asked.

To answer he would have to abandon the lovely state he was in. It would be like waking up in the morning. Or putting aside a book he was lost in. But if he stayed still perhaps she wouldn't persist.

She moved round to his right ear now. Combing. The scissor blades scything.

'Did you hear me? Have you gone to sleep?' she asked.

'No.'

'So, good year, apart from that awful business?'

She meant what had happened on the bridge. His mesmerised feeling leeching away.

'All fine and dandy,' he said, 'apart from when you locked me in the garden shed and didn't feed me for a week.'

'You should be on the stage, you know. I think there's one leaving in a minute,' she said.

The scissoring action, soothing, beguiling, hypnotizing.

'You did me a very good turn,' she said. 'Don't think I don't know what you did. I won't forget in a hurry.'

Tom returning. Catherine's whimpering, gurgling noises and her milk smell.

'Oh, Tom,' said Doreen, 'you woke her up.'

'No I didn't. She was awake.'

'Oh yeah.'

Tom sitting back in his chair.

Tom murmuring, 'And who's a lovely little girl?'

Mewling noises from Catherine, sleepy ones Ralph judged.

'You're a caution, Tom MacGraw,' said Doreen.

'And you love me,' he said.

Ralph had never heard Tom say this word. Ever. Did he mean Catherine? Or Doreen? Or both? It wasn't clear.

He felt the comb moving through his hair, pulling, straightening, heard the scissors clacking, and he just sat there, thinking nothing, letting the moment hold him.

Acknowledgements

I would to thank Jason Hartcup for his vehicular advice, Jonathan Williams for combing my language through and taking out all the kinks, knots and other infelicities, and Jason Thompson for preparing the manuscript for publication with his customary and exemplary attention to detail, exactly as he has done for me many times before. Any mistakes are my own.